HER MAJESTY'S
HIT MAN

HER
·
MAJESTY'S
·
HIT MAN
·

Allan Prior

WILLIAM MORROW AND COMPANY, INC.
New York

Library of Congress Cataloging-in-Publication Data

Prior, Allan, 1922–
Her Majesty's hit man.

I. Title.
PR6066.R57H4   1987   823'.914   86-21768
ISBN 0-688-06769-7

Printed in the United States of America

First U.S. Edition

1 2 3 4 5 6 7 8 9 10

BOOK DESIGN BY BERNIE SCHLEIFER

TO HARVEY GINSBERG
for all his help and encouragement

A U T H O R ' S   N O T E

This is a true story.
That is, I believe it to be true.
How can anybody know for sure?
But I believe it to be true.
So much so, that here and there I've changed things from the way they were told to me, to something slightly different, that is, exact locations and small things like that. Nothing big.
Except the Ending.
I don't know what the Ending of this story is.
I'm not sure anybody does.
Otherwise, this is a True Story.
That is, I believe it to be so.

—A.P.

HER MAJESTY'S
HIT MAN

O·N·E

THE TELEPHONE RANG, promptly at nine o'clock.

Jay knew, before he picked it up, that it was Mr. Jones.

Mr. Jones said, "How are you, dear boy?"

He was never able to make up his mind if Mr. Jones was gay or not. Probably not. Probably black leather and whips. Something way out, as Polanski had said to the police when they looked at the murder scene, look for something way out. He always remembered reading that. Mr. Jones would be way out. He had to be. No suburban villa in Bexley for Mr. Jones. No tea-making machine at the bedside, no snug warm wife for Mr. Jones, oh no. Mr. Jones would be holed up in a posh mansion flat, probably in Kensington, and voyage up to Soho, by appointment, to get his rocks off. Mr. Jones was not your obvious Etonian civil servant, despite the tie, which could even be bogus. No ordinary civil servant would be able to do what Mr. Jones did. Not wouldn't. Couldn't.

Mr. Jones hired people to kill people.

On behalf of Her Majesty's Government. Which, of course, made killing all right.

Jay knew what Mr. Jones meant when he said, his voice thin and dry over the telephone, "I have a small, urgent job for you, dear boy. Are you free to drop by this morning?"

Mr. Jones knew bloody well he was free.

Mr. Jones had probably put watchers on him overnight. Somebody outside right now, very likely. Not that it mattered. He

11

wasn't doing anything else. Jay smiled to himself. While you're doing that, you aren't doing anything else. Who had said that to him? Some *idiot* in the army, he supposed.

Creepy. That was the word.

Something in a fawn raincoat.

Mr. Jones had worn the fawn raincoat, not new (did Etonians ever wear anything new?), when they had first met. By design, of course. Mr. Jones had introduced himself. In a leafy Surrey lane, for God's sake. "Hello, dear boy. I'm Jones. I was talking to your old CO the other day. Spoke well of you." Liar. His old commanding officer would have spat blood. Unless he'd meant somebody at the SAS. Jay never quite knew. Mr. Jones talked like that. He implied, did Mr. Jones. He left things in the air. Jay drank his coffee black, with a lot of sugar. The trembling had stopped, he noted clinically. It would not happen again, not until afterward, and with luck not even then.

That meeting in the green and lovely Surrey lane had started it all. Jay had been in the mood to try anything. He'd just had another row with Cherry and walked out of the cottage to cool off, to get away. It had been one of their early rows, when they could still make up in bed. Not like the ones that came later, with the drink, and the horrors locked in his mind, horrors he could never talk to her about. Money had been the cause of the row. Cherry had been used to money and couldn't live without it, a lot of it. Those times seemed long ago, the cottage, the kids, the swimming pool, the dogs. All so very long ago. Yet he sometimes ached when he thought of it. Even now. Jay lit his first and, usually, his only cigarette, which would send him to the bathroom and set him up for the day. He noted that his bowels were no looser than usual. That could only be good. Lately he had begun to wonder. Would Mr. Jones ever call again, and if he did, what would his answer be?

Mr. Jones had called. And he hadn't even thought of saying no.

Which meant that Mr. Jones knew him better than he knew himself.

Well, he would, wouldn't he, the old creep?

Jay turned the five-year-old Jensen into the Whitehall parking lot, on Horse Guards Parade. The gatemen were expecting him, called him sir, and told him where to park. He could have been going in to talk to some bluff old Service Corps major about an army contract for underpants, woolen, or undershirts, cellular. In a way, he was doing something like that. He locked the car and walked quickly toward the building that held Mr. Jones. It was September, and a mild one in London. He nodded to the guardsman at the gate, and the man saluted and said, "Good morning, sir."

They always knew if you'd been army.

That, too, had been a little time ago.

He had done things, even then, that the guardsman would never have thought the proper duty of a soldier.

Jay pulled his old Burberry around him and strode toward the looming Ministry building, riding like a shabby old liner in the gray seas of Whitehall. Bloody England, going on as if nothing had changed in the world. Guardees and men with breastplates on horses, for God's sake. Sitting over their manifests, and plotting their maneuvers. Mind, we had a bloody good army, little but good. The Falklands had shown that. Granted, the opposition had been piss-poor, but just the same, the lads had done well, no denying it. Trouble was, not enough people were in uniform, or even knew what it was for. No conscription, so the country was full of potbellied boozers aged eighteen to twenty-five who wouldn't know one end of an Enfield from the other. Shirkers to a man, work-shy wankers. Still, the Falklands had shown we had some good stuff left.

He was sounding like his old man, in his head.

That could not be.

The old man was all guts and, as the American cousins would say, Old Glory.

He, Jay, was not like that. Never could be.

Odd thing, the old Burberry he was wearing had belonged to his father. Now, of course, every tab had been removed from it, and so had all the labels from every garment he wore, down to the scraped-out and obliterated maker's mark on his shoes. His wristwatch had no serial number. There was nothing in any of his pockets, except a handkerchief with no laundry mark, twenty pounds in fivers, and six one-pound coins. Wear a suit, dear boy, Mr. Jones had said, ringing off, so he had, one he'd worn before, on similar occasions. It had no grit or fluff in the pockets and had been recently cleaned. The cleaner's label had been taken off. Nice and clean. That was how he had been taught.

Jay presented himself at the reception desk inside the Ministry building. The uniformed commissionaire, with ribbons from Malaya and Suez, said, "Mr. Jones, sir? If you'd follow me, sir?"

Jay stepped into the antique lift.

Mr. Jones had tea waiting. It was Darjeeling and gave off a fragrant aroma as he poured it into shallow Doulton cups and waved Jay to a chair. "I can't stand this Ministry hogwash they bring around, so I have my girl brew up for me." Jay sat down. He had never seen any girl. He had never seen anybody, except the two men in plain clothes at the lift exit, on the top floor, who had looked at him steadily, in the way that heavies, army or criminal, always did, at the breadth of your shoulders and how you held yourself and wondering if you were trouble. Trouble? Jay smiled. He could have taken them both out in ten seconds. Only one had been armed, a small bulge under the left armpit. Shoulder holster. The other had nothing. Fresh-faced, about twenty. They didn't look Regiment. Probably Army Security. They doubtless made Mr. Jones feel safer.

Jay accepted the scented cup and a digestive biscuit.

All this fuss with the tea, he thought, so Mr. Jones does not have to shake hands.

"Are you well, dear boy?" Mr. Jones peered over the rim of his cup. His collar was stiff, his hair thin and pomaded, his skin sallow, and his suit dark and none too new. His eyes were something else. Mad, probably, Jay thought. But then you'd have to be mad to sit in this perfectly ordinary civil service office, with this worn carpet, and the curtains that did not close, and do what he did. Himself, too. He was mad to be here. It was a mad situation.

But some poor sod, as they said in the army, had to do it.

It just happened to be him, and it happened to be Jones.

Simple as that.

"Fine," said Jay. "I'm fine. What's the job?"

Mr. Jones looked faintly disapproving. "All in good time, dear boy." He smiled, showing the National Health teeth. "How is the little lady?"

He meant Angie.

"She's all right, as far as I know."

"Oh? Is she away?"

"She's at work. At the BBC. Making up some actor's face at this moment, I imagine."

Mr. Jones nodded and placed his cup carefully in his saucer. "That is still on, is it? All going well?"

"I don't talk to her, if that's what you mean. About anything that matters, that is."

"The women," Mr. Jones sighed. "They are a problem."

Amen to that, thought Jay.

He said, "Angie's no problem. She's a very ordinary uncomplicated girl who doesn't want to get married or anything like that, not yet anyway."

"Not too many like that about," said Mr. Jones, obviously not believing him. "But discreet, even if she ever . . . knew?"

"Absolutely," said Jay. "But she won't."

"No," said Mr. Jones, "of course not. That would cause . . . problems."

"Can't happen." Jay finished his tea and put his digestive biscuit back in the saucer. He had lost his appetite. Mr. Jones's bringing up Angie had done it. Angie he kept in one compartment of his mind. He lived with her, went to the movies with her, sometimes took her on drives out to the coast. Brighton usually, he was very fond of Brighton. God, he really was getting like his old man, the old boy had forever taken floozies to the place, after his mother died. Floozies, what had happened to floozies? They had disappeared with the British Empire, that's what had happened to them. No such thing any more. Angie wasn't a floozie, she was a makeup girl at the BBC, and the kindest bedmate he'd ever had. They had been together now for eighteen months and they still exploded when they touched. If the wind was in the east, anyway. That was another of the old man's sayings: "If the wind was in the east" meant sex. If he felt like it, she did. At once. If he didn't, she simply snuggled up to him. She would hold his hand and watch television with absolute contentment. She was tall, almost too tall for Jay, who was five-nine, but she had a good, slightly plump figure, which she never slimmed. Her eyes were hazel and her hair was gold. She loved him very much and would have liked to have a child by him, but she had said so only once and later pretended it was a joke. After Cherry, the selfish bitch, she was a wonderful find, all giving and not much taking. He did not love her in the mad way he'd loved Cherry, anyway at the start, but he liked her very much, and admired her simplicity and trust. He did not want anything more than that from any relationship with a woman.

As Mr. Jones said, anything else was a problem.

The wind, however, was often in the east.

Angie had kept him on a level keel for a long time now. Perhaps she was the only thing that had. The drinking had gone down to manageable proportions for a while, and the dreams had stopped for a bit. Lately, however, he had started to drink again, and there had been a few dreams, not many and not too vivid, but a shade too often for comfort. Jay shifted in his seat, suddenly eager to get on with it, get it over with. What was the old bastard going on about now?

Mr. Jones was asking him if he would like more tea.

Jay shook his head.

Mr. Jones put his fingers together to make a steeple. "About money?"

Jay sat very still and waited.

Mr. Jones passed across a slip of paper. It had a figure written on it.

"I thought that," Mr. Jones said, raising his eyebrows.

Jay nodded, hardly seeing the line of figures. "Fine."

"In the same place, naturally."

Jay nodded, again. It would go toward the nest egg. He knew how much there was in Zurich. Add this to it, and it came to thirty-two thousand. Not a fortune, but he was getting there. Soon, very soon, he would go and draw out the lot, not just sit around pretending to Angie he was working, that all he could afford was the rent of the Hammersmith pad. Two rooms, kitchen, and bathroom in the rather sleazy block, car doors banging for an hour in the morning, trees in the streets, pigeons shitting on the cars all night. When it was fifty or sixty grand, he'd call it a day, and take Angie off to Vence and buy that dilapidated old cottage. It needed work, but he could do that himself, he was very handy at the old do-it-yourself. Maybe he would even give her the kid she wanted.

That, of course, was in the future.

"Let's go, Geronimo," he said.

Mr. Jones smiled, slightly disapproving. "We are the eager beaver this morning, aren't we?"

He opened a file.

Although the room was cool, Jay, very slightly, began to sweat.

The taxi was waiting on a double yellow line on the other side of Whitehall. Jay walked across the wide road toward it, taking deep breaths. The driver was nobody he knew, nobody ever was, and didn't even turn his head as Jay got into the back. As soon as Jay sat down, the car drifted out into the traffic, along Whitehall toward Trafalgar Square. Jay put on his thin gloves, picked up the black leather briefcase lying on the back seat, and opened it. They had given him a Beretta 952 Special, fitted with a silencer. It was a .22, high muzzle velocity, explosive head. Make a hell of a mess, but inside, where it mattered. He slipped it into the left inside pocket of the Burberry and put on the pair of heavy-rimmed glasses with plain lenses that were also in the briefcase. A little disguise was better than a lot. Look ordinary, that was the first rule. The briefcase would have no recognized ancestry. There was one thing about Mr. Jones. He never overlooked detail.

Jay sat back in the seat and tried to think of nothing.

He used the old Canadian relaxation technique. First relax the head. Then the neck. Then the spine. Then the legs. It didn't do much good, but it passed the time. The taxi wound its way up Shaftesbury Avenue and took a right into Soho. The place was busy, the businessmen hurrying about, the brassy old whores smoking their first cigarettes of the day, and the first clients eyeing them up. My God, the optimism of some people. Jay looked at his watch. Twelve-thirty exactly. Another two minutes to get there. On the dot. One thing, it hadn't been a long ride to work.

The taxi came to a sudden halt.

"We're over a minute early," said the driver, through the glass partition.

"I'm not waiting," Jay replied. "I'm in and out. You be here when I do come out."

"If I'm not," said the driver, "I'll be cruising round, pick you up at the bottom of Lexington Street, as per instructions."

Jay felt a cold anger. "You be here," he said. "Don't piss me about."

The driver made no reply to that, except to say, "We're only a minute in front now."

Jay took a deep breath and got out of the cab.

He slammed the door and walked quickly into the narrow doorway bearing the gilt sign "Eastern Tours." He walked up the stairs quickly, but one at a time. The place, like everything in Soho, smelled musty and full of the sin of years, somewhere under the dark paneling covering God knew what. The tourists who came in here would have to be hard up for a holiday. Probably party comrades from the Clyde or Marxist schoolteachers from Hull, in owlish glasses, going to see the Promised Land at cut rates. Mr. Jones had said he would be unlikely to see anybody on the stairs, and he didn't. He counted them just the same. Eighteen. Say nine inches deep, each. Plenty of clearance room at the bottom. If he had to, he could jump the last ten. He hoped it wouldn't come to that. He pushed the door open at the top of the stairs and walked into the reception office. As Mr. Jones had predicted, there was nobody at the desk. If there had been, his orders were to abort. Still at an easy pace, he lifted the counter flap and walked into the office space behind the reception desk. Two men in shirt sleeves were on telephones at the far end of the office, their backs to him, one staring out the window into the street. Nobody nearer. Good. He hefted the briefcase in his left hand and turned smartly into the glass box of a private office with no name on the door. The door was open (the office was very warm) and it was a good deal darker in there, due, he supposed, to the wooden files that loomed all around the walls. The man was not where Mr. Jones had said he would be. Instead of sitting at his large desk in the center of the office, he was bending over a small filing cabinet at the far end of the room. He wore a cream shirt and his hair looked long but fashionably cut. Well, Mr. Jones had said he would be young.

At that moment a telephone rang in the outer office. The man who had been looking out the window walked up to the ringing instrument and picked it up and spoke into it. He looked toward Jay and the glassed-in office but did not seem to see anything, for he turned away again, still talking, and idly picked his nose.

Jay walked quickly and quietly across to the young man, put

the Beretta to the back of his head, and pressed the trigger. The body fell forward, into the gloom. There was almost no blood, as far as Jay could see. These Berettas were the job. He looked again, crouched low down, just to be sure.

He was still a long moment. Then he straightened up, put the Beretta back into the inside pocket of the Burberry, and walked out of the office, not too quickly. There was nobody in the reception area, and he passed through to the stairs. A very high fear threshold, that was what they'd told him, even for the SAS. Of course, nobody can keep it up forever. They had smiled, in their sinister SAS way. Jay took the last four steps at a jump, surprising himself, and then straightened up, breathed in deeply twice, and opened the door to the street.

The taxi was there.

He walked to it, still not hurrying, and got in.

The driver gunned the engine, which was running, and moved off. "Jesus, you were quick."

"Yes, I was." Jay put the Beretta and the glasses into the leather briefcase, locked it, and placed it back on the seat.

"How did it go?" The driver didn't look back. Jay hadn't seen his face clearly yet and never would.

"It went fine," said Jay, "except it was a woman."

"Jesus Christ," said the driver, still not looking round.

He dropped Jay quickly, at the Leicester Square tube station, and drove off before Jay could go through the fiction of paying him.

Jay got a ticket from the automatic machine and went down the escalator.

To his clinical surprise, his legs were trembling; he supposed, with anger.

The tube rattled on, half filled with lunchtime travelers, mostly shoppers. An Asian woman in a sari sat opposite. He looked at her with forced interest. Anything to get rid of the terrible anger he felt. What a balls-up, what a frigging balls-up. He concentrated on the woman opposite. Something about the way she sat, the slant of her face, reminded him of the desert women in Aden. Up in the Radfan, his first job with the SAS, fighting tribesmen egged on by the Egyptian and Yemeni terrorists; a hundred and twenty degrees in the day, below freezing at night, a war fought with Land Rovers and gelignite and bazookas and air backup. A war nobody acknowledged ever began or continued or ended. The Regiment had done well there, but they did well everywhere. Bloody efficient, the Regiment, then as now. He took a deep breath, catching his reflection in the tube window opposite. Fair hair, helped a little by the conditioner, as his haircutter called the dye, my God, the bloody Radfan was twenty years ago, building sarfans out of stones to keep the ice-cold air out at night, that was twenty bloody years ago, and what was he doing, twenty years after all that, but sitting on a tube train, presently stopping at Green Park, and feeling a cold anger that he'd just been involved in the biggest fuck-up, bar none, of his career.

Career? What was he thinking about?

It wasn't a career, and it certainly wasn't a vocation.

It was a war, an underground war, as real as this underground train. He was in it, as he was in this train. The rules of the underground war were simple. They took out one of yours, you took out one of theirs. If you thought it worthwhile, you took out one of theirs first. He never knew which was which and he never asked. Nothing like this had gone wrong before, although there had been moments. The girl in the Eastern Tours office could have been just a functionary, even British, though the high cheekbones had screamed Slav, as he crouched down and turned her face around to him, like a lover. Probably some innocent. It was no use caring, he told himself. All that had happened was that Mr. Jones had made a boo-boo, his first ever. It had been, Jay thought, a highly visible, a far too highly visible, exercise, from the very start. Walking in, walking out, for Chrissake, when had he ever walked in before?

In the German tavern, his very first job, he had walked in, yes, but that had been a very different operation. Nobody in the tavern had known him, how could they, he had been in Berlin only two hours, brought into Tempelhof by jet fighter from Northolt, and out to the beerkeller in a taxi. The man had been sitting alone, drinking lager in vast quantities, as they had told Jay he would be. An ordinary middle-aged worker, to look at, in his shiny peaked cap and shabby leather coat. As they had said he would, the man had gone, finally, to the pissoir. Jay wondered how he had lasted as long as he did without going. The man had been making water in the pissoir when he had seen Jay come in, look around and see the place was empty, and then reach into his pocket. The man had looked surprised, sliding down into the channel of flowing water, and, Jay supposed, piss. He had seen Jay, seen the weapon in his hand, but he had not reacted, his hands had stayed frozen at his fly, because, as they had told Jay years before, when you have the drop on anybody they take five whole seconds to react, in any way at all. And it did not take five seconds to press a trigger. He had turned around, walked out of the tavern, and hailed a taxi back to Tempelhof. He had been back in London two hours later.

Today had been different.

Today there had been people around, people who could describe him. The man on the telephone in the office, for instance. Jay got to his feet and found the tube door open and got out at Green Park instead of going on to Baron's Court, as he should have done, and reported in by telephone to Mr. Jones.

In Piccadilly, Jay hailed a taxi.

Mr. Jones was not pleased to hear he was at the reception desk downstairs. Nonetheless, he had Jay shown up to his office at once. The two heavies had nodded the bemedaled commissionaire back into the lift and searched Jay. They had done it very correctly. Jay had said, tight-lipped, "You didn't look in my jock-strap."

The big one said, "We will if it would give you a thrill."

"Whose order was it to search me?" Jay asked.

"Routine," said the big one, not meeting his eye.

"Somebody's worried," Jay said, going down the corridor.

They watched him go. They would dearly love, Jay thought, to kick the shit out of me.

He had opened Mr. Jones's door without knocking.

Mr. Jones was not happy.

"You really should have telephoned first, you know."

"Why?" asked Jay. "Would you be likely to be in a meeting?"

He wondered about that. Did Mr. Jones ever go to meetings? He had to, all civil servants did. What did he say, and to whom did he submit his reports? Jay did not know. Somebody high up, no doubt. Not ministerial level; all this was done a lot lower than that.

You take out one of ours, we take out one of yours.

Patriotism. That was the word.

They want to destroy us. They tried every day, everything from propaganda broadcasts to subverting old gays in the Foreign Service (there seemed to be an unending supply of them, probably because the public schools were still open) to murder most foul. That was where he and Mr. Jones came in, only this time they hadn't, had they?

"Bad show." Mr. Jones was at a loss without his tea, and he flapped his hands a few times before letting them fall into his lap. "Great pity."

"What now?" asked Jay coldly. "Do I go back and try again?"

Mr. Jones looked shocked. "Good Lord, no. They would be most enraged if we did that. They'll know it was a mistake. They'll know who we were after. Probably send him back home on the next Aeroflot flight. You did him a favor, or rather the girl did."

"Where was he?" asked Jay gratingly.

"How do I know? Taking a piss probably." The hands were still now, and Mr. Jones's voice was calm again. "I'll let them know by a roundabout way that it was a mistake. They'll see it like that, I'm sure."

The underground war, like all wars, Jay reflected, had its rules.

"Never mind all that," he said. "Was I *supposed* to get caught with that Beretta in my hand?"

The thought had been troubling him ever since he had crouched down next to the girl and seen her soft, surprised face. It was odd how they all looked surprised. He waited for Mr. Jones's reply.

"My dear boy, why should we do that?"

"I don't know, I'm just asking, that's all."

Outside, the traffic rumbled, a low murmur along Whitehall.

"Why," asked Mr. Jones, "should you ask?"

"I know some things. Maybe it's my time to go."

Mr. Jones smiled tolerantly.

"Not much. You don't know much. Really, you don't. And we'd never do that. We look after our people. Not as well as the other side, I admit. They make guarantees we can't match, they go to such lengths. I mean, they snatch people to barter, whenever they lose somebody. Lonsdale. Colonel Abel. Or they get them out. Blake. Burgess. MacLean. Philby."

"They're big important people. Spies. I'm nobody."

Mr. Jones put his fingers into a steeple and nodded, seemingly in agreement. "It was a sad mistake. Couldn't you see it was a girl?"

"It was dark in there. She had her back to me. Do you think I should have asked her to dance first?"

Mr. Jones smiled, but the eyes remained level.

"Why don't you collect your car and go home?" he said. "I'm never sure how safe vehicles are in London, even in the Whitehall lot. I had my car broken into last month. Just a vandal. Young black. We traced him, of course." Mr. Jones smiled thinly; he had enjoyed that. "One very scared young black boy, I have to tell you, but it was nothing, just a boy, thieving. The country's in a mess, when you can't leave your car overnight in Horse Guards. Young bastard took the hubcaps, too."

Jay said, "What's the next move? Do I get my money or what?"

Mr. Jones looked genuinely surprised. "Well, of course you do. A bargain is a bargain. But I wonder if you'd care to leave everything with me, I'll push the dirt under the carpet, I'm used to doing it, but just in case somebody did see you—as you say, it was a mite *open*, as a job—then I wish you'd go home and stay indoors with your lovely lady, until I call you, what?"

Jay stood up. "Just so long as my money is all right."

But of course it wasn't just the money.

It was the war, the underground war.

He'd once half told the old man some of the things that happened, not mentioning himself, of course, and his father had grunted, "I'm bloody glad to hear it."

Jay walked to the door. "You'll be in touch, then?"

"But of course," said Mr. Jones, smiling and bobbing his head.

As Jay left he could hear Mr. Jones muttering into a telephone, but his voice was too low to make out the words.

He walked to the lift under the disapproving eyes of the two heavies.

Jay did not go back to the flat. He drove his five-year-old Jensen carefully—he was still shaking a little (whether from fright or rage he didn't know and didn't care)—toward Holborn, and parked it in a garage behind Tottenham Court Road. He walked to the Museum Tavern, his favorite pub in all London, and was just in time to catch it before it closed, to the astonishment of the few American tourists present, at three o'clock on the dot. He drank two large whiskies without feeling the effects of either, and left with a tip from Joe, a regular researcher at the British Museum, opposite. Wellbeloved, with Steve up, in the four-thirty at Lingfield. He put a fiver on it at Barney's, the little Irish bookie's around the corner, and slowly walked the extra hundred yards to his office.

Some office. It was an accommodation address, plus telephone answering service, plus a conference room, if there was one empty. Usually there was. Jay wondered what the other clients did. His arrangement was a cover, or rather had become one. It had not started out like that. He had taken the place in hope and faith, four years before, when he was still married to Cherry, just after he came out of the army and the world was new. In association with a chemist friend he had taken out a patent on a special kind of marine paint, virtually unrottable in seawater. None of the international paint manufacturers wanted to know about it. They were in the business of selling paint that did rot, fairly often. His chemist friend had dropped out, or rather Jay had bought him out, after two years, for peanuts. He was now working for one of the said international paint manufacturers and Jay had kept the fairly useless patent, plus tons of the actual stuff, stored in a warehouse south of the river. All that was left was the various blocks of stationery, in his private cabinet, along with the bottle of Teacher's he now opened. The odd thing was, they'd had a good first year, while their product was a novelty, but repeat orders had been slow in coming. The smaller Japanese and American firms were forever showing interest, but nothing more. Still, the company gave Jay a good cover, as a businessman traveling abroad, anytime he needed it.

Jay poured himself a large scotch and drank it in one gulp, then drank another, more slowly, while he brooded over the mail that had arrived. Yet more letters from Tokyo claiming ongoing interest (who said the Japanese were good businessmen, they were terrible businessmen, they had more bureaucracy than Stalin), and one from Belfast that he did not understand, but that seemed genuine, asking for samples of the paint. It was from a small boat-repairing firm and the letterhead looked genuine. He scribbled out a note to the warehouse to send the samples. This service was included with the warehousing. He wondered what else lay in that vast service warehouse south of the river. Guns for the IRA, probably. Or condoms for the Republic. Anyway, it would be nice to make a decent sale. There weren't many these days. Ordinarily, he would have wound up the company years ago. Now it was invaluable, to cover his income from abroad. As Mr. Jones had said, his eyes for once twinkling, he could hardly do the job for the country that he was doing if he had to clock in every morning in some office or other.

Anyway, what job could he get?

In the army since he was twenty.

In the SAS for three years, the maximum for an officer.

Then, Civvy Street and Cherry wanting the lot, and he, like a bloody fool, giving it to her. Cottage, swimming pool, everything she asked for, because weren't they going to be rich from the marine-paint scheme into which, like a bigger fool, he had sunk his army handshake money?

They had not gotten rich. They had gotten poor.

They had also gotten angry, at each other.

Then Cherry had gone, with his children and his furniture and everything that he had, to the other man, a decent guy as far as he went, some kind of a city gent, bags of money, just what Cherry needed. Jay had sold the house, which, with the mortgage hardly started, hadn't come to much, given half to Cherry, and moved, with one suitcase, into the Hammersmith flat.

Jay took another swallow of scotch. It wasn't having any more effect than the whisky in the Museum Tavern. He recognized the danger signs, but ignored them. What if it had been the booze that had finally driven Cherry away, her face flushed with indignation? "Stop shouting at me, you're always shouting! It's all you ever do! What the bloody hell is the matter with you? You never used to be like this!"

She had been right. He hadn't.

By that time he'd started working for Mr. Jones.

He could not tell her that.

So he could not tell her what the matter was.

End of story.

Jay pressed the button on his desk and after a moment Vi,

who doubled as switchboard operator and secretary, came in. She was a bright and pleasant girl of twenty. Cockney, uninhibited, and very efficient. He gave her the draft letters, one to the Belfast firm acknowledging its letter and promising samples, and the other to the warehouse to send the stuff. Vi all too obviously noted the rapidly diminishing level of the whisky. Like all Cockney girls, she had a well-developed maternal instinct, which was another way, Jay thought, of saying she was bossy, in a strictly working-class, female way. Her deep cleavage and short black skirt meant nothing, except, he supposed, to Ron, her boyfriend. Certainly not to him. Vi said, "Hey, you're hitting it a bit hard today."

"One of those days, Vi."

"Business no good, then?"

Vi had quite a turnover of clients. She must wonder how I keep going sometimes, he thought. If she only knew the times I've sat here, like this, just boozing and telephoning the bookie. Except that she probably did. He liked Vi. She was honest. It was, after Cherry, a quality he found he liked most in a woman.

"Well, it's not exactly thriving, but we are getting a few inquiries and some repeat orders. I'm not broke yet."

"No?" She didn't sound convinced. He must invent a few more orders, to look right. No point in anybody getting suspicious. "The Swiss keep us going." His Swiss money supposedly came from a business concern, for "industrial consultancy services." Mr. Jones arranged it; Jay had never asked how. It simply came, as a monthly check, deducted from his total in Zurich.

Vi looked pointedly at the glass. "Not driving home in the rush hour, are we?"

"Just got to make one telephone call. Then I'll be off. I'll be back in the flat for the TV news."

He wondered how the incident at Eastern Tours would be explained away.

"How's Ron?" he asked, to change the subject.

"He won't get married, he says. Well, not yet. My mum says I'm stupid, why should he, when he's gettin' what he wants as it is?" She collected the letters moodily, stood up. "It's a problem, innit? Maybe women's lib's no good. I mean, I work, but he doesn't bother his bottom, he's still doing a bit of moonlighting, toshin' an' that." Jay knew she meant wallpapering people's homes for cash, no VAT or receipts. Vi was truly a Cockney, she simply didn't *see* middle-class people like him, although she worked with them every day. "I'll type these up now, then you can sign them and I'll post them for you."

"Thanks, Vi." Jay nodded and she left, waggling her bottom because he was a man, but it meant nothing. Jay looked at his watch, reached for the telephone, and rang Barney, the bookie. The tip had run second in a field of ten. Nothing to come. He put the telephone down and poured himself another slug of scotch, and waited for the tremors to go.

They did not go, but they almost did and that would have to do. Vi came back with the letters, and frowned disapprovingly at the even lower level of whisky in the bottle. He signed the letters and she took them into the outer office. He looked at his watch. Almost four-thirty. Time to go. The rush hour started earlier than ever these days. He didn't want to be caught in a traffic jam at Hyde Park Corner. If he went now he would miss it.

Jay bought a *Standard* from the news vendor at the corner of the street and looked through it, very carefully once he got into his car.

There was no mention whatever of the incident.

The BBC six-o'clock news had nothing either.

Jay sat in front of the flickering TV program, as usual presented partly by women. Their piping voices irritated him.

He belonged to the last generation of *men*, as Angie was forever (with a laugh) reminding him. He had never changed a diaper in his life, and he could not understand how any man could want to be present at the birth of a child. Angie had said she didn't care, he could stay away, even go away, she'd be glad of the chance. As usual with her, it had sounded like a joke, but wasn't.

Jay took another pull at his scotch—he'd started as soon as he came into the flat. Mr. Jones had probably got on to the other side and apologized and they had acted quickly, possibly spirited the body away, to surface it later as a road accident or something.

The effort of thinking must have activated the alcohol, because he began to sweat. He realized he'd eaten nothing all day, and made himself a cheese sandwich, leaving crumbs all over the kitchen table. He took two bites, and poured himself another scotch. He must have had most of a bottle by now. No wonder he was getting bleary.

This, he thought, is the way it went with Cherry.

Things got on top of me, I got pissed, oftener and oftener, and then I fought with her. The rows got worse and worse.

Finally, she got too hurt to bear it anymore and she got out.

I don't want the same thing to happen with Angie, do I? he spelled out to himself. She deserves better than that.

Just the same, this is how it was, I was like this, like I am now, this minute, in this room.

I thought I'd licked it but, seemingly, I haven't.

Of course, after a balls-up like today, anybody could be excused, right?

The telephone rang.

It was Mr. Jones.

"There's nothing in the paper or on the TV," Jay said, in reply to Mr. Jones's "How are you, dear boy?"

Mr. Jones hesitated. He had probably noticed the slur in Jay's voice. Probably? Bloody *had*, no danger. He said, "No, and let us hope there won't be. I was just checking, to see you are all right."

Jay was annoyed. He tried to keep his voice level, and thought he succeeded. "What made you think I wouldn't be?"

Again, Mr. Jones hesitated. "No reason, dear boy, no particular reason. If there's any further news I'll be in touch. Quite possibly, soon. Take care."

The dialing tone.

He always did that.

It always made Jay furious.

"Bloody old public-school fart!" he shouted at the dead instrument.

He was public-school himself but at least he had been expelled.

"Hello, darling, who was that, a customer who doesn't like your paint?"

Angie. He hadn't heard her come in. He hoped he hadn't sounded too pissed.

"Hi. You're early."

"Got fed up, sitting in the Acton Hilton and listening to directors and actors talking about themselves. Very boring."

The Acton Hilton was the BBC's studio and rehearsal building.

Angie looked around the room. "The place was tidy when I left this morning." She picked up his old Burberry. "Did you need this today?"

"It was a bit chilly," said Jay, who rarely wore any coat, even in the coldest weather. "Here, give it to me."

"It has money in it?" She handed the Burberry to him incuriously. Lovely girl, he thought, never asked too many questions.

Then she did. "Why the suit?"

"Business lunch."

"You never said." She smiled quickly, followed by a little worried frown; she'd seen how drunk he was. "Was it a good lunch?"

"Some people from Belfast. Very interested in the product."

"Oh, good." She moved away from the subject. He plainly hadn't sold anything, and she was a girl who was highly sensitive to tender male egos; she wouldn't have lasted ten minutes as a makeup girl if she hadn't been. "Go somewhere nice?"

He stared at her blearily.

"For lunch?"

"Oh, not bad. Soho. Some new place."

Why did he say Soho? In case somebody had seen him? He was beginning to be careful with her, as he'd begun to be careful with Cherry, before the end. He added harshly, "Does it matter?"

Angie flushed, as if he'd sworn at her.

"Sorry. Just interested in what you do, I'm silly that way, as you know. Look, I've got soup, homemade. You'll have a bowl on your knee in five minutes and then I'll tell you about my day and you'll be bored out of your *mind.*"

Angie picked up his jacket, put it and the Burberry over her arm, and went into the bedroom. He almost snatched it back from her, and then he remembered that it was safe, clean, there was nothing in the pockets, nothing at all, but of course, *that* was unsafe, and he suddenly followed her and grabbed the raincoat and the jacket from her and hung them at the back of his closet.

Jay reasoned that Angie would have been sure to notice there was nothing in the pockets. Possibly she'd noticed already? But her face was calm and composed. She was used to tantrums from her actors, when eyeshadow or a wig looked wrong.

"We are getting tidy, aren't we?"

"Get the soup, woman, or better still, give me a kiss."

They kissed, a long one, and he relaxed, a little.

She said, "That was nice."

He reached for her, but she broke away and was gone into the kitchen, calling over her shoulder, "Food first. Sit down and take your shoes off. Soup won't be a minute."

The soup was rich and warm and he took it slowly and chomped whole-meal bread. Angie was an artist with food and never ate junk, which he loved. He made an excuse that he wanted to watch *Panorama* and then the awful *Play for Today*, another diatribe by a writer new to television (or anywhere else probably) who churned out a chronicle of the tribulations of a one-parent lesbian family—and fell asleep, his head on Angie's shoulder.

The telephone wakened him at midnight.

It was Mr. Jones again.

He was alone on the sofa. Angie had put a blanket over him and gone to bed, leaving a note: "Filming at six tomorrow. Must get my rest."

He said to Mr. Jones, keeping his voice low, his head beginning to hurt, "Don't you ever go to bed?" It was extremely rare for Mr. Jones to call as late as this, when he must have known Angie was in the flat.

Mr. Jones did not laugh. He said, as if it were noon, "I have an appointment fixed for you. It's tomorrow."

"Where?"

"The SAS, actually. You are not to be offended. It's all-expenses-paid. Look upon it as a refresher. That's what it is, really. And although I don't want to say too much on the telephone, there'll be an excellent payday at the end of it, if you are game."

Jay thought: that's a bloody lie, for one thing. He said, "You're blaming me, aren't you? For the balls-up?"

"Not at all, dear boy, but please be there tomorrow, by four. They're expecting you. You'll meet lots of old friends. And I'll be in constant touch. Also, if you agree to go, my superiors might see their way to putting a little extra in the kitty, as it were, if you follow?" He paused. "Or else they might take another view, you see?"

Jay felt the anger and frustration and booze all mixing in his head. "Listen, that money's mine. I earned it."

"Nobody said you didn't. Please do be there tomorrow."

"You're still blaming me, you creep!"

But Mr. Jones simply replied, "Take care, dear boy," and the line went dead.

T·W·O

JAY SPENT THE three-hour drive to Hereford silently cursing Mr. Jones. The cunning old devil did not exactly have the power to make him go on the bloody SAS course, did he? Of course he didn't.

The fact remained, Jay was bloody well going, wasn't he? He could have told Mr. Jones to bugger off. Of course he could. That way, he would have put himself beyond the pale, and Mr. Jones would probably never send for him again. But wasn't that what he really wanted, to get out of Mr. Jones's game once and for all? Of course it was. The trouble was he hadn't enough money yet, in his Zurich account. Simple as that.

So here he was, going to take part in God knew what kind of pantomime, all to the greater glory of Mr. Bloody Jones, to sharpen him up, for what? Who could guess? Jay had last been at Hereford as a young subaltern, tongue hanging out at the very idea of getting into the SAS. This time it was very different. He was sixteen years older, for one thing.

Jay slowed his speed to a legal seventy (the last thing he wanted was another ticket for speeding) and tried to remember why he'd wanted to join the SAS so much in the first place.

Because he was a silly young sod?

No doubt he had been. But that wasn't all. The SAS was like sex. You loved or you just liked it. But why, he asked himself, turning the Jensen off the highway onto the secondary road from Hereford, what was so special about the SAS?

That one was easy.

The Special Air Service was, quite simply, the best there was.

The SAS was the pride of the British Army and the envy of every army in the world, copied (but not *quite,* Jay thought dryly) by everybody, even the Israelis. Every SAS trooper was the survivor of the hardest physical and spiritual examination to be found in the long history of war or preparation for war. Born in the Western Desert, during the Second World War, out of the old Long Range Desert Group, operating behind enemy lines, its men disguised as Arabs and sometimes even Germans, the SAS had become the aristocrat of covert operations. SAS men had fought in all of Great Britain's small wars since then. They'd been hand-to-hand against the terrorists in Malaya, the only Asian country to successfully resist an armed Communist takeover. They'd been in the Radfan, fighting the Yemeni terrorists in the desert. They'd lain in wait in the soft bogs of County Armagh, for the boyos to come over, and killed them when they did. They'd been at almost every hijacked airliner in Europe. Even the French, who were sure they could do everything military better than anybody else, consulted the SAS when they had terrorist trouble. When the IRA men holed up in Balcombe Street in London, cheerfully defying the armed London bobbies outside, heard on their radio that the SAS had been called in, they gave up at once, although they still held two hostages. In the Regiment, that had been held to be a very good moment indeed. In the Falklands, the SAS's exploits had been legendary. Some of the things the SAS had done there had not come out yet and might never come out. Like the way they burned a whole squadron of Super Etendards and their deadly Exocet missiles on the ground, and escaped alive.

To just be one of the happy band of brothers again for a few days, that would be an honor and a privilege, Jay thought, cursing himself for a sentimental fool, but knowing that was why he was really here, to do something honorable once again, something he could point to with pride.

Jay turned the Jensen into the SAS HQ, hidden in the suburban housing development. The military policeman checked his papers and waved him in. The place seemed, at that moment, in the very last rays of the sun, curiously domestic and safe, like the headquarters of a line regiment, with most of the troops on overseas duty.

Jay knew that meant nothing.

After all, he had been here before.

"Of course, I was told to expect you." The adjutant was young for an adj, about twenty-seven, Jay thought, but then he would be, here. "You're a reservist, I see, one of our backup people." He smiled, dark and smart, and slightly sinister, as everybody was here, with no badges of rank showing anywhere, just an army sweater and slacks. "They asked if you could be given a run, and the easiest thing seemed to be to put you on a selection course." He smiled politely. "Obviously, you've done that before, but since this is only a kind of refresher for you and not the sort of thing we normally do, well, it's all we have to offer, I'm afraid. Would you like tea or something?"

"No thanks," said Jay. Tea. Even the SAS offered you tea. The whole bloody country ran on the stuff. The adj knew he'd done the course once before, at least that was something. A somewhat unusual order had come from On High and that was all. His not to reason why, and all that. Jay hoped the aspirin would continue to work its will. He had wakened that morning with one bastard of a hangover. His eyelids had been trying to close all the way to Hereford.

The adj closed the slim file on his desk. The SAS did almost no paperwork. Nothing in there, Jay knew, would tell the adj anything other than his previous SAS experience, which was the usual three years secondment away from his line regiment.

"I see you've passed the old forty mark. A bit over the top for all this, but I imagine you keep pretty fit."

It wasn't a question. If you weren't amazingly fit you wouldn't last five minutes here. Jay knew that, so he just smiled and said, "Well, I jog a bit."

The young adj laughed at that typical piece of army understatement. He looked very fit himself, but Jay wondered if he would ever be able to do the things he himself had done. Probably not, few could, even fewer would ever be asked, and although the SAS had thrown away the old maxim that the English didn't like war and therefore they turned it into a sport, there was probably a line most of their people would draw somewhere, quite possibly well to the right side of Mr. Jones and his underground war. On the other hand, perhaps not. It was a long time since he'd been at

Hereford, and perhaps things had changed. Some odd stories, hardly any of them cricket, had come out of the Falklands. The barrack room full of Argentinean commandos who had awakened one freezing morning on South Georgia to find *every other man* with his throat neatly cut and the lone sentry dead in the snow, same way, outside, had been nothing like cricket at all. The Argentinean commandos, who were not, after all, your average peons, had promptly and sensibly held up their hands to the British paras as soon as they stepped onto the snow. It was said a team of four had done that, if it was true. Nobody ever knew if anything was true, about the SAS. That was its power. Even when you were in it you were inclined to know sod-all.

Just the same, that had been war.

What he and Mr. Jones did was something different, something way out.

Certainly, nobody here at Hereford would know anything about it, or want to. He was simply an odd bod who, for some curious reason, was being put through the hoop. Still, the adj seemed slightly curious. He looked at Jay's sweater and cords and the incipient belly the sweater's contours showed and grinned suddenly. "Don't know if I'll be up to it when I'm forty. Hope so, but doubt it. Still, the boss is more than that, and he's pretty fit." The boss was the commanding officer and got the only sirs ever handed out in this place. Everything was done to make you forget you'd ever been in the infantry or signals or wherever you came from. Here, all that mattered was time. *Don't be late* was really the motto of the SAS. Even the war memorial to the glorious dead, across the barrack square, had a clock on it, to remind everybody still walking about that if you were late, you were dead. Or RTU—returned to unit—which something like ninety percent of the hopefuls were. Be late at a meeting point *once*, and you were out. Jay wondered if they would send him home if he balled up, but decided probably not, unless he was a direct nuisance to anybody else. Not that that mattered, either. A lot of aspirants perished of exposure on the Beacons and nobody ever knew anything about it, certainly not the media. It was a dangerous place to be, and Jay wondered, through the haze of his hangover, what lay behind the decision to send him here, and what lay ahead, if anything.

Doubtless it would be revealed unto him, sooner or later.

The young adj said, "Do you fancy a drink in the mess, or will you turn in?"

It was, after all, eleven o'clock at night.

The adj had not expressed any surprise that his arrival time had been changed. Mr. Jones had telephoned or got somebody else to telephone. Jay had said, "Tell Mr. Jones I'm going to be late. Tell him I won't be there until this evening. Late this evening." If Mr. Jones was going to piss him about, then he was going to piss Mr. Jones about.

Now here he was, refusing the adj's offered drink. "I think I'll turn in. See you in the morning."

The adj nodded and smiled and called for a runner. A man appeared through the door on soft soles, silently.

The adj said, "Take this officer across to his billet. It's room thirty-six."

The soldier, who showed no rank either but had regular infantry stamped all over him (at least to Jay, who had served in an infantry regiment), held open the door. Jay said to the adj, "Well, see you tomorrow then."

The adj smiled the wan small smile and replied, "Of course. Sleep well."

Jay knew better than to start a conversation with the soldier as he carried his small bag across the ground toward the quarters. However, he could not resist a comment. "My God, it's like the Hilton compared to the last time I was here." It had been Nissen huts then, and primitive ablutions, and, he remembered, people used to get quite tanked on days off. Now, he'd heard, nobody did, ever. It was all too serious for that, the world having changed the way it had.

The soldier grinned and showed two side teeth missing in the gray, shaved army face. "That must have been a long time ago." Probably a sergeant, Jay thought, he had left out the sir, so possibly an instructor, possibly *his* instructor, or one of them, taking a fast look at him. Nothing here was what it seemed. He began, very slightly, to tune his perceptions up a notch. This promised to be a rough ride, bloody rough.

"It's pansy soldiering now, by the look of it," he said deliberately, as they walked into the building, which was brand-new, or looked it, and very modern, with plastic floors and freshly painted banisters and walls. The War House had obviously decided the SAS deserved it, after Queen's Gate and the Falklands.

"Not exactly," said the soldier, stopping outside room 36 and handing Jay the key.

"No, I don't suppose so," said Jay, turning to open the door. "I'll say good night, then—"

The corridor was empty.

Jay switched the light on. It was a neat little room, narrow, with an army-issue cot and a chair and a dressing table. A camouflage-type uniform hung on a hanger behind the door, and a pair of boots stood, like sentries, alongside the bed. A Kalashnikov rifle lay on the chair, unloaded, genuine or a copy, he couldn't tell which, everybody was copying them these days (including the Czechs, who then sold them to the IRA) because they were so good. Ammunition was stacked next to the weapon. Jay checked that first. It was all right, and it was, of course, live. Everything was, here. It was the real thing or forget it. Jay extracted from his bag, and threw on the dressing table, an old woolly hat. Nobody wore regimental headgear or army-issue pisspots here. It could get wet and windy where they would, sooner or later, be going. Over the camouflage uniform, behind the door, was slung a webbing belt containing pouches with extra ammo for the Kalashnikov and emergency rations, which included some Coca-Cola-like cans, of a kind he hadn't seen before. He put them all back where he found them and took from his bag a set of thermal underwear, including long johns, he'd bought at Harrods on his way out of London. These he laid nearby on a chair. He stuffed two thick pairs of woolen socks into the webbing pouches, which were pretty full as it was, and took off his sweater and slacks and got into bed in his shorts.

He lit a cigarette, inhaled, and lay back on the pillow, his hands behind his head. Here he was, all tucked up like a nice little boy on his first day at school. What a load of bloody nonsense it was. More like his first day in the punishment block for being a naughty little boy. Jones had obviously decided that the official version was to be that *he* had boobed, most certainly not Mr. Jones. He'd once seen a cartoon, pinned on an office wall, with the caption "Assistant Heads Must Roll." Plainly, he was an assistant head, and Mr. Jones was in the clear. He still could not believe he had agreed to all this bullshit, coming back here after all this time. He should have taken the next plane to Zurich and drawn his money out and then told Mr. Jones to get stuffed.

Jay drew on his cigarette and sighed. There was nothing like enough money, that was the trouble. The underground war should pay its participants high, but it did not. He wondered if there was a standard UK rate. Probably, and lower than anybody else's, he'd wager, in tune with the times. Probably the CIA paid a lot more, and they did more of it. The Israelis, in their underground war against the PLO, probably paid Israeli Army pay and nothing else. The Russians, who had a hit squad in every embassy in every big city in the Western world, probably did the same but gave their guys accounts at Marks and Spencer or Saks Fifth Avenue as a bonus.

The thing to remember: We had to do it to them, if and when they did it to us. It was that or, as the American general at NATO had said, roll over and play dead. Jay had no doubt whatever how he felt about that. He considered all left-wing peace campaigners to be wimps and uncomprehending tools of Soviet expansion. Some of them all too comprehending, in fact. They would not know the time of day until some Soviet conscript hit them in the teeth with his rifle butt.

The thing to remember: He didn't do the job just for the money.

Not even for the power, as he suspected Mr. Jones did.

He had no power. He was a pawn, but they couldn't do without him. He was a patriot, more of a patriot, even, than his bemedaled old dad, because there were no mentions in any dispatches for the combatants in the underground war. Jay reached out to his slacks and took from the hip pocket his very slim silver flask, property of his grandfather, who had been a soldier too, and finished off the contents in a long, slow swallow: Help him to sleep, and he'd get no chance to put it to better use. He remembered the first time he'd come to this place and how eager he had been to show them he was made of the right stuff. What an innocent idiot he had been, but then you were, with Sandhurst and the line regiment your only experience.

It had been a rude awakening here, but then it was for everybody.

In those days, nine people out of ten had been returned to unit. Obviously, none of that had changed, and the other three guys in his team (it would be a unit of four, in SAS it always was) would be trying to do what he'd been trying to do, all those years ago: get into the Regiment.

He'd got in, and very proud he'd been. Of course, he'd come well recommended. Two courts of inquiry, exonerated both times. Not many lieutenants in a line regiment could boast that, for God's sake. His father had been astonished he got through them. "Par for the bloody course, again." He had been expelled from school, and he had joined the army as a private soldier and taken a commission through the ranks. No need for it, the old man had grunted, just showing off, that's all. He had come to the notice of the SAS after the second court, because that had made most fuss. It wasn't every day a second looey in a line regiment broke the neck of a great hairy paratrooper with a karate chop. The bloody fool had startled him, suddenly appearing like that, and behind him to boot, brandishing a bloody rifle as if he meant to use it as a club. What was he expected to do but react like a soldier, which he had.

The chairman of the court, an old bemedaled half-colonel, who reminded him of the old man, had seemed bewildered at the use of the karate chop. As Jay told his brother officers, who thought his whole behavior a rather bad show, the old half-colonel would probably have preferred a straight left. That, on top of the previous court, which involved the untimely death of a machete-brandishing idiot in Guyana he'd taken out with a single revolver shot (the raving lunatic was only trying to take his head off, that was all!), had been too much, even for his long-suffering CO, who had, Jay was in no doubt, stirred up the interest of the SAS. His CO had then suggested to Jay that he apply for the statutory three-year officers' course. No officer stayed longer than that, at SAS. Only the regulars, some of whom seemed to stay forever and were privates, corporals, or NCOs in their own regiments but just SAS troopers here, stayed on and formed the backbone of the various specialist units. The officers came and went and under emergency conditions *never* went in first. In direct contrast to the Israelis, who in consequence had a very large casualty list of officers.

The SAS believed in experience first, and only the regular teams had it.

Also, in the SAS, it was not thought clever to get yourself killed.

Your whole training was to do it to the other fellow.

Jay put out his cigarette and felt a sudden shiver of apprehension. He shouldn't be here, for Christ's sake.

Or maybe he should?

Maybe he should have seen that the figure in the gloomy office at Eastern Tours was a girl. A couple of years ago, he would have. Which, supposedly, was why he was here. To sharpen him up.

The point was, was he up to it? Could he cope with the stress and speed of it all? It might be an idea to fail deliberately, but the idea didn't appeal to him. Pride or something. Anyway, he'd told Angie he'd be away a week. He'd said a sudden call-up of a section of the Territorial Reserve, and she had accepted it, albeit with a little surprise, as he hadn't mentioned the possibility before. She'd been rushed, listening to him on a telephone at the film-location hotel, and had simply wished him well, and see him soon. Thank God for that girl and her lack of questions. He'd get the paranoia and booze out of his system, if nothing else, here.

For now, better get some shut-eye.

Jay turned over, closed his eyes, and slept at once.

The telephone roused him two hours later.

Groping for it in the darkness, he just about heard, through a haze of sleep, but with every nerve jangling, the crisp words, "Outside, in your kit and with your weapon, at the lorries, in four minutes."

The telephone went dead. He looked at his watch and swore.

He got out of bed and put on the thermal underwear and the camouflage kit and the boots and the woolly hat and grabbed the Kalashnikov and raced out, slamming the door behind him. All over the building he could hear other men doing the same, but no real noise, because everybody wore soft-soled climbing boots and nobody swore or shouted, as they would in any similar army situation. This crowd had plainly arrived at Hereford knowing something. His extra knowledge, he hoped, might save him.

He was at the lorries, running flat-out all the way, in three minutes forty-seven seconds flat.

* * *

The three-tonners rumbled through the dark and rainy night toward the Brecon Beacons. The Beacons, hilly, bare, and inhospitable, were the SAS playground. Jay thought he recognized the bleak, bumpy roads and double ruts, even in the dark. He sat and looked at his three comrades. One was an oldish—well, thirty-five—signals sergeant, here to get into the signals section of SAS. The second was a frail-looking Glaswegian slum rat of about twenty, who'd done two tours in Northern Ireland and had to be tougher than he looked. The last was a young lieutenant from the Northumberland Fusiliers, who, astonishingly, had a slight Tyneside accent. In Jay's day most officers had the statutory standard voice, or they faked it. This young man—Jay placed him at around twenty-two—was slim and fit-looking and probably a sportsman. Good, quick reflexes, and an air of expectancy and confidence. Nonetheless, Jay thought him likely to be the weak sister of the quartet, he couldn't really have said why. Time would tell, anyway.

The three-tonner bounced its way along the high hill road. They would soon be there, if he was right. Nobody talked; they had exchanged the few vital facts about themselves, in a whisper, when they left the Hereford barracks and wound their way through the housing development in which the barracks was incongruously set. Then they had fallen silent, allowing their nerves to recover from the shock of being wakened at such an ungodly hour. Jay, alone of them, had not been surprised. One of the watchwords of SAS was surprise. Like, always try the back door first.

It had been taught to him good by his first SAS instructor, a seasoned old Jock, no doubt now pensioned off, by the name of Nair. Jay looked at the others. Each aspirant had an orange canvas bib hooked over his camouflage uniform, with a number on it. Jay's number was 13. He had made no comment when it was handed out to him. He had thought: special treatment, then? But he had shown nothing.

Maybe, he reasoned, it was because he'd been here before, and they knew it. Maybe and maybe not. With them you never knew. He glanced at his watch. Two hours, forty minutes. They had to be somewhere in the Beacons by now.

The signals sergeant whispered, "Where are we?"

Nobody answered.

There was no point in telling him. He could say, "The Beacons," but if the silly sod hadn't found out where SAS trained before he came, then he was a prime favorite for RTU at any time, probably soon. He began to wonder if he did not have two weak sisters in his group.

The Jock said suddenly, "Wherever we are we're gonny get pissed on when we get oota this truck." The rain sheeted down on the canvas to underline his words. "It's the cowin' Brecon Beacons, it's like Salisbury Plain, only it's more bare-arsed. It makes the Plain look like Torquay."

"When did you go to Torquay?" Jay asked, surprised.

"One summer," said the Jock. "I was working in the kitchen of the Imperial Hotel. That's when I decided to join this mob." He spat a load of what Jay realized was tobacco juice over the tailboard of the three-tonner, toward the jeep that closely followed, holding officers and instructors.

"It used to be chefs, noo it's officers," said the Jock. "Prima fuckin' donnas."

We have one here who is going to be all right, thought Jay, if nobody else is.

The three-tonner stopped. The rain sheeted down.

"Everybody out of this vehicle," whispered a voice in the darkness. Somehow that voice was familiar to Jay. Nobody in the SAS ever issued an order in an ordinary army voice. This one was Scottish and he was not surprised to see, when he climbed out, that it belonged to Company Sergeant-Major Nair, who had been his instructor at Hereford all those years before.

This struck him as a coincidence, and Jay did not believe in coincidences.

"Hello, Mr. Nair," he said. "I thought you'd be at home in Rothesay counting your grandchildren."

Nair's seamed and craggy face, which looked as if it had been cut by a thousand bloodless razors, peered at him in the darkness. "So we've come back for more, have we? Well, well, well."

Good try, Jay thought, but you were not surprised enough. He began to feel a little afraid and more than a little angry.

Nair said, "Well, on your bikes, you know the drill!" He handed Jay a piece of lavatory paper with a map drawn on it. "Follow that. Be at your rendezvous point at oh-nineteen-thirty hours on the dot." He smiled, a terrible sight, consisting of a full set of National Health teeth fit to rival those of Mr. Jones. "And ye eat the shit paper right after ye've read it."

"Why, has it been used?" Jay asked.

"I'll stay and watch," said Nair. "Ye have one minute to digest the information."

The other three men crowded around Jay as he read the map by flashlight. It showed no land contours. There was a hill to climb. There was a stream to follow, due east. There was a long stone wall to hang on to and leave when it petered out. There was a plantation of firs to find, due north of the wall. There was no scale of distance. He glanced at his watch. Four hours to do it in probably meant hard yomping. That was all.

"Time's up," said Nair. "Chew it, man."

Jay rolled the toilet paper into a ball and swallowed it.

Nair smiled the terrible smile once more. "Don't be late, or you're returned to unit."

"Wouldn't mind fuckin' goin' back noo," said the young Jock.

"Where are ye from, laddie?" asked Nair, with interest.

"Glesga," said the Jock.

Nair let out a long, slow approving breath. Jay wondered how old he was.

Jay said, "All right, let's move."

Nair waved, the truck moved, the convoy moved.

They stood in the dark at the side of the road and watched it go.

"Did anybody remember anything about that fuckin' map?" said the Jock. "Because I didny."

"I have it all, if nobody wants to argue?" said Jay. He waited. Nobody spoke.

"It's all yours, Major," said the Jock.

"Captain, actually," said Jay in a posh voice, and they all sniggered. "All right," he added, "I think it's this way, straight on up this hillside."

"It would be," said the Jock, but he was the first to the top, sleeting rain or no. That took them almost an hour.

Jay stood with them, looking into the cloudy night. He felt, momentarily, exhilarated. He also felt so exhausted that he might die at any moment from the sheer pain and stress of it all. He took in deep breaths, looking upward for the North Star. There it was.

He looked east for the stream. He couldn't see it. He moved ahead of the others. "The stream was marked as being on top of the hill, but it won't be. It'll be some way down. By the North Star, I reckon we go east, this way."

"You're the boss," said the Jock.

They found the stream thirty-five minutes later, much lower down the other side of the hill than he'd expected it to be. The map, deliberately, had shown no contours.

The water was ice-cold, but they drank some. Their water bottles were full, but they had a raging thirst despite the cold. The stream was about four feet deep, and fast-flowing.

"We have to ford it," Jay said. "We are going to be wet everywhere from now on."

"The crummy sods," said the Jock. He slipped, grimacing, into the icy stream. "It's lovely once you're in."

Silently, holding their weapons above their heads, they forded the stream, waterlogged and frozen.

I'll either die, Jay thought, or I'll survive.

Before them, the night stretched, implacable, and a keen, biting wind numbed their faces.

"I've never volunteered for anything in ma life," said the Jock. "D'ye think I mebbe made a mistake this time?"

"Keep the noise down," said Jay. "They could have people posted. You never know."

They struggled on, over the rough, boggy terrain, into the darkness.

Jay popped his second benny after an hour of yomping. The efficacy of the first one, which he'd taken surreptitiously, as soon as he knew for sure it was an exercise and not just a stunt to keep everybody sharpened up, was beginning to wear off. He hadn't needed the stuff sitting in the three-tonner, but he wasn't to know they'd drive right into the heart of the Beacons, way past Senny-bridge. The new pill soon took effect, and his legs, which had gone leaden on him, felt suddenly lighter. The others, being younger, seemed to be bearing up well. If I have to keep this pace going for three or four days, I'll be chock full of Benzedrine before the end of it, he thought. He did not allow it to worry him. Everybody was on something, or had been in his day. The thing was to pop it at the proper rate, so you didn't get manic and shoot somebody's foot off. The powers that be didn't seem to know or care if you were on something. He supposed that people were showing willingness by taking the stuff, as far as the powers were concerned. Certainly, in the various actions he'd performed with the SAS, they'd had no sleep, and the only way to do without sleep was to take the bennies. He'd made sure he had a supply in his pocket when he left London.

"Where are we, sir, any idea?" asked the Jock.

Jay grinned wryly. At least somebody realized he had leadership qualities.

He squinted at the stars through the scudding cloud. The rain had stopped, but since they were all wet through, it made no difference to how they felt. "We're on course," Jay said. "At the end of this wall, we turn east, which is that way." He pointed hopefully in what he was fairly sure was the right direction. He'd seen the North Star clear enough, and it was the one to go by. "We should be all right."

The old signals sergeant (who was probably ten years younger than Jay was) said, "Do we have to keep up this speed? We'll kill our fucking selves."

"We do," Jay replied. "They expect it."

"I tclt ye," whispered the Jock. "Never volunteer."

The young lieutenant spoke. "I suppose we should push on?" He sounded very tired. He had the build of a sprinter. This terrain was for workhorses. Jay looked again at the signal sergeant's face. It was ashen. "We take five minutes. I think it's all downhill from now, anyway." He had no idea whether it was or not, but they did seem to be on the slope of a mountain, and the stream ran silvery, downhill. No point in ending up carrying the sergeant, or, worse still, leaving him. That would mean he'd be RTU'd at once. On the other hand, one minute late and they were all RTU'd anyway. For himself, he did not mind.

He squatted on his haunches, as the others found stones to sit on. The young officer was plainly very tired, his poncho slipping on his shoulders. The sergeant looked as if he would never get up again. The young Jock lit a cigarette taken from a piece of greaseproof paper and sucked in the smoke, keeping the flame cupped.

Jay said, "Is it dry?"

The Jock offered it to him. "Want a drag?"

Jay took one, courteously, although he really didn't want it.

The bennies were helping. He would make this first rendezvous or bust. What happened after that, well, he'd meet it when it came. He handed the cigarette back to the Jock and asked, "How was Ireland?"

"A craphouse, as usual," said the Jock. "I didny mind the bandit country. I just got a wee bit sick o' being shot at in Belfast."

Jay nodded. He'd been in Ireland in the earliest contingents. He'd lain in a field in Armagh, not moving, for two whole days, covered with shit and straw, waiting until the farmer, who spotted for the other side, was sure there was nothing on his land that shouldn't be there. On the third day the boyos came, and then it had been war. He could hardly move when he first came out of that hole in the ground; the earth and straw were everywhere, in his mouth, nose, ears. But it had worked. They had bagged a couple, staggering under the sudden shock of the bullets, as they walked across the moonlit field. Only boys, barely out of their teens. Tough shit. Them or us. He had been full of bennies then, as he was now. He looked at his watch. "Time to move."

They all stood up.

"Here we go." Jay started forward, and they fell into line, the young Jock bringing up the rear. Jay had seen soldiers like him before. They never went point; that was flashy. But they could always be depended on to cover your arse, which was just as important, possibly more so. He noticed that the Jock turned and looked back every twenty paces, sometimes more often, and he thought: the little bastard has it.

The wall ended in a shambles of rock. Whoever had grazed sheep up here was an optimist. Even in summer, there could have been very little pasture for them. He pointed and the others followed him as he marched. They went down the bare hillside so far and fast that he began to fear they were off course. He could see nothing but dark night and darker sky, and the cloud was thicker then ever and it had started to rain again. The water ran into his eyes (thank God he'd brought the woolly cap, which absorbed some of it) as he strained to catch a glimpse of the promised fir plantation, plainly designated on the toilet-paper map. They trudged on, cursing in low, monotonous tones as they turned an ankle or stumbled to their knees in the dark.

The young lieutenant asked mildly, "Are we on course, do you think?"

Jay detected the note of utter weariness in his voice. He isn't going to make it, that one, he thought. But he was too tired to do anything but whisper, "Has to be this way. Any other way is uphill, and even fir trees won't grow on a summit, in this place."

He hoped that was right; it sounded right.

They slipped and slithered down the side of the mountain, cursing more loudly now, forgetting the fact of silence, at the far end of their energy, especially the young officer. Jay was sure he was on nothing, the signals sergeant too. The Jock probably didn't need anything, he was just naturally tough, a survivor from birth, in the hard streets of his native city.

The hillside suddenly became steeper than ever, and they careered forward, throwing their weight back, almost at a run, small stones scattering before them in the blackness, and Jay thought, I've steered them wrong, we're going over some cliff face or quarry, this is too steep. Like the others, he slowed, or at least he thought he did, and he was on his backside and still sliding down and cursing and he could feel the others behind him doing the same, and then, just as he thought balls to this, I'm giving up, wherever we land, that's it, just at *that* moment, the steep shelf ended, and they were on firm ground and the plantation of firs loomed, miraculously, in front of them.

They stayed on their backsides and just looked at it.

Jay consulted his watch.

"We're ten minutes early," he said. "Bad manners." The others laughed softly.

"The trouble is," he added, picking himself up, "we have to walk through this wood first and we've no idea how far it is."

It took them eight minutes and they reported to a jeep, with Nair and the adj sitting in it, with two minutes to spare. Three other teams were already there; two more were adrift and RTU'd.

CSM Nair noted their numbers and times.

"Lucky Thirteen," said Jay. "Can we eat now?"

Nair said, "Not yet. A brisk wee walk first, five miles or so, to another site where a wee bit more exercise awaits ye."

Jay almost hit him.

* * *

The next two hours passed in a haze of sweat and exertion. They fired, at half-targets in the half-light, with the weapons of their choice. Some men, Jay noted, had the standard Franco Belge FN self-loader, others had tommy guns, one man a sawn-off shotgun, which was, in proper partial atonement, a Purdey. They ran up and down steep hillsides, taking whatever cover there was, with the instructors among them, somewhere, always the voice of CSM Nair, his Glaswegian voice distinctive and grating and, seemingly, specially directed at Jay, who, as far as he could see, wasn't doing anything dramatically wrong. Jones, he thought, he's behind all this, he's the reason I'm suffering all this shit, why don't I just pack it in, tell Nair and everybody else, even the mild-looking CO, a smiling killer if there ever was one, to shove it up their assholes.

Something held him back. It was a kind of test, he supposed, and he'd always been good at tests. Even the sweat running down his back in cold sheets, when he knew he hadn't another bead of sweat in his body; even the ache in his calves and his thighs, and the hammering need for sleep that abated only when he popped another benny; even this did not break him, for no reason he could really explain, except that he enjoyed it. It was mad, crazy, and totally off the wall, but he enjoyed it. It was as simple as that.

"All right," shouted CSM Nair, after what seemed several hours. "You can stop and eat, if ye want to. Ye ha' ten minutes."

Most of the men were too tired to eat.

Neither the young lieutenant nor the signals sergeant opened their cans of emergency rations. The young Jock, on the other hand, pulled out his Coca-Cola-like tin and tore at the plunger. A sort of explosion took place inside the can (chemical, Jay supposed), and after half a minute, the soup it contained was hot. Jay followed the example of the young soldier and found the soup a lifesaver. It went down his throat with more appreciation than, say, the mushroom at Simpson's in the Strand, which was the best he knew. The young lieutenant just lay with his back against a rock and watched. The signals sergeant did the same, only his eyes were closed. Jay also ate two biscuits and a bar of milk chocolate and drank a little water from his canteen.

"All right," Nair shouted suddenly. "All parties will form up, and at the trot, proceed half a mile south to the burn, or if ye're English, stream. Don't ask its name, it hasny got one. Go!"

Jay and the young Jock got up with a grunt. The others were slower, and, looking at Jay, the young lieutenant grimaced. Jay took a benny from his pocket and slipped it into the man's hand. For a moment the young lieutenant hesitated, and Jay thought: he's the kind of young Steerforth who might report me. But all he heard was a whispered "Thanks." The man turned away and brushed his hand across his mouth, and Jay knew he had swallowed the pill.

Thanks be buggered, he thought, I need you, laddie.

He knew what was coming next; he'd done it before.

Obviously, they loved the log so much they'd never made it redundant.

"Some burn," said the Jock, gazing at the foaming and fast-running torrent before them. "It's mair like the Clyde."

"Can everybody swim?" Jay asked.

It was, as they said, the sixty-four-dollar question.

They all nodded that they could. That was something.

CSM Nair was shouting at them. "All right!" He stood, his seamed face impassive, amazingly fit for his age, his instructors all around him, NCOs to a man, permanent staff here, the toughest bunch of military instructors known to God. Well, that was as it should be, always provided you weren't the one they were being tough with. "All right, you see in front of you six railroad ties. Each one has a single handcuff attached to each corner." Nair paused, and almost seemed to smile, then thought better of it. "One for each man. Every team of four takes a log. The idea is to take the log across the wee burn and then through the assault course on the other side. The record for this exercise is eight minutes, thirty-four seconds." He still did not smile. "I was one of the team that made it, some little time ago, I may say." He paused, then screamed, "Go!"

Jay said quickly, "Nobody try to lift that log! I'll go to the front, take the right side, left hand." He nodded to the young Jock. "You take the other, at the front. You other two, left and right at the back."

They did as he bid them, put on the handcuffs, and waited.

All around them the other teams scrambled.

Jay said, "I've done this before. Trust me. Now, *lift* the bloody thing—it's heavy now, but it floats in the water. Go!"

They lifted the log, which was very heavy indeed.

"Here we go, in step, left right, left right, at a run, go!" shouted Jay.

They did that, too.

"Into the water, me and Jock, we'll hold it there, while you two rear men slide in on your bellies. Go!"

They did that, and they were the first team in the water. It was cold and fast and tore at them, but the log floated, as Jay knew it would.

Eight minutes, thirty-four?, he thought.

That was the moment when he first saw the girl, sitting in the CO's jeep, a pair of binoculars to her eyes. His gaze simply went that way, he did not even know it was a girl for sure, except that she was wearing a sheepskin and had nothing on her dark hair.

I must be bloody imagining things, he thought. It must be the bennies.

"Right, pull for the shore," he yelled. "Let's break their fucking record for them!"

Once they got out into the water the log had a life of its own. It took them fast, downstream, and from the cries of alarm of the other three, Jay knew they were shocked by the sudden power of the current. There was a stunted clump of gorse on the opposite bank, and Jay turned the log into the current, shouting to the others, his mouth half full of water.

"Into the current, face the current, swim against it, there's four of us!"

The Jock replied, "It's a guid job ah went tae the swimmin' wi' the school or I'd be drooned by noo." A wave of fast-moving water took him in the face, and he gasped. Jay thought: he'll keep his mouth shut from now on. He'd better, I need him.

If the two of them could move the log around into the current, the other two, at the back, only had to shove and stay afloat. Slowly, painfully, Jay and Jock turned the log around in the swift current, which tore at their clothing and filled their combat boots and threatened to drown them altogether. Jay could not see that anybody was doing any better. The chances were most teams would settle for going with the tidal wave of water and only realize, too late, that sometime they had to strike for the other shore, and that meant not just staying afloat but fighting for every foot of water, all the way over, and that took time. The log, pulling and bucking as the water hit it, swerved this way and that, but Jay and the Jock held on, pushing, swallowing the water that came over the log, half submerged most of the time, until finally they could feel the extra power of the other two men behind them.

At that point Jay knew they were in with a chance, not of just getting across but of making good time. He didn't know where the strength came from, probably the bennies, but somehow he began to lead the log and the team directly into the current, giving a little ground, hoping to gain landfall not too far down from the gorse bush. They were making good progress in the freezing water, provided nobody gave way.

When somebody did, only yards from the bank, it was, unexpectedly, the Jock: "Ma hand's lost its power," he gasped. "I canny holt on tae the bastard log."

"Yes you can," shouted Jay. "Just *keep* it there!" His own mouth filled with icy water, and he reached out to the bank, which, thank God, had a shelf, and somehow, in a last, sudden, desperate push, as the log made a sudden swirl of its own and the young lieutenant screamed in sudden agony, they pulled the sleeper up the shelf and onto the grassy bank. The young lieutenant was still screaming. Jay knew that his shoulder was dislocated.

It did not occur to him to abandon the attempt.

They fell around the log, on their hands and knees, throwing up the water they had swallowed. The young lieutenant stopped screaming and sat like a stricken animal, holding his left shoulder with his right hand.

Jay gasped, "You'll be all right. We'll help you over the obstacles."

The young lieutenant did not reply.

At least, Jay thought, he didn't say no, and he could have been excused if he had. Not that it would have mattered to Jay, either way. He was going to beat that record, he was going to shove it in their faces, he was going to enjoy that. He retched the last of the water from his freezing lungs and glanced back. None of the other four teams was better than halfway. His eyes went to the slight hill where the CO's jeep stood, and to the figure of the dark-haired woman, if it was a woman, in the sheepskin coat, with the binoculars to her eyes, but before he could be sure of that or of anything else, the voice of Nair, and the other instructors, rent the air.

"C'mon, Thirteen, what d'ye think this is, a rest home? On yer feet, man, on your feet the lot o' ye, c'mon, c'mon, c'mon, beat the clock, beat the clock, wull ye?"

"Ignore these bastards," Jay said quietly. "Just do as *I* say. We get up and we trot to the first obstacle. It's dead easy, but we reverse order when we get there and send the rear end up first, right? Now, on your feet, *go!*"

Somehow, they all stood up.

Jay looked at them.

They'll never make it, he thought.

"Take your time by me, and ignore these clowns!" He saw Nair's face tighten, if that was possible, and could not resist adding, "Their record is shit. We're going to take minutes off it. Left, right, left, right!"

At a ponderous trot, and with the instructor's voices screaming in their ears, but mostly Nair's now, because the others had turned their imprecations and entreaties toward the teams still struggling in the water, they carried the log toward the first obstacle.

God, it looked high.

The wall before them was built of thick wooden planks and was twenty feet tall. There were two ropes draped over it. A fit man on his own could have scrambled over it easily enough, hand over hand on one of the ropes, but four men carrying a railroad tie had problems.

Jay tried hard, through his exhaustion—his limbs were shaking violently and all feeling seemed to have left his body—to remember how they had gotten over it the last time. He closed his eyes and, ignoring the screams of Nair ("What the hell are ye waitin' for, laddie, it's only a wee wall! Come on, Number Thirteen, what's holding ye up?"), he concentrated. It was all complicated by the young lieutenant's arm. He didn't look at the man, he didn't want to see his pain. The thing was to get over this bastard wall. The rest, as he remembered it, wasn't easy, nothing here was, but it was possible.

Finally, Jay said, as the signals sergeant made a move, prodded by Nair's voice, "Ignore *him!*"

Then he took a deep breath and said, "Listen, the lieutenant here, and you, signals, go up first, the lieutenant up the right-hand rope, which he holds on to with his right hand. His left hand is on the log, but since it's useless, Jock here and I will take all the weight. We won't let it drop, because if we do your arm will be useless for a long time. Right, let's go!"

Slowly, they inched their way up the wall.

The log was a dead weight between the Jock and Jay, but somehow they bore it, on their shoulders, as the two front men pulled themselves, by inches, to the top of the wall. Once or twice the young lieutenant cried out in pain, but it seemed to be nothing he couldn't bear. Twice the signals sergeant lost his footing on the wall and twice he regained it. "Keep going," Jay whispered hoarsely. "We can do it!"

I think I'll die at the top of the wall, Jay thought. If we ever get there, I'll die.

He didn't.

They all four sat atop the foot-thick wall, the log poised between them. Jay grinned weakly at the others. The signals sergeant looked whiter than ever, and the young lieutenant was a pale shade of green. The Jock was a half-drowned slum rat. Somewhere, in the water, Jay had gashed his head, probably a blow from the log. He had felt nothing. The blood trickled warm down his face.

Nair and the other Instructors shouted and raved behind them.

Jay no longer even heard their words.

The team had to get down the other side of the wall without hurting the young lieutenant; that was the aim. If they did hurt him, he'd pass out and then they'd try to carry him, and it wouldn't work. Jay said, "Jock and I go down first, reverse order. We take the weight of the log. You follow, on the ropes, slowly, a pace at a time. Go!"

They did it, but they hurt the lieutenant.

It happened in the last few feet. The Jock's wet boot slipped on the wood of the wall and the log hurled down fast, before Jay could hold it firm. The young lieutenant screamed. Jay held the log long enough for them all to fall to the ground on the other side of the wall. They lay there in an untidy heap. Jay looked up, through his exhaustion and the trickle of blood that was now getting into his eye. If we got over that bloody thing, we're home, always supposing the lieutenant can go on.

He forced himself to look at the man.

He was not reassured.

The young face was greener than ever, and he was retching steadily, in short dry heaves. The other two didn't look much better. The Jock's eyes were closed, and the signals sergeant stared ahead, at nothing.

Jay knew he'd have to get them on their feet now or they'd be here for ever.

"All right," he shouted. "Everybody up!"

Slowly, they got to their feet, raising the log by inches as they did so. Finally, after what seemed a very long time, they were all standing, the log at hip height.

"We put the log on our shoulders now," said Jay, not looking at the young lieutenant. "And it stays there, over the rope swing that comes next."

Don't think about any of it, he told himself, just do it.

"Forward, go!"

With himself and the Jock at the head, they moved over the open ground, the log at shoulder height, like zombies, Jay thought.

All the way, Nair and the other instructors screamed.

They called everybody by the numbers on their backs, and to Jay it seemed that they shouted "Thirteen!" more often than any other number.

"Go back and shout at the others—they're behind," he mouthed.

But the words did not come out, they died on his lips.

At the swing, they had a dilemma.

The swing had two ropes, and the obvious way, if they had all been fit, was to take a rope each side of the log, back up to gain momentum, then leap forward, holding the log on their shoulders.

They tried it, and the lieutenant screamed and they swung back, still on the wrong side of the watery bog, which lay beneath the rope and the bar from which it swung.

They tried it again, and the lieutenant screamed again.

The Jock whispered, "Good try, but we've had it, boss."

Jay croaked, "Had it be buggered."

He girdled one of the slack ropes and looped it around the young lieutenant's arm. He then hooked it firmly around the log. He looked into the man's face.

"All right?"

"Why not 'One mighty swing and we're free'?"

Jay laughed. They all laughed. It was a cracked, hollow sound.

They backed away, and at a yell from Jay, they charged forward, uttering, in unison, a racked, terrible scream. The ropes flew before them, the young lieutenant screaming louder than any of them. They let go the ropes and fell forward on the other side of the bog, still yelling, all but the lieutenant, who was now unconscious. They lay on the ground for what seemed a long time, but was probably less than a minute. Then, very slowly, Jay loosened the rope that held the lieutenant to the log and threw it back into the bog.

Nair called across to them, "Are ye givin' up noo?"

Jay give him two fingers.

They carried the young lieutenant the last hundred yards to the CO's jeep. In the jeep stood the young adj, a stopwatch in his hand. The CO sat motionless in the driver's seat, and next to him was the girl in the sheepskin—and it was a girl, thought Jay, in wonderment—looking at them without expression. Offended, Jay shouted at the adj, "What is this, a Roman circus?"

The adj said, "You've broken the record for the course by twenty-two seconds."

"Well, of course we have," said Jay.

They lowered the young lieutenant's inert body to the ground. Nair's voice came from behind them.

"Why is that man lying there sunning himself on the grass?"

Jay stood up, or as far as he could

"Get an ambulance for him, CSM!" he yelled. "And do it now, and that's an order, soldier!"

Nair said nothing and did nothing. The adj stepped out of the jeep.

"I rather think the fellow needs one." He smiled briefly at Jay. "Well done, old boy."

"Fuck you, too," said Jay and sat down again on the wet and muddy ground. He accepted a lighted cigarette—astonishingly still dry—from the Jock. The signals sergeant stared ahead and made no reply when Jay asked if he was all right.

The Jock said loudly, "Officers and chefs, there's no bloody difference." He drew on the cigarette and passed it back to Jay.

By the time Jay had drawn on it too, and looked up at Nair, and said, "Well, we broke your record for you, three men and a cripple," and Nair had looked back expressionlessly, and the adj had looked away politely, or even painfully (how could one ever know with them?), the jeep had moved off, driven by the CO, with the girl—if it really was a girl—as passenger.

All that Jay could remember about her was that she was beautiful.

The next day they got a replacement for the young lieutenant, who was of course RTU'd and sent to hospital. The replacement had expertise, and was probably an instructor, although he wore a numbered canvas bib like the rest of them. Jay anticipated all that came from then on: the attacks, with live ammo, on the stone cabins, to simulate street conditions, the instructors marking every team and every individual for speed and initiative. He even managed to last out the dreaded hill test, in which men carried stones in their backpacks up and down, up and down, under the screams of Nair and the others. To get through it, Jay simply popped another couple of bennies. The signals sergeant strained his back and dropped out, a bloody shame after so long. He just sat down, looked reproachfully at Nair, and said, "That's it, you can have it." And Nair signaled a jeep to take him back to Hereford, then back to his unit. "Well done—don't forget you broke their record, they'll never forgive you for that," Jay called.

He never missed an opportunity to stick it to Nair.

It gave him some of the same exhilarating feeling he'd had when he'd tried to burn down his public school. Bloody nearly succeeded, too. He might have gotten away with it if he hadn't started the fire in the chapel. That had been stupid, because there wasn't much to burn. After that, he'd gone to finish his schooling at a progressive establishment, recommended by his old headmaster because it was built to accommodate such adventurous spirits as Jay. "Adventurous" was not the word his father had used. All that feuding with the prefects hadn't been made up by his entering the public school boxing championships two years running and winning both times. Yet that fact had probably saved him. Officially, he'd been allowed to leave, but his father always insisted he'd been expelled. The fire business was hushed up. The progressive school had been soft and easy, and he'd liked it. He'd felt at home. He stayed only a year and wished he'd never gone anywhere else. The school's motto, "We turn out happy people, even if they're only happy postmen," made sense to him. It had been better anyway than the running fights with the prefects and masters at his public school, which was like the running fight here, with Nair and the other instructors.

It was simply a matter of when.

It came on the last day of the exercise, when his team was "taken prisoner," in a sudden sweep around the stone huts. The team that took them by surprise was all instructors, led by CSM Nair.

"All right, you're prisoners. You, Thirteen, step forward," shouted Nair, a Kalashnikov in his hand. "Hands on head, everybody!"

They laid down their weapons and put their hands on their heads.

Jay stepped forward as instructed.

Nair said, "You were given information at the briefing. Tell us, what was White Section's objective?"

"For God's sake," Jay said, "stop playing cowboys and Indians."

It was then that he noticed the steel cabinet. It was inside one of the stone cabins, and bloody incongruous it looked.

It was ordinary War Office issue, and as soon as he saw it Jay knew what it was for. He said, "I quit. That's it!"

A sudden rush of the three instructors—Nair stood back—bore him into the cabinet, and the door slammed. It was extremely dark inside, and Jay shouted, "Stop this load of nonsense, you cretins."

The pace sticks and weapons began to rattle on the outside of the cabinet. The din inside was horrifying. Jay took his sodden handkerchief from his pocket and tore it into shreds, with his teeth, the sharp noise in his ears getting worse by the minute. He knew this could always be defended as an anti-interrogation exercise, if any excuse was ever asked for. Nobody would now convince him he wasn't being singled out, and yet, and yet . . . he had broken their stupid record, and that could be enough to spark off something like this. As the noise thundered and hammered in his head, as the blows on the outside of the cabinet increased, he managed to get the pieces of sodden cloth into his ears. At least that would stop him from being actually deafened for life. He pulled the woolly cap down over that, and then he put his hands over his ears and pressed as hard as he could.

It didn't keep the noise out, but it helped, a little.

The hammering seemed to go on forever.

The sickness came sooner than he expected, and he retched up the emergency food ration he'd eaten an hour before. He crouched down and tried to hide from the noise, but it was useless. In real circumstances he could see how anybody might give in. If he didn't know this was a rehearsal and not for real, he'd give in himself. The distinction, he noted, was considerable.

The hammering went on, and after a while it was all he could hear. His whole nervous system started to react to it, and he waited for the next blow, in pure agony, the sweat drying on his body and no way of being sick again because there was nothing to come up.

At last they stopped. He had no idea how long he'd been in there.

He heard a key turn in the lock of the cabinet.

Slowly, with a superhuman effort, Jay pulled himself erect and braced his back against the wall of the cabinet. When the door swung open he was ready, even if he was only just conscious. CSM Nair opened the door, and the sudden daylight struck Jay sick. He swallowed the bile and stood, swaying, as he accustomed himself to the light. Nair stood three paces in front of him.

Jay slumped, as if to fall, and as Nair stepped forward, Jay lunged toward him, bringing up his head very sharply, and butted Nair full in the face. He felt the teeth go, and, he hoped, the nose, and then he knew nothing but blackness.

When he came to, he was in a jeep and the young adj was feeding him brandy. There was nobody else in the jeep, but he could just hear, as if through cotton wool, firing across the hillside, and he knew that the others were still going on with the whole stupid shooting match. Jay felt light-headed, but the brandy helped.

The young adj said, "I think you've done enough, old man.

Good show, really. The last thing was a bit silly, but the chaps got carried away somewhat. Nair's spitting blood, but not much. His teeth were false, of course, but it was a nice try." He gave Jay a cigarette, lit it for him, and drove him back to Hereford, at a slow, convalescent pace, as if Jay were an invalid, which in a way he was. Jay refused any treatment, and slept ten hours in his bunk. He got up to find a typewritten note on his pillow, and his weapon and uniform gone. The note instructed him that he was released, as of now, and wished him good luck. A scribbled P.S., in what was obviously the adj's hand, said he'd be hearing from Nair's solicitors about the teeth.

Jay grinned, and dressed very slowly. He felt much better, if still a little deaf, and somehow proud that he'd managed to get through it all. He decided he would eat breakfast on the road somewhere, and, still feeling somewhat fragile, he walked out to his Jensen, got in, and tooled it to the front gate. He handed his release note to the gatekeeper, who looked at him a long moment, and then said dryly, "See you again, sir?"

"Not," said Jay, "if I can help it."

He turned the Jensen out through the housing development. Back into civilization again, he thought, back into dear old England again, and that includes Mr. Jones. He turned left for the London road.

T·H·R·E·E

Marty wondered about Jay.

Was he right for the job?

She drove her rented Chrysler along the Embankment toward Chelsea Cloisters and tried to add up the pros and cons. To begin with, she was prejudiced in his favor, as any woman might be, just on account of the look of him. The other *mechanics* she had seen, on grainy black-and-white in Mr. Jones's viewing room, had looked what they were, but this one was different. Or anyway he looked different. The job, as far as Virgo had told her, needed somebody who had the extra quality of not looking the part. This man had no distinguishing features that screamed mechanic, other than a slightly broken nose, obviously well reset, that, according to Mr. Jones, he had picked up in a rugby game at his school.

Sitting in the dark viewing room, eyes on the man walking along a Kensington street unaware that he was being filmed from a vehicle that seemed to be hunting for a parking space, Marty concentrated. This man was light on his feet, well but quietly dressed, in dark jacket and gray slacks, the extra fitness plainly there, but only to the expert eye, to others a young executive perhaps, or even a successful salesman. He did not look the ex-soldier, which she knew he was, from the dossier ("for looking at, not taking away, I'm afraid, my dear") that Mr. Jones had provided her with, and which she had read with very considerable interest, and a feeling of excitement, almost sexual, ridiculous because she had never met the man. The overwhelming impression was: he could be right. The bumbling Limeys, so aptly represented by Mr. Jones, had come up with the goods first time.

"No names, I'm afraid, my dear girl," Mr. Jones had said, indicating the file. "Just call him Jay, shall we? It's his real name anyway. Need to know and all that. If your masters in Virginia are interested, naturally there'll be more." Mr. Jones coughed discreetly, and she wondered how much he knew, if anything, about her and Jack Virgo. Probably something, these talent runners all knew each other, and not just on one side of the fence, either. Sometimes she felt it was all a great big boys' game and that she was in it more or less by accident. Yet she knew it wasn't accident that had put her in the leather chair in Mr. Jones's viewing room in the very small and discreet viewing theater in London's West End, any more than it was accident that the man called Jay was up there, for her judgment, on the screen.

God, he looked dangerous. Quiet, but knowing what she knew, very dangerous. Or did she feel that *because* she knew? A thrill had gone down her spine and ended, as ever, between her legs. There was something about him that reminded her of her first lover in the Company, Gene Collier, who had been killed in a secret operation in the Middle East, like so many others. She had known him only two months, slept with him only a few times, and then he was gone. It had been Jack Virgo, inevitably, who had taken her out to dinner and told her about Gene. She had been Jack's secretary then. They had gone to bed together that night, for the first time but not, my God no, not the last.

Jack Virgo. To him she was still a secretary.

Even when he promoted her into the field and then out of it, back to Langley. Probably because of that.

Jack. She seemed to have known him all her life.

Well, she had, the part that mattered.

Marty drew on her cigarette. Mr. Jones coughed, he probably disliked women smoking, or just women, she'd sensed no masculine vibes at all, and with her looks she expected masculine vibes as a matter of course. She felt, for a moment, a fleeting fellow feeling for this man Jay, whose taskmaster and paymaster Mr. Jones was. Jones was the British equivalent of Virgo, and she did not, any longer, care for the breed. They did not take the risks, out in the field. Jack Virgo once had—he'd been in at the Bay of Pigs fiasco and, miraculously, survived it—but not for years. Jack had been behind the desk, running operations, for a long time now. Her own small experience in the field (Nicaragua, Grenada) had given her a sympathetic eye for those who did the work. She did not find them boring and quite possibly expendable, as Jack Virgo did. Virgo told her: don't fall in love with the talent.

Marty knew he was right, but looking at Jay striding along, a fit and dangerous animal, she thought: I'm glad Jack doesn't know how I'm feeling just looking at him. He'd go ape, the pale eyes would narrow in the fleshy face, the balding head would gleam with sweat, and she'd be treated to yet another lecture on the way those who worked for Jack Virgo had to behave.

They had to behave as much like Jack Virgo as they knew how.

They had to do everything Jack Virgo's way.

Or else.

Or else, what?

Marty had wondered that, a hundred times, about Jack. If she left him, actually left him, applied for some other job in the Company, in some other division, away from Jack's influence and power, which was considerable but not universal (she'd had offers, oh yes, she'd had offers), what would he do? Run after her? Talk her around? Threaten her?

Whichever way, she had never put it to the test.

Fifteen years now and still his woman.

Or so he thought.

Marty composed herself, with a secret smile. Jack Virgo wasn't here, was he? She was his emissary, trusted or not. There wasn't very much Jack Virgo could do about that. The whole thing—whatever it was—was too hot for Jack to come over himself and do the looking. So he'd sent her, carte blanche. Well, that was how she would run it, her way.

Still, looking at the man called Jay, having read his folder, she felt again the *frisson*. She wondered what he would be like in bed.

"He doesn't look very army," she said to Mr. Jones, sitting, no doubt very bored, in the smoky darkness of the viewing room.

"No, not really. He didn't fit in, in his own line regiment, where everybody was, well, more or less your common or garden soldier, as it were. He's a bit of a loner. That's why he got into the SAS. They don't like great gregarious heroes."

So, this man answered Jack Virgo's other demand: get me a

guy with resources, somebody who can work on his own, maybe even help plan the job himself, somebody special, not your average mechanic.

The film flickered on for a few more minutes, then shut off abruptly. Mr. Jones intoned into a microphone, "Thank you, Bob, that will be all." Marty lit another cigarette, and Mr. Jones coughed again but did not comment. She wondered how much he knew of Virgo's proposed operation and realized, again, and with increasing irritation, how little she knew herself. It was extremely possible, the paranoid way Virgo worked, that Mr. Jones knew more than she did. The operation had to have some British connection, didn't it, or why were they in on it? On the other hand, Virgo had told her that he wanted somebody absolutely not known to anybody at the Company. For that he could have gone to the French or the Germans, and he hadn't. They, of course, would stand out in an American situation more than any Brit would. If it was an American situation. She didn't know. She didn't know shit.

"Is that everybody?" she asked Mr. Jones.

They had watched four pieces of film, she had looked at four dossiers. Jay's had been the last. It was no accident, Marty felt. Mr. Jones was a creep at a hundred yards on a dark night, but she had an uneasy feeling he did few things without deliberation.

"That's the lot, my dear girl."

"The last one's the only candidate, really."

"Well," said Mr. Jones, obviously pleased, "I rather thought that myself, actually."

"SAS? Isn't that unusual?"

"Yes and no. He was an officer, so he stayed only three years. The men stay longer, forever, it seems, the best ones." The voice in the darkness sounded proprietorial. "Matter of fact, I recruited him myself."

"Really? I'd like to meet him. Would that be possible?"

Mr. Jones, in the darkness, seemed to brood.

"Well, yes, but I'd rather it wasn't a formal meet. I mean, I take it you can't offer him anything yet, that is?"

He was reminding her that Jack Virgo had the last word, in that very polite, yet steely, English way. Marty replied, "No, I can't, and I'd rather hoped that any approach to whoever we decided on would be made by your people."

"That," said Mr. Jones, with extreme caution, "was not my understanding, dear lady. I had thought Mr. Virgo accepted that this would be a most secret Company operation and that all we would be doing would be putting the operative your way, as it were. All arrangements, fees, and so on would be strictly between yourselves and whoever you, as you say, select."

"Well," said Marty icily, "if you don't want a formal meeting, how do you suggest I assess this man?"

Mr. Jones cogitated a long moment. When he replied, he seemed to be talking to himself. "I wonder," he said, "if it would be possible for you to see him in action, as it were?"

"In action?" Marty was startled. "Where, in action?"

"Well," said Mr. Jones, "with the SAS people, actually. He's doing a sort of refresher course down there." He sighed. "I don't know if my influence stretches that far, but if it does, then how would that appeal to you, um?"

"It would appeal to me very much," said Marty.

Marty turned off the Embankment toward Chelsea Cloisters. There were all sorts of safe houses, owned or rented by the Company, all over London, but Jack Virgo had insisted that she use none of them. He wanted her visit strictly private, no Company involvement. He would get into the game personally, when the time was ripe. Meantime, her mission was to keep a low profile and find the right operative for the job. She had, accordingly, taken formal leave and flown into London, as if on a short holiday, telling people she was catching up on a little cheap shopping. The state of the dollar vis-à-vis the pound made that highly believable. The large hotels were always full of lookouts of every kind, with receptionists in the pay of newspaper reporters and God knew who else, so Marty had taken rooms at Chelsea Cloisters. It was a large apartment block, you could get lost in it, and nobody ever talked to you. That was one good thing about the Brits. They might be poor these days, and in a hell of a mess politically, not having made up their minds whether they were going to be a left-wing banana republic or a monarchist free-for-all, but they had the manners of the old world, anyway in London. They respected privacy. Jack Virgo said they'd sit still for anything, unemployment, strikes, union blackmail, crippling taxes, as long as you left them alone in the privacy of their gardens. Jack thought the Brits were finished, especially if a left-wing government got in, with their policy of closing down all nuclear bases, progressing probably to all other bases, and telling the U.S. to go home. If the Brits go, Europe goes, he said. Then it's time to leave, it's time to pull up the drawbridge and think Fortress America.

Jack Virgo thought the Brits were through, but hoped they weren't. He would do anything he had to do to keep them in the game.

The game, to Jack, meant the war against the Soviets. Against their foreign allies, the Cubans, the Nicaraguans, the Angolans, or any other client state. "These KGB guys," he would say, leaning back almost admiringly, his cigar glowing in his face, his large glass of Southern Comfort in his hand, "they got it made. They report to nobody except their bosses, no newspapers, no media hawks for them, no sir. They do as they like, they kill, they kidnap, they subvert, the whole works. And what do the U.S. media do? They equate the Company with the KGB. We do a little of the same thing, and it's 'dirty tricks' and 'un-American,' and it's 'throw the files open and let Joe Public see what we've been keeping under our vests for years, let Joe Public come in and browse through our offices,' for Chrissake! And we stand still for it. Carter did that. The media forced him into it. Kennedy wasn't bad. Lyndon came around. Nixon was great. He and Henry understood the war." Virgo based his opinion of all presidents on their attitude toward the Company. "We're back in the game, baby," he had told Marty, lying back in bed, the pillows plumped behind his head, bourbon in hand. He was always loquacious after sex.

"The other side can do as it likes and nobody objects. Kill people. Anybody they like. Of course, they use clients, no guy ever comes up and shows his KGB card and then takes a shot at the Pope! But it gets done. They're good, they're very good. But we can do it, too. If we don't, we might as well pack up and go home and wait for the Cossacks. Because if we don't defend ourselves, we're dead." He had drawn deeply on the cigar. Marty could not think who else, except Jack Virgo, would smoke a cigar in bed. It was all part of the Southern macho thing. Yet Jack wasn't all steel. He had his bad dreams like everybody else. She'd held him in her arms and heard him cry out, in his sleep. But awake, he was all action. He pointed the cigar at her. "Listen, Marty. The Israelis know how to run an underground war. They play it hard. Mossad got every one of those Arabs who killed the Israeli athletes at the Olympics. Every last one. They had to wait, but they waited. All right. If the Company ever tried to mount an exercise like that, the shit would hit the fan, the media would go crazy."

Marty had brought him back to the point. "If our top brass found out? About this operation. Would the shit hit the fan then?"

"Yeah, yeah," said Jack Virgo, "if they found out. Which is why . . ." He pointed the cigar at her again, what did he think it was, another prick for God's sake, he'd just used the other one. Their sex these days had a lot of violence in it, it was a thing of biting and scratching and sweat. Jack Virgo was not a finesse man. He would have considered that fairy. So they lived hard and loved hard, and most of the time it worked, in its way, because it was all there was really, and she came with him, when he gave her time, which that evening he hadn't. Marty was sick of his point-   ·
ing that foot-long cigar at her, sick of a lot of things she didn't admit even to herself, and she said, interrupting him, "Look, Jack, is this Brit thing totally your own? I mean, does any-body else in the Company know about it, do our top brass know about it?"

Virgo's eyes had narrowed to slits and then opened wide, his favorite innocence gambit.

"No, they do not."

"Then," said Marty, "I think I would reconsider. It could cost you. You know how they feel about independent operations."

"This won't be independent. It will be, if I was KGB, what they would call adventurist. Isn't that what they accused Khrushchev of, when they threw him out, adventurism? Well, I don't mind that. That's fine. I'll tell them when the time is right to tell them. Me and old Nikita, adventurists? I like it."

Marty said, pushing for information, "It could still cost you, Jack."

Virgo had smiled. "Look, baby. In this ball game, in the Company as it is now, with its full complement of liberal shits, am I right, anything could cost me. I'm interested in what is good for my country, I'm interested in you going to London and finding me the right man, that is all you have to do, nothing else. I would go myself, but that could blow it, and this thing is too big to blow, so I have to trust you."

Marty replied, "And you hate that, don't you?"

Virgo said, "Sure I hate that. Every time I let somebody do something important for me they ball it up."

"When did I ever ball anything up?"

Virgo warned, "Don't let this be the first time, is all."

"Can't you go to our top people with the problem?"

"Baby, we cannot because top people would be horrified at what I propose, they would puke over their Calvin Kleins at what I propose, they wouldn't recognize the necessity, they wouldn't want to be implicated, they would shit themselves. So it's me who does what has to be done, and let the chips fall, because then it'll be too late, it'll be over. And all you have to do, Marty, is find me the right guy to do it, the right guy against the world."

And that, Marty reflected, was as much as she knew.

Marty turned the Chrysler into the parking lot at Chelsea Cloisters. It was twenty degrees warmer in London than it had been out on the Brecon Beacons, but the visit had been more than worthwhile. Whatever strings Mr. Jones had pulled, they had been the right ones. She had sensed a certain reserve in the commanding officer, who seemed much like any other soldier, until you saw that he wore no ribbons, no badges of rank either, and was very quiet and thoughtful in manner. Like Jay, a sort of loner, she supposed. There had been no names, so, like everybody else, she had called him sir. She had stayed the night at a local hotel and reported to the SAS HQ only for a one-day visit. The CO had driven her out to the Beacons in his own Land Rover. She had taken his advice, given over the telephone, to wear something warm. It was well she had; she could still feel the numbing cold.

Marty got out of the Chrysler, locked it, and went into the Cloisters. She took the elevator up to her flat and let herself in, poured herself a large vodka, and only then threw off the sheepskin coat and the long suede boots that had kept her, if not warm, at least not totally frozen out on the Beacons.

The log business, God. The man they called Jay had done well, a great show, no doubt of it. He'd shown initiative, and, more, he'd broken their record. When he threw it right in the old instructor's face he'd looked not so much a mechanic as a genuinely angry man, not deadly and uncaring, but a sight too caring.

Marty sipped her vodka and stretched her feet toward the electric fire, which she had switched on as soon as she came in. It had been an experience, and she had learned a lot. If Jack Virgo had seen these Brits in action, he would have been cheered, but she doubted if Mr. Jones would extend the invitation. The CO, with that dry English cough that preceded any personal or delicate remark, had said, "The only lady visitor we've had, I believe." He had pointed toward the team of four men, struggling with the massive log. "Anyway, that's your chap, at the end there."

He hadn't asked what her interest was, or who she was.

Plainly, Mr. Jones, if he cared to use it, had pull.

Marty tried to organize her thoughts about Jay.

All right. He had the form, as the Brits said. He had done things that were not on paper, not even in the dossier Mr. Jones had handed to her. That contained personal details, like his army record, jobs held, women he'd been married to or lived with— there had been some mention of a girl, a makeup artist or something. He lived in West London and ran a small business, probably a blind. There had been an indication of his background, schools, languages, experience with weapons. "First-rate in almost all small arms. Also explosives, but has not yet used that facility in the field." Mr. Jones had added, "These chaps get a good grounding at the SAS. He's the only one I've recruited. Most want to retire and grow roses."

Not surprising, Marty thought, after what I've seen this week.

Still, was Jay right for the job?

Marty mused. He was brave, he had initiative, he looked as if he could pass for a gentleman, or anyway somebody respectable, if he had to. That had been one of Jack Virgo's points. "No shambling bums. No psychos, especially no psychos." She had questioned Mr. Jones about that, and he had made a steeple of his fingers and replied judiciously, "Well, of course, nobody absolutely normal exists, my dear. Everybody has something, some hang-up, sexual, physical, fiscal, something that wouldn't, taken out of context, be generally regarded as absolutely normal. But no psychological problems, as such. Shows signs of strain lately, of the kind one grows to accept in these, ahem, operatives, yes." Mr. Jones had unsteepled his fingers, looked at them, and then steepled them again. "All SAS types are somewhere near the edge, in what I believe the medical types call a psychological scenario. Our man conforms to type, in that respect." He paused. "He does this job, partly for the money but also because he believes himself to be a patriot."

"Really?" Marty couldn't keep the surprise out of her voice.

Mr. Jones smiled. "Unfashionable, I know, but there you are. Mind you, he isn't good with money, so the money always matters. Don't spoil him, though. Our rates are somewhat lower than your own, in all things, I fear. One wouldn't want the dear boy to get dissatisfied, what?"

"You said he'd been showing signs of strain?"

"Well, yes, he had." Mr. Jones coughed dryly. "That was why I felt he needed that, er, refresher. Not that they would teach him anything he doesn't know. Just, he was relaxing rather too much. He has a girlfriend, and, well, he might have been getting a little settled in his ways." He added hastily, "Of course, he simply went back as a reservist, which, technically, is what he is."

Marty pursued the point. "That worries me." It did. The man she'd seen seemed to have all the *bottle,* as the Brits put it, in the world, out on the Brecon Beacons; but what she wanted him for was something else. She knew, or rather Virgo had told her, that mechanics burned out, like pilots or football players or nuclear physicists, or anybody who did anything amazing with his body or mind or both.

"I wouldn't want somebody with a problem," she had told Mr. Jones.

"No problem, dear lady. We intend to go on using him. If that influences you in any way."

"It does." Marty had felt relieved. Still, she pressed. "If you're sure I have nothing to worry about in that regard?"

"Absolutely nothing, my dear. I assure you."

I'm glad you assure me, Marty had thought, but you don't report to Jack Virgo, and I do. Marty got up and poured herself another vodka and then sat down again in the electric fire's glow. She felt sleepy—the knife-sharp air out on those hills went right through you—and forced herself to concentrate. All right. The man Jay. Mr. Jones had not said exactly how many jobs he had done, but she felt, somehow, he was hinting at around six, which was good enough. He looked great, and he'd been stupendous, on the Beacons. He was undoubtedly the best candidate of the four. She could hardly go back and ask Mr. Jones for another batch. Maybe there weren't any more.

Marty could not think why she shouldn't pick up the telephone right now and tell Jack that she had found the right guy for the job, whatever it was, and catch the Boeing back from Heathrow tomorrow. So what was bugging her?

Something.

Marty slowly sipped the last of her second vodka.

The something was all too obvious, if she just thought about it. This man Jay reminded her of Gene, now dead. Jay had also looked at her a very long time, as she sat in the CO's jeep only a matter of yards away; in the jargon, they had made eye contact. She had certainly been rooting for him to make it, and when his team had staggered across the finish line, carrying the boy with the dislocated shoulder, she had been very tempted to scream like some teenybopper with damp panties. Maybe that was the problem, the damp panties?

Marty considered it, sexual attraction, and rejected it at once, but not the idea of it. It was the idea that was worrying her. This man Jay was the talent, and she was nowadays a talent spotter, and in some ways, with Virgo's help, a talent runner, a controller. One day she would show them that it wasn't absolutely necessary to be a hard-drinking all-American boy like Jack Virgo to run operatives, to rise to the top in the Company, though no woman had ever done it. A few, granted, held important jobs, but not top jobs. Not surprisingly, Jack Virgo had laughed tolerantly at her complaint: "It's like the U.S. Army, baby, only we don't have to have a Commandant of the Waves. It's the last bastion of male chauvinist piggery."

He had added crudely, "Women have their uses, of course."

Marty knew he meant as honey-traps and snoopers, in and out of important men's beds, as spies and sometimes as recruiters and even as street operatives. She'd done it. She'd seen the Company guys in Nicaragua, hiding in some fleabag hotel, waiting for the Sandinista supporter, the tall young guy who looked as if he'd never eaten a poor meal in his life, to arrive, all jewels and lovely wife and fancy left-wing politics. It had been a kidnap ploy that had never materialized; somebody had tipped him off. There was no such thing as good security down south. Those republics were rotten all through. Just a shade better than the Marxists would make them, but that was all. She'd told the male operatives, "No running to my assistance, no shit like that, I've done the course, just as you have. I won't run to your aid. Don't run to mine."

They had grinned and said nothing.

Marty had known that in a pinch, they'd have done more for her than for any man.

Jack Virgo too had grinned when she told him. "I asked them to look out for you. They were only doing their job."

Marty had felt like raging at him, but she hadn't. It would have done no good. Soon after that, he'd pulled her back into the office, to help him run people, calling it a promotion, which it was. She'd done well for a girl from Brooklyn who'd passed the civil service exam and got a posting to Virginia as a secretary, and taken it from there. Now she actually sat in on some important meetings, not the ones where policy was decided but anyway the ones where fairly important decisions were taken, and when she spoke, the men in their shirt sleeves took off their horn-rims and listened. Possibly they did it because Jack Virgo was her protector and boss. For whatever reason, she was accepted.

If this job went wrong, her head as well as Jack Virgo's could be on the block. Marty wondered why she had gone along with Jack without questioning him in more detail.

Marty had worked hard, and slept with one or two people she'd rather not have slept with, to get where she had. Jack Virgo was the main one, but there had been others. She had also worked her sweet ass off to do it, so that Jack Virgo couldn't throw it in her face that he'd done it all for her: got her on the courses, talked up for her at personnel boards. Jack made no secret of their sexual relationship, but nowadays that kind of thing hardly mattered. Jack was married to a Southern heiress, he had a posh life-style, the big Southern *Gone with the Wind* mansion, the three obligatory kids, two daughters at Vassar, a son at the Point.

Jack Virgo and Marty had a thing, a long-lasting thing, but just a thing.

To Jack Virgo, that was all it was, all it had ever been.

One day, he hoped to sit in the top seat at the Company, no matter how he denied it.

If that ever happened, would they still have a thing?

Marty doubted it.

She crossed the room, looking at her watch as she did so, picked up the telephone, and dialed transatlantic, followed by the digits that she knew would cause the telephone to ring on Jack Virgo's desk in his study, at his home.

He answered, and he sounded sleepy.

"Jack? Marty. Hi."

"Hello there, Marty." Jack was always cautious, especially with calls to the house. He had said no calls to the office. Yet any call could be intercepted in one of the Company's routine checks on personnel. Even calls to Jack Virgo, a head of division.

"Jack, I've had a look at that merchandise we talked about. Boy, are prices cheap compared with back home! Do you want me to go ahead and buy for you?"

There was a pause at the other end of the line. She could almost see him, sitting in his study, surrounded by books he had never read and magazines he had no time even to glance at. She had been to his house once, on an invented Company errand. At least she had called it that; she really wanted to see his wife. Elvira was a Southern beauty, and she had been very charming to Marty, but Marty suspected that Elvira knew about her and didn't give a damn. She rather liked Elvira, who seemed scatty, but wasn't. Still married to Jack after twenty years, she had to be smart. And rich. Marty waited for Virgo's reply.

"Are you sure it's the right choice?"

"Absolutely sure."

"Do the Brits you've talked to recommend we buy?"

"They recommend, very highly."

"And you say what?"

"I say go, as of now."

Again, the hesitation. "I don't know. It's a risk."

"So it is. What isn't? What do you want me to do?"

Jack still hesitated, then said, "Look. I have to come over. Say the weekend, Friday late."

Marty didn't know why she was surprised. Jack had said this was important. Why should he take her word? She said, "If that's the way you'd like to do it."

"It's a big purchase." Jack was going through their cover, that she was buying diamonds for a birthday present for his wife.

"As you like. Shall I do any more?"

"Enjoy London. Or maybe have another meet."

"I haven't had a real meet yet."

"You haven't?" He sounded incredulous.

"No, I haven't. You said—"

"I know what I said. I'll call you when I get in. See you Friday."

The telephone went down.

Marty sat staring at it for almost five minutes.

It rang again. It was Mr. Jones. "Hello, dear lady. How did your trip go?"

"Oh, great. Very useful."

"You've made your decision then?"

"No . . . not absolutely. My boss is coming over."

"Oh?" Mr. Jones sounded testy. "When?"

"Friday."

Mr. Jones coughed dryly. All this coughing, she thought. Why don't these Brits just come out and say a thing? "Just as well—we have a job for Jay ourselves," Jones said.

Marty was coldly angry. "Hey, one that could go wrong?"

"No chance of that, dear lady," Mr. Jones said briskly. "Only a day's work."

"Just the same."

"Well," said Mr. Jones, "if you people can't make your minds up?"

"We'll talk again Friday." Marty said goodbye and put down the telephone.

Men, Mr. Jones and Jack Virgo, the goddam sons of bitches.

That night she dreamed of Jay and the log taking him into deep water. In the dream she plunged in, to rescue him. She woke up and laughed and went to sleep again, dreamlessly.

F·O·U·R

THE JET LANDED at Aldergrove at exactly ten minutes past eight in the evening. It was already dusk, this late September day, and Jay wondered where the summer had gone. They'd been stuck in London since May, Angie on her television shows, and he on, well, other things. All summer, except for the business trips, and they could hardly be called vacations. He looked out moodily at the gloom of Ulster. A fine rain was falling, and the tarmac glistened wet. The pilot switched off engines. Jay took the plugs out of his ears and clambered out of the observer's seat. He tapped the pilot's shoulder in farewell and allowed the two mechanics, who had appeared from nowhere, to help him to the ground. The flight had taken twenty-six minutes from Northolt. Jay shook himself and pulled the Burberry around him. He was wearing his dark business suit under the raincoat. He carried no weapon, as yet. There had been special instructions about that. The lights of Belfast had glittered innocently beneath them as the jet had coasted in to land, but Jay knew it was not a city in which to carry arms until you intended to use them.

Mr. Jones had been very firm on that.

Mr. Jones had also been very apologetic. He hated to have to do this to Jay, but there it was, something extremely urgent had come up, and Jay was the obvious man for the job. The remuneration would be fifty percent above the usual, in view of the haste of the thing, so soon after Jay's refresher. How had that gone— had he enjoyed it?

74

"You don't enjoy things like that," Jay had replied. "You survive them."

Mr. Jones had smiled urbanely. "Yes, but I think you'll feel, as they say, the benefit, what?"

"I don't know about that," Jay had replied. "All I felt was so tired I slept for two days. Until you called me, in fact. I was intending to go away for a few days to recover."

"Really?" said Mr. Jones. "Where?"

"Does it matter?" Jay had been irritable, and why not? "Brighton or somewhere. Angie's had a heavy summer, and so have I!"

Mr. Jones had looked disapproving. He had only wanted to know where Jay was going, it was a perfectly innocent question, from one gentleman to another. Of course, Jay was not a gentleman. Mr. Jones had sighed, and said, "Then I suppose we'd better get down to briefing. The jet is standing by for you. You should be out again by midnight and back here in the early hours. Just call me. I'll be up."

"Here?"

"Oh, yes. I have a few things to do. Matter of fact, we had somebody else chalked in to do it for us, but he said no."

"Don't blame him," said Jay. "I'm not too happy about the venue. Things can go very wrong over there. It isn't like West Germany or Cyprus or somewhere. There are a lot of eyes."

Mr. Jones steepled his fingers. "That's why the money's a little better, dear boy. Now, as to details . . ."

The more he talked, the less Jay liked it.

So many things could go wrong in this place.

Everybody was watching.

Everybody was trigger-happy.

A sudden violent act here was not out of the ordinary, so people were ready, they were tuned-up, expecting trouble. He'd been worried then, sitting in the Whitehall office, trying to imagine the scene, and he was even more worried here, standing on the wet tarmac, the soft Irish rain slowly soaking into his Burberry. He hefted the leather sample case in his hand and stared into the gloom.

As if on cue, an unmarked Land Rover appeared out of the darkness, from the Flying Control area. It stopped on the apron. The shadowy figures inside did not emerge. Bloody security, Jay thought. In this place it starts as soon as you set foot on the soil. He shivered. It was the memories of the province that bugged him. He'd done a tour in this forlorn place, in Belfast itself, as a young second lieutenant in his line regiment, then SAS in Bandit Country, for a couple of months. Nothing about it was attractive. He liked the Ulster people, who were marvelous and friendly to the lads, especially in the Protestant districts. The ghettos of the Falls were something else. He didn't know the answer here, but he guessed that O'Neill and Lynch, representing moderate Ulster and moderate Republic, had been getting too friendly for anybody's comfort in the sixties. It had been beginning to look as if North and South could live together after all. Not that they hadn't, in reasonable amity, since '22. It was the extremists who seized the opportunity to blow up the civil rights campaign out of all reason. And it was the extremists on the other side who faced up to them. One way or another, the chance had been lost, and now the only thing that could ever really work, in his view, was partition. As in Cyprus. As anywhere, where two groups of people on the same island couldn't agree.

Meantime, there was an underground war, and people who believed on both sides of the fence that they were quite sincerely in the right died. Every day and every night.

He walked toward the Land Rover and got in the empty seat next to the driver. All that was academic. The Brits were on one side, and that was that. What was behind his errand he did not know. He never knew.

"You picked a lovely evening for it, old chap."

The Brit at the wheel was a *guardsman,* a Coldstreamer. Over six feet tall, long blond hair, fair mustache, unmarked army uniform, no badges showing except the rank of captain, the haw-haw manner of the breed. Jay didn't like that; he'd been hoping for Army Intelligence at its quietest, not its most bloody obvious. In a rear seat sat a corporal in glasses, Intelligence Corps by the weedy look of him, and a local Belfast accent when he spoke, which was simply to say "Good evening, sir," but Jay caught the soft intonation.

Jay felt a *frisson.* He could see the need to be in uniform; at least part of the way, it opened all doors. He could also see the need to have local people who knew the ground. But they posed problems. They had families, living locally somewhere, they were get-at-able, dangerous, a risk to all kinds of security. He did not show his face, any more than he could help, to the corporal. He said, "I want to be back here at around eleven-thirty, no pissing about, is that all arranged?"

"Oh, absolutely, old boy." The guardee tooled the Land Rover to the airfield perimeter and headed it toward a gate, not the usual passenger gate but one manned by army personnel. They recognized him and waved him through.

So much for security.

Jay couldn't resist it. "No check at the gate?"

The guardee smiled pleasantly. "You don't want MPs peering into your ugly mug, do you, old chap?"

"Where is it?" Jay said.

The guardee swung the Land Rover onto the Belfast road. "Under the cushion on the back seat. Right side. Behind the passenger."

Jay said, "Fine. Is there anything I should know?"

"Oh, yes," said the guardee. "Quite a bit, if you can bear it."

"First of all, where?"

"The city, where else? Breathe the nice clean country air while you can. You'll know we're there by the smell. The great unwashed. The arse end of the world, that's our destination."

As they drove sedately into the beleaguered city, the guardee's voice droned on. It sounded, on the ground, even worse than it had in Mr. Jones's office, where all things were reduced to matters of policy. This was the street where duty was done. Jay had to remind himself of that.

It was all a matter of duty.

Somebody had to do it.

He'd drawn the card, that was all.

Jay sat morosely in the drafty Land Rover as it buzzed along the Irish roads. The evening traffic was heavy in the city. If the Eastern Tours job had been public, this was even more so. And it was to happen in this edgy, all-seeing city, not blinkered, safe-seeming, soppy old London.

Here everybody would get a good look at him, and afterward they would be bound to put the jigsaw together. He didn't like that one bit. Mr. Jones had quickly reassured him. No need, ever, to go back, dear boy. This is a one-off. Strictly a one-off. Mr. Jones smiled, as if the phrase was one he had lately learned, which it probably was. All Mr. Jones had to do, Jay thought, was to sit in his office and wait. If he was out there he'd shit himself. For that matter, he was not too happy, not happy at all. He'd recovered from the Brecon Beacons, but he still carried a few bruises and there was still a strip of plaster across his forehead, from where the log had hit him, in the struggle in the water.

"Been over here before?" asked the guardee.

Jay said noncommittally, "Yes."

The guardee said, "The Regiment?"

Jay knew he meant the SAS. The guardee had clocked him correctly. Maybe he wasn't a complete idiot.

He did not reply.

The guardee said, "I thought of it once, but they seem to like me in this job."

Jay said nothing to that either.

They were moving out of the brightly lit shops of central Belfast now, and the streets were becoming darker and smaller. Here and there a shop was deserted, with wooden planks across the windows, or barricaded behind gratings and heavy locks. Huge tower estates loomed from time to time, and they were twice stopped at checkpoints. Army patrolmen looked in at them, their camouflage overalls bright green and brown, their weapons glinting in the lamplight. The guardee showed his papers on these occasions, and they were waved on. All this time, the guardee talked.

After two or three miles, the streets became deserted, lights burned in the houses, and there was a feeling of being watched. They turned abruptly into a slum-clearance site, and drove in bumpy blackness for a full minute. The guardee had switched his lights off. He seemed to have finished his briefing. It was pitch-dark. Jay got out of the vehicle, quickly and quietly.

The guardee's voice carried to him in the darkness.

"You got all that, old boy? All quite clear?"

"Yes," said Jay, low. What was the idiot shouting for?

"I'll come with you part of the way."

"You fucking won't," said Jay coldly.

The guardee stayed where he was.

"You can't miss it. It's not much of a place, glorified bar-cum-boardinghouse."

Jay said, "The only thing I haven't got is the name."

"I think I should guide you, at least across this site. It's a few minutes to the road."

"You'll do nothing, prick. The name?"

The guardee, very coldly, told him.

Jay thought, He sounds like one of the prefects at school, when I got out of line. He felt suddenly up, keen, ready. The spell on the Beacons had put the edge back on him.

He began to walk toward the lights.

Finney's bar was high-class for the area, although it was situated near a slab of semi-slum high-rise. The ten-minute walk had taken Jay into an area of solid houses, some with gardens. There was a neon sign spelling out "Finney's Hotel & Bar" in blue tubing. It seemed respectable enough. Jay did not know anything at all about this part of the city and did not want to. His briefing had been simple. He was to go in the bar, find his man, and then proceed according to briefing. He went in, walked straight up to the bar, and, still holding his briefcase, full of paint samples and genuine-seeming letters inquiring about the stuff, asked for a large scotch.

He made no effort to disguise his accent.

Finney, the landlord, if it was Finney, a tall thin man with a mop of wavy gray hair, asked, "Would that be with water?"

"As it is, please." Jay laid an English pound coin on the bar. The conversations around the room had faded as he spoke.

"It's a poor ould day." Finney put the drink in front of him.

Jay downed the scotch in one gulp.

"Ye needed that one," said Finney, with a rise of the heavy eyebrows.

"I did. Trying to sell paint to you people is very hard work. I'll have another and one for yourself."

"Sure, I'll have one bi the nock," said Finney, helping himself to a bottle of Guinness. "You're a salesman then, sir?"

"For my sins," said Jay, looking around now. The room, which had gone silent, was buzzing with quiet conversation again.

Finney wiped the bar with a cloth. Like barmen in England fifty years ago, he wore a long white apron. There were no women in the bar, and only a dozen men, half of whom looked as if they could have been salesmen. Finney's next remark confirmed the point.

"We get a few in the selling line staying with us." He was looking at Jay very steadily. This city, Jay thought. Eyes everywhere. "We have the rooms above."

"I'm staying in the town. A bit pricey. I'll remember next time, maybe."

"Your first trip, then?"

Questions, more than he'd wanted. But this was a better way than creeping into a corner. Front it out, they'd look once and then, if you seemed all right, they'd leave it alone.

"Yes, I was over talking to a fella interested, seemed worth it. He's coming in to meet me, all being well. If he turns up." Jay looked at his watch. "I could have got home tonight otherwise."

"Ah, you have to hustle for business these days, sure enough, sir."

Before Finney could ask if the person he was to meet was a regular customer, Jay picked up a *Belfast Telegraph* from the counter. "Can I?"

"Help y'self, sir. Sure there's nothin' in any of them to cheer a man up."

Jay nodded his thanks and went across to a corner seat with his drink. He stared around. Nobody was looking at him. The place was thickly and brightly carpeted and had Victorian iron rails to the stairs, obviously to the rooms above. The other door, he had been briefed, led to a men's room in the backyard, a relic of the days when this had been a simple bar. That was his way out, obviously, at closing time, which—Jay looked surreptitiously at his watch—was in forty-five minutes exactly. It was a very long time.

Jay read his *Telegraph* for five minutes before glancing over it at the other occupants of the room. Four looked like visiting salesmen, two from the South, to judge by their accents, two Brits, as out of place as he was himself. They seemed to be businessmen and were locked in close conversation, referring from time to time to sheafs of paper covered with figures. They did not pay in cash for the drinks Finney brought across to them. Plainly they were staying in the place, and the drinks were going on their bill. That reassured Jay, but not altogether. If he had known that twelve people, at least, were going to get a very good look at him, he would have vetoed this operation at the start. He was half inclined to abort it as it was.

The only thing stopping him was that he'd gone this far, and the guardee and his corporal were moving around, if they stuck to the plan, and there was no way of contacting them, none at all.

Forty minutes to closing time, and yet this looked like a bar that, with its hotel-style licence, might never close. The man was not in the bar; he'd seen that in his first look around the place. Apart from the visiting businessmen, the rest were locals, less sharply dressed but of some small affluence; shopkeepers and the like, he guessed them to be. Most were drinking Irish or Scotch whisky and porter or Guinness chasers. Some smoked pipes. It was a comfortable place of its kind, a good cut above an ordinary Belfast drinking bar. The sort of place a man in a good way in the scrap trade might frequent. They had told him almost nothing about the man except that, and how he looked.

Jay sat and thought: This is bloody stupid. I ought to finish my drink and get out.

He had decided to do exactly that when the man came in. He was wearing the distinctive cap, a very light tweed, almost white, and a dark blue suit of thick worsted, the sort a Belfast workingman of his age might wear, if he got on in the world a bit. His face was fat and his manner jolly, but his eyes were everywhere, and Jay's first reaction was, he's no mug.

Finney was greeting him. " 'Evening, Joe." He deftly placed a large glass of Irish and One by the Neck in front of the man. "Thon's a poor ould day."

The man sipped his Irish and poured the stout himself. "It is, oh yes, indade it is."

Finney gestured toward the corner in which Jay sat, looking over his *Telegraph*. "Goin' to try your luck then, Joe?"

The man laughed loudly, causing one or two of the locals to look up and smile. "Bejasus, I could use some. I reckon ye have the thing fixed itself."

Finney shook his head. "Not at all. It's ready for a big payout."

Jay allowed himself to relax. He turned and looked in the direction toward which Finney pointed. In the corner stood a huge slot machine, its dials softly glowing.

The man said, "Givvus a fiver's worth of coin, I'm gonta get even with this skin tonight!" Finney promptly put a blue bag of coins on the bar counter. "I thought ye might go mad," he said, "so I got them special from the bank for ye."

The man put a fiver on the bar, took the packet of coins, and advanced on the slot machine. Finney brought his drinks across and put them on Jay's table. "I hope ye don't mind, sir? Himself's just gonta give the machine a bit of arm, y'see?"

Jay thought, I cannot believe this, I simply cannot bloody believe it. He smiled and said, "Not at all. Sure."

"Ah, thank ye, sir." The man emptied the coins out of the bag onto Jay's table, which was the nearest to the slot machine, simply a happenstance, but one he did not care for, did not care for at all. The man dropped several of the coins onto the floor, and Jay picked up one that had rolled under his feet and offered it to the man.

"Thankye, sir, ye might give me luck if ye spit on it!"

Jay spat on the coin and gave it to the man.

The locals in the bar laughed. The businessmen went on talking to each other. It occurred to Jay suddenly that they could be backup, they were young enough. Nothing had been said either by Mr. Jones or the guardee about backup, but then it wouldn't be. Need to know. If his back was being covered, that could help, in this city.

The man placed the coin Jay had given him among the others and began to play the machine. The intermittent shuddering of the thing was tedious; the stack of coins began to dwindle, despite occasional small wins. Jay crossed to the bar, got himself another drink, and wordlessly took it back to the corner.

Finney said as he served Jay, "One of these days he'll do it."

Jay sat and sipped his drink as the pile of silver coins went down. They were surprisingly soon exhausted. The man looked at the machine for a long moment, than at Jay, and said, "I'll have this ould skin this night if it's the last thing I do on God's earth."

Jay smiled a smile he didn't mean.

This, he thought, is getting very, very dangerous.

The man went across to the bar and laid another fiver on the counter. Unblinkingly, Finney handed him another bag of coins.

The man returned to the machine and began to feed in the coins.

Jay looked at his newspaper. On only one occasion had he ever talked to a subject. That had been in Cyprus, and he had been accompanied by a Cypriot who was there to finger the man, and he had not understood what the two of them had been talking about anyway. He had guessed the subject to be some sort of gun-runner. Cyprus was a great place for that, and for a dozen other activities that might end, for its participants, violently. For the subject it had ended very violently, at the back of his workshop. The finger man was posing as a salesman, as Jay was tonight. They all three went out the back to demonstrate the sample, which was some kind of small electric drill. Jay had done the job from behind, as the subject craned over to see the finger man demonstrate the drill. He had turned unhurriedly and walked out, leaving the rest to the finger man, and found the small car parked where they had said it would be. He drove down the mountain roads to Limassol, and an hour later he was on a flight to Heathrow.

Jay had not liked it then, the talking to, or rather listening to, the subject, and he liked it less, a great deal less, in this place, full of eyes and ears.

The machine next to him clanged and hissed, and he forced himself to turn from time to time and look at the man. The large white tweed cap was pushed back from the man's face now, and he pressed the buttons and pulled the lever with maniacal fervor. "I'll have the beatin' of this fella yet, surely to God I will, if there's justice in heaven itself!"

The second lot of coins was almost gone, and the rest of the room was watching with some sympathy when the man hit the jackpot. The coins cascaded into the receptacle in a clicking avalanche of silver. The man shouted and swore and danced, and everything in the bar stopped. Even the two businessmen looked across. The regulars crowded around the man and laughed and clapped him on the back and shouted their delight.

The man stood, quiet and somewhat dazed now, as he collected the silver pieces and laid them out in rows, with the help of his friends, on Jay's table. "You don't mind, do ye, sir?" The man called for drinks on the house for everyone in the bar, and Finney said, "By God, Joe, ye did it, at that! Are ye givvin' your winnings away already? How much is it, anyway?" Finney seemed as pleased as anybody, and Jay thought: I really should abort this; they'll be talking about this night for a month.

He indicated to Finney that he'd have the same again, a large scotch. The locals all took their specials, but the two Brit businessmen declined politely and went on talking. The man's friends totaled up the jackpot and told the man, who was by now sitting bemused at Jay's table, that his winnings came to thirty-seven pounds, even.

"Will ye have it in notes, Joe?" asked Finney kindly, as to a drunk.

"I will not," said the man. "I'll have it in me cap and show herself the sight of it when I get home. I have only the hundred yards to go, so I do, and she's forever givin' me the length of her tongue about the gamblin' and bettin', so I'll just demonstrate to her it isn't all losing!"

The man looked at Jay and winked.

Jay smiled back and sipped his whisky.

The man sat for a very long time, looking at the money. Then he began to pile it into his white tweed cap. To Jay's surprise, the cap held it all. It was a very large cap indeed, with a tweed bobble on the top of it.

Finney came across to supervise the work. He placed an Irish in front of the man and asked, "What you gonta do, Joe, now you've won the jackpot?"

It seemed to be a serious question. The man looked surprised. "D'ye know, that's a helluva ting? What ammant I gonta do?" He looked at Jay and raised his glass. "Your health, sir."

"And yours," said Jay, drinking his whisky.

"You brought me the luck," said the man, with the solemnity of a half-drunk. "It was yourself spittin' on the coin did it."

"No," said Jay. "That coin went a long time ago."

"No matter," said the man. "You're the stranger. It's well known a stranger's spit brings ye the luck." He touched his brow with a hand like a ham. "You'll have another, Mister . . . ?"

"No thanks," said Jay. "I'm supposed to be talking business with a man, if he ever turns up."

The man said, "Well, tomorrow's another day. Business can be done anytime, but it's not every day ye win the jackpot."

"That's true," said Jay, thinking: only fifteen minutes to closing time, and the guardee said he always goes home prompt at closing time, it's a thing with him. Jay added, "I don't have the luck." It was true; he didn't back many winners and he had dozens of bets on horses every month.

"Is it the horses with you?"

Jay nodded. Anything to keep the conversation general. How had it got this far?

The man placed a finger along his nose. "I hear one from time to time. When the boys are takin' one over." He smiled, the sharp eyes blurred with drink. "Takin' one over to win, y'know what I'm saying?"

Jay had forgotten. This was the land of the horse.

"Well, I get plenty of tips, but they're never any good."

The man sighed. "Even the jockeys don't know. They're the worst judges, the jockeys. It's the trainers ye need to hear from. They know. If anybody knows."

"I never meet any trainers," Jay said. "I'm strictly a guesser."

"Then ye'll lose your money." The man touched his winnings, brimming over the edge of the ridiculous cap.

"I do." Jay was telling no less than the truth.

He liked to gamble. He always had. It was one of the reasons his army pay had never covered his expenses, one of the reasons he'd gotten out of the army when he saw there wasn't much prospect of promotion in his line regiment. The card games, the drinking, the racing losses, the mess bills, what a catalogue.

It was, he supposed, one of the reasons he was sitting here.

He said, "I enjoy a bet. So why not?"

The man, who showed no signs of moving from the table, leaned forward. He was drunker than Jay had realized. But he had a question, and it was a good thing Jay was prepared for it.

"What line of business are ye in then, if I might ask?"

"Paint. I'm over here trying to sell it."

"You staying at the hotel here?"

"No, no, I'm in the city."

"Ah. Well. If it's business y'have to look the part, am I right now?" The eyes, that had gone bright for a moment, clouded again. Jay, who could drink most of a bottle of whisky at a sitting, and who was blessed with a head of iron, felt as if he had not had a drink all evening. He glanced at the clock above the bar. Ten minutes to closing time, and then he was out. If the man hadn't gone by then, Jay had an alibi. Or anyway, an explanation: The man stayed in the bar, he showed no sign of leaving, and, besides, he'd been too visible. It would serve. It would have to serve.

The man said, as if Jay had contested the point, "Business is important, sure it is. But so is living, aren't I right?" Jay nodded; the man was getting maudlin, he would to God he was somewhere else. The man took a wallet from his pocket. From it he fumblingly detached three or four color photographs taken, by the look of them, on a cheap Polaroid. He held them for Jay's inspection.

Oh, my God, no, Jay thought. Not this.

He began, very seriously, to dislike the man.

The man said, the photographs spread out like a hand of cards, "Four childer I have, mister."

"Nice family," Jay said.

"That's Joseph the eldest, and Mark and Mary and the little one, Charley." He waited for Jay to comment.

"Very nice." Jay had said it a hundred times to men in the army. He had never carried phtographs of his kids, even when he had them. Now there was nothing in his pockets except the fake wallet and business cards that said he was a paint salesman. "Lovely family," he added, his whole body chilled now, with anger, which should have been directed at Mr. Jones and the guardee, but had somehow turned in toward himself, and then outward, towards the man.

The man put the photographs away and said, "How about yourself? Any childer?"

"Two. A girl and a boy."

Always tell the truth, they had told him. Or as near to it as you can. The truth sounds right. One truthful remark among a dozen lies can help the lies, make them palatable.

"And how old's the wee fella?"

"Six next birthday." It was the truth again.

The man said, "Well, there y'are, the same age as my wee fella. Ah, they're a blessin' to a man, a family, they are just." Jay nodded. It was all he could do. The man took from his pocket a turnip watch in silver, obviously an heirloom of no real worth. He consulted it. "Just time for a last drink. I doubt your business acquaintance is coming tonight, it's nearly closin'. But don't despair. In this country, sure, it means nothin', nothin' at all. To-morrow's another day." He raised the hamlike hand, but not his voice. "Can we have two of the same there?"

"You can, Joe," said Finney, who had caught the almost con-versational tone of the order and bustled across with the drinks. He put them down and stared at the coins in the cap. "Are ye really gonta walk home with that wee cap filled up the like o' that?"

"Certainly I am," said the man, and winked at Jay in salute. Jay drank his whisky and said nothing.

"Begod," said the man, "ye can take your whisky, for an Englishman."

Jay smiled and picked up his case. "I'll have to say good night."

"If you're going back into town you'll need a taxi," Finney said.

"No, thanks. I hired a car. It's just up the road." This was get-ting worse. He had to get out, now, out and away from this insan-ity. "Is the gent's out the back?"

Finney said, "Sure, if you're leaving, sir, you can get to one out there. There's another inside, but that way you're on your way home, are ye not?" He raised his voice. "Time, gentlemen, for all those who have a home to go to!"

The man drank his whisky and smiled at Jay. "Good night to you, sir, and may ye back many a winner this season."

Jay smiled back automatically, nodded, hefted his briefcase in his hand, and swept out of the bar. To his relief, none of the regu-lars seemed to be leaving, and the businessmen were still talking. The darkness and the cold air hit him. He went into the men's room, which was a stone-built pissoir dating back to God knew when, and urinated, thinking out his story. He would stick to his decision. There was no point in changing his mind now. The job was off. Too much *danger*. It was as simple as that. He began to work out the directions the guardee had given him. He would get out of here, very quickly, walk to the corner of the street, two hun-dred yards along, before the Land Rover arrived, and then he'd just jump in and tell them no go. The man would still be in the bar where Jay had left him.

They'd be furious, the guardee anyway. The corporal didn't

matter. Nor did the guardee, really. He was only a dogsbody, following orders. Mr. Jones would be tricky, but in the last analysis, Jay's decision was final, wasn't it?

Jay came out of the pissoir and took a deep breath of damp air. The rain had stopped, and there were a few stars to be seen. The high that he had been on, the psychological residue, he supposed, of the Beacons, had quite gone. He felt relaxed, and easy with himself, now the decision was made. A few difficult moments ahead, but nothing he couldn't handle, although he'd never aborted a mission before. Still, there had to be a first time.

He stepped out of the yard into the street.

The flickering neon sign, "Finney's Hotel & Bar," illuminated the street for fifty yards or so.

At the very edge of the light, walking, none too steadily, into the darker patches farther on, was the solitary figure of the man.

It *was* him, without doubt; he'd drunk up and gone straight out the front door. Jay followed, walking very quickly, scanning the street ahead for any sign of the Land Rover. There was none.

Jay slackened his pace. The man was going home, with the cap, containing his jackpot winnings, in his right hand. Jay smiled. Bloody good luck to him; he'd be happy tonight, anyway. They might send somebody else, probably would, to do the job, but what the hell. He felt, for a fleeting moment, an insane impulse to run up to the fool and tell him to disappear, get lost, save himself, but that was, of course, simply not on. All that was on was to let him get to his home, a row house in the next street, and disappear from the night. Obviously the guardee, for all his shit, was late, and just as well.

At that moment the Land Rover came fast out of a blind entry. It had no lights showing, and the engine was spluttering, cold. Late, Jay thought, cursing inwardly, probably been there for hours, alerting the whole neighborhood. The Land Rover cut across the road, the engine loud with choke, the guardee and another man (not the corporal, no glasses), both in uniform, jumped out, very fast, leaving the Land Rover by the curb. They laid hands on the man, one on each side of him, in the classic way of all arresting officers. Jay sprinted the fifty yards toward them, and in the time it took him they had all but gotten the man into the front seat of the Land Rover. He was protesting, and at the crescendo of his protest (Jay could not hear the words, his heart was pounding in his ears, Jesus, did nothing ever go the way it was supposed to?) the cap suddenly came out of his hands and the hundreds of silver coins wheeled and danced and bowled along the pavement.

The men all stood and stared at them.

The coins ran on and on and spun and stopped. Nothing else moved in the dark street.

"Thon fellas is lost," cried the man. "Look what ye done!"

"Shut up, you!" The guardee thrust the man hard down into the front seat.

Jay thought: What a balls-up. He said, very low, "Forget it— I've been rumbled in that place. It's no go!"

The guardee stared at him uncomprehendingly. "What are you talking about? We have to get out of here." He held the door open, and Jay got in the back, fast, next to the Intelligence corporal in the glasses, who looked apprehensive, as well, Jay thought, he might. The other man, the sergeant, ran to another vehicle, at a point twenty yards up the road. The guardee got into the driver's seat of the Land Rover, shouting, "Eyes front, you!" to the man sitting next to him, and gunned the motor. They tore, lights off, out of the street.

"Me jackpot money," the man shouted. "It's gone!"

The guardee said, quietly, "Shut your fucking mouth."

"Put your headlights on. You'll get us all killed," said Jay.

The man tried to twist around. Jay saw that the sergeant, the one who had gone, had put handcuffs on him.

"Eyes front, I told you!" said the guardee, backhanding the man across the face with his free hand. After a few hundred yards he put on his lights. Jay felt better. Soon he would get a chance to explain, to reverse all this, to call a halt, to say, forget it, I'm very probably remembered back there, or I will be, sooner or later. A cold sweat spread over his body. The relaxed feeling had gone. The high had gone. All he felt was cold.

If he aborted the operation, the man would go free. He would also see Jay, and identify him, which he possibly hadn't done yet. Of course, he'd heard the voice. No two voices alike. He'd go back to the bar, sooner or later. He'd talk, compare notes, doubtless report to whoever his superiors were. Jay thought, it's possible I can do something, it's still possible, I can get the guardee to stop, and get out, talk to him, discuss it. He sat, very still, behind the man, as the Land Rover sped along the deserted roads.

The man was protesting mildly. He seemed to be sobering up, fast. "What d'ye want me for, sure I'm nobody, I'm only a wee businessman selling a bitta scrap iron."

The guardee said, "Just a few questions, downtown. You've been downtown before?"

"Sure I have," the man said, "and they've always had to let me go, am I right? I done nothing, I done nothing at all, ye'll be wasting your time like ye did before, so you will!"

The guardee said, "Now, you know you're a quartermaster and I know you're a quartermaster, so just keep your mouth shut or we'll shut it for you!"

The man slumped in his seat, muttering, "I done nothing, I tell ye, Jesus help me I done nothing." But he seemed, to Jay, slightly reassured. He'd been downtown before. He could cope.

The Land Rover buzzed on through the dark night.

No vehicle followed them.

Slowly, they found their way out of the mean streets, up into the high road that fringed the city and the hill that loomed over it. The road was misty and deserted, with high hedges, on both sides. It was then Jay knew there was no turning back, no way of changing anything. It was a balls-up, but it wasn't his fault. It was Mr. Jones's fault. Or the guardee's. But not his.

The Land Rover came to a shuddering halt.

The man peered forward. "Where are we? We're not on the way to the station, are we?"

The guardee said icily, not looking at him, "Just get on with it, will you?"

Jay took the Webley from under the seat (a Webley, for God's sake—were they mad, in this situation?) and put it against the man's head. He did not stay to see what a mess it made, because he knew. "What stupid bastard left that for me?" he asked quietly, tossing the weapon into the guardee's lap. "Where's my car?"

"Fifty yards up the road," said the guardee. "Jesus, what a mess." The corporal with the glasses vomited on his boots.

Jay did not look at them or at anything at all.

He picked up his sample case and walked the fifty yards to the

Ford Fiesta. The key was in the ignition. He had been told the way to the airport (straight on for six miles, follow the signs) and that somebody would be waiting for him at the gate.

Jay started the engine and drove off at a moderate speed, into the soft damp night.

Jay found the jet fighter waiting in the dark at Aldergrove. Same plane. Same pilot. If the man was curious, he didn't show it. Jay fitted himself into the observer's seat, the mechanic waved, and they took off in a sudden swoop. Flying in one of these things was nothing like sitting back on an airliner. It was hairy. The lights of Belfast were laid out below them, like a fairyland, and then they were over the Irish Sea. Jay closed his eyes, fighting the force of the takeoff, and tried to relax, the Canadian way, but his spine was like steel. The deed had been done, but what a mess. He was still shaking. His old ability to dissociate himself from the action, to stand outside it while he was performing it, to see it all coldly, professionally, was, he felt with some slight panic, gone. For a moment there, in the Land Rover, he had very nearly not done it. He had almost tossed the Webley to the guardee and said, "Do it your bloody self."

Then the training had taken over.

Why, then, was he feeling like this?

The jet fighter climbed, and Jay's stomach rumbled. He hadn't eaten for ten hours. He didn't feel hungry anyway. He didn't feel anything. A deed that should have been easy had become very complicated. Why not wait until the man left the bar to pick him up? Why, a lot of things. Because, was the answer, it had to be the right man, there had to be no possibility of a mistake, and in a dark street there was always the possibility of a mistake, especially from a motor vehicle, especially looking across a road. Yet, *he'd* been exposed, and that was unforgivable. Worse, he'd talked to the subject, and that was inconceivable, impossible. The cheap Polaroids of the man's wife and children, very ordinary people, danced in his mind. Jay took a grip. He had to stop *this*. He-simply-had-to-stop-it. He had to think of nothing, absolutely nothing at all, until he reported to Mr. Jones.

Jay sat and thought about nothing, as the fighter zoomed across the Irish Sea, climbed a bit for the hills of North Wales, and set down at Northolt almost to the minute, as per schedule.

Jay touched the pilot on the shoulder by way of thanks (they had not exchanged a single word) and found his own way across to his Jensen, resting in the parking lot. The elderly RAF intelligence officer who had seen him off, called after him in the darkness.

"All go well, sir?"

Jay called back, "Yes. Fine. Thanks. Good night."

The RAF intelligence officer called back, "Good night, old chap."

That man, Jay thought, had no idea what it was all about either. Just an apparatchik obeying orders. He drove the Jensen along the airfield perimeter and out through the gate, where he was waved through by the RAF sentry without being stopped. They'd been told to do that, been given the car's registration number, no doubt. He didn't like that, but didn't suppose it mattered, really. No point in getting paranoid, not more than absolutely necessary, anyway. He drove halfway back to town before he stopped at a public telephone booth and called Mr. Jones.

"Yes, dear boy, how did it go?"

He could have been asking a cricket score.

"It went bloody awful. It was a shambles."

"Really?" The opening batsmen could have both been out for a duck apiece.

"Yes, really. Too public, and a piece of hardware like a cannon. Whoever selected it should have shot himself in the foot with the bloody thing."

"We're talking a mite too specifically," said Mr. Jones reproachfully. "But anyway, I take it the deed is done?"

"Yes, it is, and I'm not happy, I'm not happy at all. It was a complete and utter balls-up."

There was a long silence. The batsman was appealing against the umpire's decision. Very bad form. Mr. Jones said, "I'm sorry to hear that. There was a little backup for you, y'know?"

Jay thought: the two businessmen. Another two people who knew his face, marvelous. Jay said, "All I need is the IRA on my neck."

Mr. Jones was silent. This was plainly inexcusable. This was refusing to walk when given out. He said icily, "How do you know it wasn't the other side?"

Jay was aghast. "A Loyalist? If I'd *known* that—"

"But you don't know, do you, dear boy?" Mr. Jones added,

"Perhaps you'll go home and get a good night's sleep, and then give me a call tomorrow and come in? There's something else, something very exciting, and, I imagine, profitable, in the pipeline."

"You'll be fucking lucky," replied Jay bitterly, and hung up.

F·I·V·E

JAY SHOOK THE WATER out of his eyes and pulled himself onto the grass. The Mediterranean sun beat down on him, and his body absorbed its warmth greedily. God, it was so good to be here. The pool was a minute one, built by an old army acquaintance of Jay's, and the water had to be drawn from the nearby stream, causing the local French population to shake their heads. Weekly baths were a rarity around here. The peasants were still the same peasants wartime RAF flying crews were warned about, should they bail out over France. "If these people smell of onions and garlic," the RAF leaflet had read, "and don't seem to wash or shave all that often, don't show distaste or disapproval. They are peasants, of a kind we have not had in England for over a century. And remember, they are our allies and can help you." The villagers down the twisting country road still smelled of onions and garlic. There were a few Parisians who owned odd cottages here and there, but not enough of them yet to make the village chic. No doubt that would come. Meantime, the small stone cottage (only two rooms, flagged floors and an antiquated stove) was to be enjoyed. Apart from the pool, the old colonel hadn't modernized it at all. "I liked it the way it was, the day I walked into it, in 'forty-five. I bought it for a couple of hundred pounds I'd made on the black market, and I've been here ever since. It's yours when you think you can afford it."

Then the old boy had died suddenly, of a heart attack.

His daughter wanted twenty-eight thousand pounds for it.

Jay had first refusal.

It was Jay's dream to live in this place.

The problem, as always, was the money.

If he bought the place, he had two choices. The first: he had to find some kind of work in London, which, with his Zurich money (which he'd use as purchase price), would mean he could modernize it, and let it out to visitors for some part of the year, coming over for a few weeks at most, when he wanted to. The second: he could just buy it, live in it as it was until his money ran out, and then see.

He had calculated, with the Zurich money as it now stood, that he could live here for three years without working. Looking around, as he lay propped on one elbow on the grass, he thought: A bit primitive, but why worry? Isn't it the answer?

Angie waved from the doorway. "Lunch is ready, darling."

He'd forgotten Angie. In the dream, he had always thought of being on his own here, living, like a French peasant, off the land, planting vegetables, keeping chickens, growing a beard, smoking Gauloises, drinking the local wine, going native. Peace was what he needed.

He also needed a woman.

He had to recognize that.

"Coming," he called, pulling himself to his feet.

Face it, Angie could not come and live here. Angie was a city girl, and she had a city job that she loved. It was a pipe dream, it could never happen. Forget it.

Jay walked, the scrubby grass tickling his feet, into the dark cool of the kitchen. There was a large whitewood table, left by the colonel, just as he'd found it, forty years before, now covered by bottles of Vittel and the local red, and dishes holding sausages and cheese and the sardines bought in Vence two days ago and still fresh, kept cool in the vast pantry. Long rolls, from the village baker, a two-mile drive but worth it, lay on the table, and there was a tang of fresh-ground coffee in the air.

Jay felt better and tried not to think of Mr. Jones.

One thing was for sure: the old bastard would be thinking about him. Wondering where he was. Jay laughed out loud, and Angie turned to him, smiling, and he kissed her. The kisses here in the sun were different from the boozy, sexy grapplings in the London flat. Here it all seemed very natural and easy, the lovemaking part of the sun and the water and the food and the wine. Jay felt relaxed, in a way that he had not felt since, he realized, the last time he was here. That had been three years ago, when he was still trying to forget Cherry and the kids.

The kiss began to get serious, so he slapped Angie on the bottom—she was wearing only shorts and a silk shirt—and said, "Food first, woman!"

"Promises, promises!" Angie broke away and sat down, waiting for him to help himself before she started. He thought what a really nice girl she was, and how even if he didn't feel about her the sick jealousy he had always, until now, recognized as love, she really was admirable in almost every way. Very good in bed, willing and adventurous and not at all shy, a great turn-off with him. Pleasant, easygoing, good company. No bad habits. She smelled good, a turn-on with him, and she forgot sex the moment they got up, and turned into a nice, conventional English girl of her kind, neither upper nor lower, but somewhere in the middle, educated decently at one of the old girls' grammar schools before the comprehensives ruined them; father in a bank, home a semi, in Surbiton; then that most English of institutions, the BBC. He had to admit it, perfect wife material.

Trouble was, he didn't need a wife.

What could he offer a wife?

Nothing, except danger and possibly death, his death.

"You're not eating." Angie was looking at him with concern. "Aren't you hungry?"

"Ravenous." Jay ate a garlic sausage and drank a glassful of the rough wine and felt better. Angie didn't expect marriage, or anyway rarely mentioned it. She was thirty-two, that was all, and if he hung around her much longer it was going to leave it a bit late for her to find somebody else. Big problem, that. He poured himself another glass of the red and thought: I'll think about it seriously, when I get a chance.

"Is something wrong?" Angie's blue eyes were wide.

He pressed her hand. "No. Just relaxing. I needed this."

She laughed. "You come breezing into the flat, and three hours later we're on the plane."

"When I get an idea, I act on it."

He had. As soon as he'd hung up on Mr. Jones in that kiosk on the London Road, he'd decided to do this, come here, think things out. He had stood in the flat and pretended he'd had enough of London, and what about her?

Angie had looked puzzled but determined. She had sensed his desperation. She was good at things like that. She said, "I have an idea. I'll make a phone call in the bedroom."

Five minutes later she was back.

"I've talked to my establishment officer at her home. I told her in absolute confidence that I was pregnant, and going away to fix things, negatively." Angie was straight-faced. "She'll cover for me with my head of department. I'll be replaced on the show, but no questions are likely to be asked. She was very sympathetic."

The freemasonry of women, Jay thought.

"What," Angie had asked, "shall I pack for this place?"

"Not much," Jay answered. "It's ten miles from Vence, but you may never want to go in, except to shop. Cannes is thirty-odd miles away if we feel like a night out."

"Sounds heaven," Angie said calmly, and kissed him. "When do we go?"

"Now," Jay had answered, "before I change my mind."

He had booked seats for Paris, in Angie's name, from a discount shop in the Earl's Court Road, one way, that very evening. They had caught an Air France local for Nice from Paris and had rented a car, again in Angie's name, at the airport, and driven directly to the cottage. The cottage keys were held at a nearby farmhouse.

The English colonel's daughter (who lived in Reading) was too mean to modernize the place, so nobody except Jay and a few eccentrics would rent it, even in August. In late September it had been empty for weeks. The daughter had asked Jay, when he called her to arrange things, "Are you going to buy it? I might drop the price a bit. Daddy always wanted you to have it, you know."

"I'll think about it." Jay had put down the telephone, in the post office in Earl's Court. He had a strong suspicion his own telephone was bugged. Anyway, the journey had been uneventful. No followers, he was pretty sure, but, of course, having Angie with him, he had not taken the kind of precautions he would have taken had he been on his own.

Mr. Jones would wonder where he was, and if he wanted to find Jay badly enough, he would probably, sooner or later, find him.

Jay said, "Enjoying your hols?"

Angie grinned. "Loving it."

"Worried about the job?"

"Don't care if I never go back."

It was lightly said, but it seemed to need an answer.

"I've always meant to buy this place," Jay mused.

"Buy it? Is it on the market?"

"Yes—cheap, too."

Angie looked around and made a face. "Well, in winter it might be rather dreary." She smiled. "If you decide to, I'll come to cook for you."

Jay said nothing to that.

He ate his sausage and then some cheese and drank some wine, which he diluted with the Vittel.

Angie cleared the plates and brought the coffeepot to the table. The coffee was hot, black, and strong, and they drank it from French breakfast bowls. She said, "You know, darling, I do have a little money from the parents' house." She was alone in the world now, her parents both gone, inside a year. "It's quite a bit really, I suppose."

Jay had never discussed his finances with Angie. She knew he had some money coming in from his business, but she also knew he wasn't rich. He wasn't exactly poor, either. There was the money in Zurich, after all.

And here she was saying, if you haven't got the money, I have.

His heart warmed to her.

"I think I'd be able to buy it. They aren't asking much. The problem is, living here. What does one do, all the year?"

Angie looked startled.

"You're thinking of living here?"

Jay said stiffly, "I was. Stupid, what?"

Angie didn't reply. She gazed at him a moment, then put her hand on his. "There is something wrong, isn't there, darling? Is it the business?"

Jay moved his hand away from hers, and was sorry he did it, but he didn't put it back. He hated lying to Angie, which was why he almost never discussed his fictional business with her. He said, "No, no, nothing like that. I suppose I am a bit fed up, tired of London traffic, muggers, strikes, people who can't be bothered, bureaucracy, unions, television, football hooligans. I sometimes think England's completely finished, and all I want to do when I feel that is get away from it."

Angie stared at him in surprise.

He'd never said anything like that to her before.

It was, however, all too true.

"England seems pretty much the same as ever," she said slowly. "To me, anyway."

"It isn't," Jay replied grimly. "Next thing it'll go non-nuclear. Next thing it'll be Finlandized. Next thing it'll be in the Soviet sphere of influence."

"You don't honestly think that?"

Jay lit a Gauloise.

"I honestly do."

She was silent a long moment.

"You do, don't you? You really do!"

"A lot of people can see it coming. Some people even do something about it."

"Who do you mean?"

He shrugged it away. "I happen to love my country. What it was, the greatest empire since Rome. All that. It was something to be proud of. Now it's all social workers talking about racial equality on Channel Four."

"You're a little Englander, Jay." Angie laughed tolerantly. "I never knew."

"Makeup girls aren't supposed to know such things." Jay did put his hand on hers. "They're just for going to bed with."

Angie didn't respond with a laugh, as he expected her to. She looked serious.

"Do you really want to leave England? Come and live here?"

"I've dreamed about it for years." Sitting there, drinking the coffee, slighty muzzy from the wine and the sunshine, Jay felt it, for that moment, to be a possibility. "Just go native, live for ourselves for a few years, to hell with England and telly interviewers who think everything the Brits do is wrong."

"Would this place be any better?"

"For a while, perhaps. Ten years. Then we see."

"But we have the Americans."

"They'll go home if we leave NATO. And we might. All it would take is a few million votes. And we'd be on our own."

"My God," Angie said. "You make it sound hopeless."

"It isn't hopeless," Jay answered. "And some people know the alternatives. It's just a matter of keeping up our guard."

"You're talking about a Soviet invasion?"

"Infiltration, more like. They've got West Germany well penetrated already. There they're into the secret service, army, politics. In the United Kingdom, their placemen are in the unions, some very deep. And a lot of nice, caring opinion-makers who'd find a night out drinking with a Liverpool football supporter a terrifying experience assist them at every turn." Jay knew it was the wine that had loosened his tongue. He laughed to make it all seem nonsense. People always talked too much on holidays, often about politics, when there was no television to watch.

"Forget it, it's boring. I'm sorry. Let's talk about something else, shall we?"

"I never knew you thought so much about politics," Angie said.

"Only on holidays with lovely women."

"The way you talk. I think you believe all that."

He laughed again. "Only some of it." He stood up. "I feel like a visit to Cannes."

Angie stood up too. "Shall I put something else on?"

Jay shook his head. "I have a friend there, actually. It's business."

"You want to go on your own?" She looked surprised and hurt.

"It's business, Angie."

She began to collect the dishes, to stack them in the sink. Her shoulders drooped. He felt like a shit, but he had to get away, he had to stop talking to her; if he wasn't careful he was going to tell her what he did and why he did it. He kissed her on the cheek— she didn't turn around from the sink—and picked up the car keys from the table.

Ten minutes later he was on the road to Cannes.

He wondered if Willa was in port. He needed to talk to somebody. She would understand; she was the only person in the world who would.

He would buy Angie a present, something expensive, in Cannes, he decided.

Jay drove on, along the dusty road, toward the sea.

The *Colonel's Lady,* a forty-foot cabin cruiser, bright with paint-work and gleaming brass, one of the old wooden jobs, full of hard work but worth it, built on the Hamble seventy years ago, lay berthed in the old port at Cannes, and to Jay's profound relief, Willa was on deck. He saw her from a hundred yards, and it was all he could do to stop himself from shouting his pleasure. Willa's body, heavier than he remembered—but it had been three years since he'd seen her, after all—was wrapped in a jersey and denim shorts, and her feet were bare. Her dark eyes, framed by the black, curly hair (with some gray in it now), should have widened with surprise, but they didn't. It took a lot to surprise Willa.

"What the bloody hell are *you* doing here?" was her greeting.

"Couldn't come to the cottage without looking you up."

Willa threw him a bottle of French beer. "It's cold, I've just taken it out of the water." Jay caught the bottle and grinned. It was good to see the old girl. Old girl—they'd been lovers once, for a season. Willa had been the colonel's lady then, and once he and she had stayed, surreptitiously, at the cottage; but the old boy was dead and gone now; it was all a long time ago. Jay had felt bad about it at the time, but not bad enough to stop, until he had to. Willa, he supposed, was the nearest thing he'd ever had to a mother. There was a fifteen-year age difference, after all. How old had he been, twenty-three? A second looey, and Willa not just a brother officer's wife but the colonel's wife. Not the same regiment or anything—the old boy had been in some secret intelligence job—but bad form, however you looked at it. Yet, at twenty-three, it was forgivable, surely? Looking back, he could hardly believe the affair had ever happened. But it had, and he had talked to her, a lot. Willa, after all, was the only one who *knew.*

He had come running here because there was nobody else he could talk to. Maybe the whole trip was for this talk, this few minutes (for it could not be long; he knew enough about boats to realize Willa was preparing for sea) they would have together? Maybe he'd engineered it all, just to hear Willa say the words he knew, sooner or later, she would say. Get out while you can, run.

The problem would be telling her he was still in.

"Who's the girl?"

He stared at her. "What?"

"Who's with you? At the cottage? You wouldn't come here without a girl."

Jay laughed. "What makes you so sure?"

"Because I know you." She coiled a last rope and stood looking down at him, her whole body bereft of sex for him now, thickening and middle-aged (how old was she, fifty-five?), but pleasantly so. With the colonel dead these ten years and the divorce forgotten, Willa had made a new life for herself, out here, on the boat.

Well, if she could, he could.

"Her name's Angie. She works in television. She's nice."

Willa grimaced. "You've given up on whorish bitches then? It's about time."

Jay knew she meant Cherry, but he didn't rise to the bait. Anyway, Willa was right. She was right most of the time.

Jay, knowing now why he had come, felt he had to postpone the moment. Work up to it slowly, think it through. He drank his beer and avoided her eye, which was remorseless.

"How's trade?" he asked, gesturing to the boat, one of a long row of similar craft berthed against the quay. Laughter and music filtered from some of the other boats. Brown girls in bikinis lounged on the decks with older men (a man had to be rich to own a boat, or even rent one, here) in attendance. It was a fun place, Cannes. The problem was, how long could he safely enjoy it?

Willa was answering his question. "Trade's fine. Most of my clients are oil-rich Arabs. They get sick a lot and cut the trip short. That's profitable and I get an extra few days in port. That's why I'm here now. You're lucky to have caught me."

"Predestined." Jay grinned, and so did she. It was one of their old words, a woman's word, so probably used by Willa first. They'd been together, what? A few snatched nights in cheap London hotels, one trip here. He couldn't remember if the sex had been any good. He knew he'd been nervous and she'd taught him a lot. He'd always been confident with women, after her. In a sense that's all they'd had, a few dozen hours. Yet he'd told her, the last time he was here, on his own, about the jobs he did for Mr. Jones. She was the only one he'd ever told.

That, he thought, suddenly desperate, had to mean something. He asked, "Still happy, doing all this?"

Willa lit a Gauloise and threw him the pack. "I settle for content these days."

"Ah, yes. Content. I've heard that's very nice."

Willa inhaled deeply, like a man. "Content is something you'll probably only ever hear about." Her eyes stayed on him, implacably. "How much are you paying that prissy daughter of mine for the cottage?"

"Fifty a week, English."

Willa snorted. "Silly young cow, could get three times that if she tarted it up a bit. Right out of the way, though. One good thing about it."

Jay smiled, feeling a trifle sheepish. That first and only foreign week together, in the cottage, had been in late October. It had started to get chilly, especially at night, but they had not minded, or anyway Willa hadn't. Even then, he'd wondered at the ease with which she'd been able to stay there with him. After all, it was her husband's place, she'd slept in it with him as a young bride; how was such an act possible for her? He'd wondered then at the cruelty of women in love toward those they no longer loved, and he wondered again now. Willa was a decent woman in the strictest meaning of the word, and yet she could take her lover to her husband's dearly beloved cottage. She had explained herself briefly. "It's been over between us for years, in bed. Now we're just good companions."

However, the colonel wasn't as good a companion as all that. He'd left her one day, Jay never knew why. Probably grew tired of being tolerant about the lovers. Jay had never known, for sure, whether the colonel knew about himself and Willa. Probably not; there had been a lot of others, and their affair had lasted no more than a couple of months. Just the same, thinking about it made him feel bad.

"Do you have a job?"

Trust Willa. Straight at it.

"I've got a little business."

"Doing what?"

"Selling paint."

"Paint?"

"Yes, paint, that sticky stuff."

Willa looked disbelieving, but said no more.

Jay stared across the port toward the old town, bathed in the soft late-afternoon light of the Midi. The summer visitors were going, especially the French, and the place looked less like Blackpool on Bank Holiday than it did at the height of the season. He'd heard they had a drug problem now. Did anything stay the same, anywhere?

"Never miss England, I suppose?" he asked.

Willa snorted. "What, that shithouse? London's full of tourists all summer, worse than this place. Piccadilly's full of druggies, Leicester Square's full of winos, the theaters are full of Japanese. There's no society life. Even the army has officers with Geordie accents. If you speak decently everybody stares at you and sniggers. The young men look like tarts and the young girls look like male prostitutes, everybody's sniffing coke, and most people swing both ways. I can't bear it anymore. I shan't go back ever again. Sod England."

Jay felt suddenly defensive. This was just what he'd been saying to Angie, but Willa was different. Willa was army. Willa was the Aldershot Tattoo and the Changing of the Guard. Willa was Cheltenham Ladies' College and coming-out balls. If Willa had given up on England, then maybe it *was* too late.

"Some of the old England's still left," he said.

Jay, like his father, the old hero, never thought of England as Britain. England was being English, an idea one could be loyal to. British was like being a Brit, a nobody, these days. It was Saxon versus Celt, and Jay was a Saxon. So was Willa. They spoke the same language.

"Some of it may be, out in the country, I daresay," said Willa briskly, "but the cities are finished. It makes you cry." Willa shaded her eyes and looked along the marina. Jay wondered if she was expecting her Arab clients soon. He felt uneasy. He had to talk to her. Still, he could not bring himself to begin.

Instead, he said, "All that's true, but there's still something left of the old England. It comes out when we need it. Look at the Falklands. Men in the shipyards who'd strike because another workman picked up the wrong tool worked around the clock to keep the ships sailing." He wondered if that meant anything, but it had to, it must. "We have a small army, but it's good. Bloody good." He grimaced; he was sounding more like his father than ever. "The people of England are still the same as the men who fought at Agincourt. Our hearts are still in the trim." It was one of the old man's phrases, that.

"The bowmen at Agincourt were Welsh," said Willa. "Nowadays, they're all out on strike, asking for communism yesterday."

"You're wrong. We have a future. We must have. We can't pour a thousand years down the drain."

Willa smiled. "We've done it, dear. We used ourselves up in the war, spent all our gold, all our credits, finished it broke and bloody near beaten ourselves. The Americans picked up the pieces, including a lot of our markets. The Russians took half of Europe and waited for somebody to stop them and nobody did."

Jay said, "A lot of people feel as you do, and I admit the socialist experiment has damaged the social fabric a bit."

Willa laughed. "A bit? You're joking."

"And I also admit that having no conscription has meant we have football hooliganism instead. Those lads owe nobody anything because nobody's ever asked anything of them."

"What's your answer?" Willa demanded. "A few assault courses, a short haircut, a nice clean uniform?" She snorted. "They wouldn't even wear a uniform, most of 'em. They'd stage a sit-down strike. Jay, it's over, darling, it's all downhill from now on, it's all industrial disputes, social security, gay bars, bingo, and bisexual telly personalities, why kid yourself?"

"Because," Jay said, "it can't be allowed to be just that."

Willa said nothing. There was a silence in the bright sun, the only sound the water lapping against the side of the boat.

At last she spoke. "You think it's your duty, don't you? To see it isn't."

Jay said nothing. Let her think what she liked.

But of course it was his duty. If it wasn't his, whose was it? The state needed protection while it sorted itself out; surely any silly bugger could see that.

"You're still doing it, aren't you?" Willa asked. "That awful job of yours?"

At last she had spoken the words.

After a long pause, Jay answered her.

"Yes, I am, actually."

"Ever since we last talked?"

"On and off."

"For that same creepy old guy?"

"Yes."

Thank God he'd never told her Mr. Jones's name.

"When did you do your last job for them?"

"A few days ago."

Willa nodded. "That's why you're here. I'm the only one who knows, the only one you can talk to."

Jay looked down at the deck. This was even shittier than he'd expected.

"Something like that."

"You haven't told the new girl, Angie or whatever her name is, have you?"

"No."

"Then don't. However tempted you are, don't." Willa's voice was low and quite different from the one she'd used until now. "I can take it, I'm just an old army wife, a tough old bag, nothing upsets me anymore. I heard a lot from Davy too, about his war and afterward, when he was in military intelligence, and some of it was very naughty."

She lit another cigarette, and he could almost see her thinking. Why had he ever told her? He'd been drunk, of course. When had it been? Just after the Cyprus business, the first time he'd actually talked to a target. Now he'd done it again, in the Belfast bar, and it had affected him the same way. He'd seen the faces, both times, and both times he'd run to Willa. Jay began to sweat in the hot sun. He wasn't thinking straight. Why had he come here? Anybody could be around, the watchers might have been put on him, he was involving her, putting her in danger, Angie too. Jay fought down the familiar rising tide of paranoia—panic, sweat, then a deadly coldness—and stood up.

"Sorry, I'm way out of order. I shouldn't be bothering you with all this. Forget I came."

Willa looked up at him. "Did something happen this last time?"

He nodded. "No point in telling you what. It just threw me, that's all."

Slowly, she said, "There's a point, love. There's a point when you have to stop being a proper little patriot. There's a time when you have to say: I'm out."

Jay nodded. It was true. Put that way it sounded very like bugging out, but it was true.

"I know," he said. "It's a matter of how."

"They won't make it easy for you."

"I know."

"They'll keep on using you. They'll use you one time too many, it's their nature—and their job—to do that." Willa's voice softened. "Why don't you get out while you can? You've done enough for your country. If you're even *thinking* about getting out, go!"

Jay looked down at her. There really was a lot of gray in her hair now. He felt a sudden tenderness. He leaned over and kissed her on the cheek.

Then he stepped off the boat onto the quay.

"Thanks. Nice to talk. I'll see you again before I go back."

"I'll be off today, probably back next week sometime."

"I'll call by again." He didn't think he would. "Must go now."

"Yes. Of course." Willa called after him, as he turned away, "Come here anytime. It's the safest place. Out on the water."

He stopped and turned. "I'll remember you said that."

Willa nodded but said no more. He could feel her eyes on the back of his neck, all the way along the quay, until he turned past the little row of cafés, with their checked tablecloths, into the town. He felt as he'd felt when his mother sent him back to school, after the holidays.

The next week was a time out of life.

Mostly Jay and Angie stayed in the cottage and lazed. Angie cooked once a day, usually steak or fish and a salad; otherwise they just ate bread and cheese and cold sausage. They drank the local red and lay stretched out in the sun on the scrubby grass, or they slopped around in the pool. Few cars ever came along the track in which the rented Renault stood. The hedge around the cottage was thick and high; they could see nobody and nobody could see them. They enjoyed each other's bodies, mostly by night, but sometimes by day, and their lovemaking was tender and seemed to reach new heights of contentment. Angie said once, as their bodies parted, out on the grass—sex had taken them by surprise—"I never knew you could be so nice."

"Nice?" Jay didn't think of himself as nice, never had.

"Well, thoughtful. Gentle."

"Why, aren't I usually like that?"

"Usually you're exciting and demanding, and that's fine." Angie regarded him thoughtfully. "Here you're like another person."

"Which do you like best?"

Angie thought a long time before she answered. "This, I suppose. There's a tenderness in it."

"Well, I'm glad you're glad, whatever it is," Jay grunted, his eyes closed, the hot sun beating down on his naked body.

"Is there any reason for that, do you think?"

"What?"

"Why you're so nice and gentle here and so rough and dangerous in London?"

Everything was all so nice and womanly that Jay almost told her, there and then.

He remembered, in time, Willa's words. He kept his eyes firmly closed. "Business worries. The old firm hasn't been doing too well. I suppose I could have talked to you about it, but I didn't want to worry you."

"Are you sure that's all?"

"Yes."

"There's nobody else involved? No other woman or anything?"

"No other woman."

"I wondered," Angie went on, "if you'd been seeing Cherry."

Jay laughed. This was easier. The sudden, insane temptation to tell all had passed. "I haven't seen my ex-wife or my ex-kids either for nearly a year."

"Why don't you ever take the kids out? You're entitled to have them one day a week and for holidays."

"I never know what to do with them. There's nowhere to go but the zoo. It just got more awkward every time. They were editing everything they said, keeping the other guy's name out of the conversation. I used to love them, worry if they got colds. All that. Now, weeks go by and I never think of them. She went away with another guy and she got my house, my money, and my kids. It's a mad, mad world, my masters."

Still, Jay did not open his eyes.

Angie said, "When they grow up you'll be able to talk to them."

"Like an amiable stranger, yes, I suppose so."

"You miss them though, don't you?" Angie said.

"Of course I miss them," Jay said savagely. "But it's no good missing them, it helps nothing."

"I'm sorry. I just wondered if it was that."

"Absolutely not. Let's just forget it, shall we?"

"If you say so."

She sounded very sad. He supposed she knew that he hadn't told her the truth. He knew in that moment the awful reality: he would have to leave her.

If she stayed with him, sooner or later, the way he'd been behaving, the drinking, the dreams (which had utterly stopped, out here), she'd suspect, or he'd be tempted to tell her, and he must never do that. It would be an act of terrible cruelty. The fact was, face it, it was becoming impossible to live with Angie, as it had been impossible to live with Cherry. He remembered the old colonel's words, here on this very lawn, long years ago, talking about his years in intelligence. "You see, Jay, most operatives in the game, in the underground war, behind desk or gun, have to be bent. Unless you're bent, not just obviously homosexual, but well, let's say a child molester, whips, porn, orgies possibly, unless you have had, at some time something in your life you've had to cover up, possibly *all* your life, some dark private secret, how will you know how to smell out the enemy's dark secrets?"

Jay had listened, as if to an abstract thesis. It had sounded almost like that, from the wise old bird, gray hair, aquiline features, pipe, very British and soldierly and tolerant, telling it like it was, really, all quite simple if only you thought about it, what? "The thing is," the old colonel, still married to Willa then, had gone on, "it's no use recruiting nice people to do business with nasty people. I know, I've recruited a few myself. You have to find somebody who's a bit bent, but not, if you'll pardon the expression, a nutter. You can usually tell by the sex. All criminals have bent sex lives. Prison probably helps the process, but they'd be bent anyway. What we're looking for are people who believe in what we're doing but are smart enough and, in a way, a strictly limited way, rotten enough to look at a KGB operative or whatever and not exactly think or act like a churchwarden, what?"

Jay had laughed. "What are you trying to do, Colonel, recruit me?"

The old colonel had looked thoughtful. "You could do it. I've no doubt of that. All I wonder is, are you bent enough?"

"Sexually, are we talking about?"

The colonel's voice had still been detached. "Yes, I suppose we are. That's the litmus test, as I say. I mean, you seem all too ordinary in that department to qualify." He had poked around in his pipe with a dead match. "Of course, people are very deep where sex is concerned. One can always be surprised."

Now, after all these years, Jay wondered if the colonel had been recruiting him. Mr. Jones had never said who had (he wouldn't, would he?), except for the absurd fiction about his old commanding officer, which the colonel had never been. So had he, in fact, put Jay up, for that most exclusive club?

Why would he do that?

The answer was all too horrifyingly plain: Jay had been sleeping with his wife.

But that meant the old boy had waited years.

It was possible.

It was more than possible. It was bloody likely.

Jay felt the paranoia creep over him. The usual symptoms of claustrophobia (although he was in the open air) forced him quickly to his feet, plunged him into the pool and out again. Toweling himself dry, he called to Angie, "Tell you what, let's dress up and go into Cannes, eat a good dinner somewhere, and lose a few francs at the tables. What do you say?"

"I say whoops, let's go!"

Angie's face broke into a smile of pure delight. She loves me, he thought, and I can't make her suffer for it. I don't know how I'll tell her it's over, leave her a letter, probably, go out of the country for a bit, anything rather than look at her. In that moment, he realized how very much he cared for her. He would not say love, for love meant Cherry and lies and deceit, and he would never have that kind of love in his life again, the price was too high. He felt a profound sense of despair. This young and lovely creature had been in his life for far too short a time. Wisdom said, let her go, and surely to God he had learned some of that by now.

The conversation with the old colonel came back to him. Was all this so bloody hard for him because he wasn't bent?

He said, "We'll go to the Coq Hardie and then to the little casino. We might even win money, who knows?"

Even as he said it, he had a slight uneasy feeling everything was a mite too public, a mite unwise, but what the hell, he had to get out of here, stop Angie's questions, forget everything for a while.

"Put on your best dress, and I'll dig out my jacket and shirt. And a tie. They won't let us in the casino without a tie!"

Angie put her face close to his and kissed him. "I do love you so."

He felt an absolute shit.

He said, "Let's go, Geronimo!"

They ate and drank and gambled the night away, and dawn found them back at the cottage, in that euphoric state when sleep seems a ridiculous idea. They sat in the kitchen and drank black coffee and reviewed the evening. The Coq Hardie had given them escargots and coq au vin and lemon sorbet and then they had watched the old men playing boule, on the sandy lots, for a while. In the little casino (it was still early) they had found a lone gambler playing roulette against the house, and winning, and Jay, greatly daring, had followed his bets and won sixty pounds English before the man consulted his diarylike systems book and gave up. Jay took this as an omen and played carefully for the rest of the night. Roulette mostly, small bets for small returns (did gamblers never realize that the house *loved* roulette?), and the first streak of light from the Mediterranean found him still ahead. The casino wasn't busy, it was the end of the season, there was an air of quiet boredom about the place. Even the regulars were smiling sadly at each other. Angie didn't bet much, she didn't understand the lure, and contented herself with sitting drinking lemonade, looking at the people, the high-priced tarts and the seedy regulars. Cherry would have been irritated and fretful after the first hour, especially if she had lost money, which she probably would have, being a foolish gambler. Jay was unused to this kind of solicitude and affection and wondered how he would live without it.

These thoughts went through his mind as he looked at Angie across the kitchen table. She wore a simple white sheath dress, and her tanned skin glowed. There was a bloom about her, and Jay felt a pang. She'd enjoyed the evening because she'd been happy, just to be with him. It was as simple and uncomplicated as that. It was the love a woman feels for a man while she is waiting to see if he will give her a child. Jay crushed out his Gauloise gloomily. "Time for bed, I suppose."

Angie grimaced. "I don't feel tired. You?"

"Not really."

"I enjoyed today. I felt we were very close."

"You did?"

She nodded happily. "I've never expected anything of us. I know you're a private person and you've had sad times in your marriage. I don't want to pry or anything, but I feel that, well, there are things you haven't told me about yourself. You say it's the business, but I don't really believe that. You never seem to bother about the business very much." She hesitated, "You go to your office so rarely I sometimes wonder if you have a business to go to." Angie smiled to take the sting out. My God, he thought, if only she knew.

Jay took a deep breath. It was time to cut this off.

His decision was right. She had to go, for her own good.

"Look, Angie. I don't know what dream you've been dreaming, but I have no real problem that you should worry about." He added, "Not unless you can think of any."

He didn't know why he'd said that, but it had an effect on her. Tears came to her eyes.

Jay had never seen her cry before.

"What is it?"

"I missed my last period."

"What?"

"I know, it's probably nothing. I've missed before, sometimes when I get a very heavy workload it happens, and I have been busy."

Jay just stared at her.

Angie said in a low voice, "I can't remember missing taking a pill, but I could have. There's a theory women do, when they really want somebody's child. After all, we shouldn't be surprised, it's what nature put us here for."

Jay found his voice. "You can't remember missing? Don't you have that date thing, day-by-day thing?"

"Yes, but I sometimes do miss taking it. I mean, I have in the past, once or twice."

Now, Jay thought, we're hearing it.

There was nothing for nothing in this world, as his father had always told him. With some satisfaction. He waited for feelings of outrage and anger, but to his surprise, they did not come. Instead, there was a sudden concern and a tenderness. He stretched out and took her hand. "It'll be all right. One way or the other."

"I could still work." Angie had, womanlike, obviously thought this through. "I can find a nanny. I can live with you. Or, if you'd rather not, I'll move out. But if I am pregnant, I want to have it."

"I know, I know." Jay stood up, and she stood too, and he kissed her gently and put his arm around her, and they went into the bedroom without saying anything and took off their clothes and got into the large feather bed with the brass posts that dated from the colonel's time. Jay lit a cigarette.

Angie laid her head on his arm and closed her eyes. She said, "It might never happen, darling." Two minutes later she was asleep.

Jay lay, his eyes smarting from the bright early-morning sunlight filtering into the bedroom, and smoked his Gauloise. He knew one thing for certain. He could not, and would not, abandon this girl, who was obviously the best thing that had ever happened to him.

The question was, how would he fix things?

Plainly, he had to tell Mr. Jones it was all over.

Then he had to find a job in London.

If he could.

The alternative was to come here, to hell with the rat race, buy the cottage, and live at the lowest possible level. He didn't much like the idea of Angie working anyway. All that happened was that the kid suffered. No, the best idea was to camp out here for the first years, see what happened. Tart up the cottage (he could do that himself) and, if they had to, go back to London then. He had a very strong feeling that the second alternative was the only possible one. If he stayed in London, sooner or later Mr.

Jones would be on the telephone, and there would be an offer, and he'd need the money and then it would be Cherry all over again.

No, face it, this place was the answer.

It would give him rest and peace and they would have enough to live on, if only just.

Jay was surprised at how coolly he was taking all this. It told him one thing: As Willa had said, he was looking for a way out.

What the hell, this was a very real situation, and he hadn't engineered it, had he?

Jay looked at the sleeping girl, disengaged her arm, and turned over onto his side. He fell asleep almost at once, and later he did not remember her getting out of the bed, but he did remember her voice saying, "I'll drive down to the village and get us some fresh bread. It'll be lovely and warm."

He must have grunted and fallen asleep again, because he remembered nothing at all until the deafening blast and the sheet of flame and all the windows of the cottage shattering and showering him with glass; and he knew long before he ran out into the road and found what he feared that it had been a car bomb, probably worked on a trembler, and that it had been intended for him, and that he had no problem with Angie any longer.

It was only after he had been violently sick that he saw the white Irish tweed cap lying on the grass, fifty yards up the road.

S·I·X

Jay rang Mr. Jones from Charles de Gaulle Airport.

"Dear boy, where are you?"

"Don't you know?"

"I know you're on a naughty hols with your girlfriend."

Jay felt the bile rise in his throat, and swallowed it.

"You sure you don't know where?"

Mr. Jones chuckled. Or it sounded like that.

"My guess would be somewhere in the south of France."

"So you do know?"

"Somebody recognized you, far too late, of course, as having gone through on a flight from Paris. Where are you now?"

Jay said slowly, "Stop asking questions, and for once in your life, listen."

There was a reproachful silence. Mr. Jones was hurt.

Jay said, "I have to say this in code. We are talking about my companion. She's met with an accident."

"An accident?" Mr. Jones waited.

"Call it an accident. Ring the French police at Cannes and they'll give you details. I had to get out."

Mr. Jones asked, "Was it a deliberate accident?"

"Yes."

"Any idea who?"

"Not unconnected with my recent trip."

Mr. Jones seemed to take a while to digest that. "You saw nobody, I take it?"

"They left a trademark, to let me know. Or somebody know."

"What did they leave?"

"A cap."

Jay could see the pearly-white Irish tweed cap, lying on the grass in the bright sun; he could smell the stink of burned flesh. The bile came into his mouth again. He spat it into his handkerchief. He was operating, as they said, on automatic pilot, he was going through the actions, doing everything he'd been taught.

"This cap? You'd seen it before?"

"On a man's head, yes."

"It's like them." Mr. Jones sighed. "Very dramatic."

"Which bunch was it?" Jay very much wanted to know, but he knew Mr. Jones would not tell him.

Mr. Jones would not tell him.

"Forget any ideas of revenge, dear boy. It's over."

Jay said, "It happened in a car. I want you to get somebody over there. Posing as a relative, brother or something. Identify the body or the clothes or whatever. Get her a decent burial. Do a mopping-up job."

"Well," said Mr. Jones, "let us see what we can do, shall we?"

"If you don't do it, then I go to the French police and I tell them everything. They'll be very interested."

"They'd hold you for murder, probably," said Mr. Jones academically.

"Let them. I want this thing done."

"Well." Mr. Jones sighed again. "I suppose it's in our own interests, anyway."

"And keep the British police out of it."

"Don't worry. Now, when do I see you, dear boy? We have to talk, you see. I have a most important commission for you, in the offing." Mr. Jones paused. "Of course, this unfortunate business has complicated things, but we can probably, as you say, do a mop-up operation."

Jay stared out of the telephone box, feeling the earth shift. Outside, the jet engines screamed, and Mr. Jones was, for all he knew, tracing the call. "Are you mad or what?"

"I'm sorry, dear boy, I don't understand."

"I loved that girl, and she's dead, and you're talking about another job. Are you entirely, absolutely, certifiably mad? My fucking cover is blown to buggery, at least one terrorist organization knows what I look like, so it won't be long before they all do—and you burble on as if nothing has happened!"

"This job," said Mr. Jones, as if he had not spoken (spoken? He had *screamed*!), "this job is away from all that, something very big, very different."

Jay thought, I do not *believe* this.

"You stupid shit, I'm blown, I'm finished, can't you get that into your head? Take me off the books or the computer or whatever the fuck I'm on, it's over! If I ever hear your voice again, it'll be too soon!"

Jay slammed the receiver down on its cradle and found he was trembling more than ever. Worse, even, than immediately after the blast. Then, he had to act. He'd known he had from ten to twenty minutes, depending on how far away the nearest farm worker was. He'd thrown everything into one suitcase, cleaned fingerprints from the obvious places, and got out, tramped across the field to the nearest main road and begged a lift from a farm truck, pretending a taxi that never came and a plane to catch at Nice.

The farmer had understood his schoolboy French, and had plainly been too far away, in his new but already filthy Peugeot pickup, to hear the explosion, for he had asked no questions, and had dropped Jay in Vence without talking about anything but the genius of Michel Platini, the French soccer player.

Jay had taken a cab to the airport, and two hours later, on his false passport (he always carried a spare), he was in Paris. Mr. Jones didn't know about this particular passport, which identified him as Joseph Carter, salesman and paint importer. He didn't know about a number of things. Or Jay hoped he didn't.

Jay pulled his ticket from his pocket. It was the only thing he was carrying, except a slim briefcase and money in his wallet. The case containing the rest of his clothes lay in a locker in the airport. He was wearing a suit and a cream shirt and a silk tie, exactly what he'd worn in the casino the night before. Was it only two in the afternoon now?

Angie was dead. Face it. The burning flesh, the sun, just put them away, put the picture away. You can take it out and look at it later.

For now, automatic pilot. Do the right things.

Jay looked at the departures board and saw that his Zurich

flight was due out in fifteen minutes. He found his boarding pass
and walked through passport control. He took a seat in the smoking section. Once the plane was airborne, the stewards served coffee and a pastry, and he forced himself to eat, a mouthful at a
time. He drank the coffee black, and tried to think. The question
was, had the boyos posted a lookout at the cottage to see if he was
eliminated? Or had they trusted to luck? Or hadn't they cared
who got it, as long as somebody did? Plainly, it was all activated
by some kind of tip-off. A sudden thought came into his mind; the
intelligence corporal in the jeep, on the Belfast road, the one who
had vomited over his boots, the one with the local Belfast accent.
Jay brooded, staring down at the snow-tipped Alps. That guy had
seen him, could finger him. It was possible. After that, what? A
leak in Mr. Jones's department? Always on, these days. Whitehall
simply wasn't safe. Everything got out, to television or the papers;
why not this, to the terrorists, whoever they were? He still didn't
know which side had come after him. Not that it mattered anyway. The point was, they had.

Were they still on his tail?

He could not be sure, but he had done a few clever things and
seen nobody obvious. He hadn't had time for anything too elaborate. Speed had been the keynote: get clear. Only one or two people had seen him. Angie had usually gone into the village alone,
to shop. Since he had left nothing in the cottage and she had
rented the car in Nice, it was always possible the local police
would only slowly figure out he'd been there at all, and they'd be
very short on descriptions.

He brooded. It was also a possibility that the people who had
rigged the car knew they hadn't got him, and would queer his
pitch with the French police. But if they did, they would be playing outside the unwritten rules of the undergound war. The rules
said you never implicate local police. The underground war was
not the business of clodhopping local police forces, or of any regular law-enforcement agency. It was only the business of governments, as a last resort, and everyone would deny ever waging it.
The casualties were known only to the combatants. How many
died that way each year was impossible, Jay thought, to compute.
Israelis killing Arabs on Parisian boulevards; Arabs killing Israelis
in London restaurants; Libyans killing other Libyans outside
mosques in Regent's Park; Provos and Proddies killing each other

in Belfast slums; Basques and Spanish undercover men killing each other in French and Spanish border towns; KGB and CIA everywhere. By bullet, knife, poison dart, car bomb; by accidents that were not accidents. In subways in New York City, or in falls from tall buildings (a KGB speciality) in Moscow. Or by cyanide pistol or poison umbrella in Hamburg or London. He did not feel, somehow, that the French police would receive any anonymous letters.

The Swissair jet prepared to land.

Jay collected his newspaper and small briefcase. He felt a little safer. Soon, once the business in Zurich was over, he would be an ex-combatant in that war. There was no way that Mr. Jones could use him. The talk of a job was simply to get him back to London and debrief him, and fix up his exit permit into the real world, complete, no doubt, with warnings about the Official Secrets Act. Walking through the terminal at Zurich airport, Jay found that he could now think about what he would do when he got clear of Mr. Jones.

Europe was too dangerous, in every way.

The United States was a possibility, but he needed a place that was hard to get into, where people had to carry identification, look, and prove, what they were, and didn't mind doing it. A society enough on its toes security-wise to keep out people who might be looking for him.

As he reached the Swiss immigration desk, Jay had made a decision. He would take his thirty-five thousand pounds and fly to South Africa, later that day. He would contact a very useful old friend in BOSS, the South African secret service, see if a couple of strings could be pulled to make him a temporary resident. Since he wasn't penniless, he could pay his way for at least three years, and he could (with his old friend's assistance) be a South African citizen inside that time. They weren't looking to throw white people out. They needed them. It might be every man to the ramparts, any decade now.

Jay told the polite Swiss immigration official he was in Zurich on business, and walked through customs into the bright Swiss sunshine, and hailed a taxi.

He told the driver the name of the bank and sat back for the rocket launch that constituted a taxi ride in Zurich. The driver took his Mercedes down the divided highway into the old town with total coolness, but at a speed that troubled even Jay, who liked fast driving. The land of the cuckoo clock looked as peaceful as ever. The burghers in the streets, undisturbed by wars in living memory, walked their boulevards in the certainty of an even more profitable peace, or war, to come. It was said that during the Second World War the Gestapo had plainclothesmen in Zurich, checking out any German national who might, unpatriotically, estimate his money would be better off in Zurich than in Munich, in the bomb-blasted winter of 1943. The penalty, of course, had been execution. Some had risked it.

Here, money didn't just talk, it screamed.

Jay entered the portals of the bank, and bypassing the counter downstairs, made his way up to the second floor. Here, in a warren of small private offices, the real business of the bank was transacted. In these rooms, minor and major Nazi officials, international swindlers, terrorist gun-runners and ordinary businessmen—who did not like the idea of working a hundred hours a week to give most of their profits to their governments—discussed their affairs. He wrote his account number on a card and passed it to a girl clerk sitting at a desk. In excellent English she asked him to wait in Room 3.

Room 3 also had a desk, a small one, and two chairs. He stood at the window, looking out toward the Zurichzee. He could just see a corner of the great blue lake. There was no queue for the boats, for a cool breeze blew over the city, but the sun still shone, and tourists could be seen, wandering idly in the streets.

The door clicked open behind him, and Mr. Simon stood there.

Mr. Simon was a Swiss, but he spoke, to Jay's sure knowledge, Italian, English, and French, besides the local Swiss German. Zurich was still a German city. People were well-behaved, polite, correct. Mr. Simon was very correct. He shook hands with Jay, whom he had met only twice before, remarked (because Jay was English) on the weather, and put a folder in front of Jay.

It contained, Jay knew, the statement of the account.

"I will stay, if you wish." Mr. Simon looked curious. "You may have questions, perhaps?"

Jay was a little surprised. Mr. Simon normally left him to peruse the statement and returned later. Quickly, Jay opened the folder and thumbed through the contents.

The room swam.

The bastard, the bloody bastard!

"The account has been closed, all funds withdrawn, as you see." Mr. Simon was simply being helpful.

But, naturally.

You did not allow combatants in the underground war to leave the battlefield anytime they thought fit, did you?

Jay waited until the room had stopped swimming. Then he said, "When did this happen?"

Mr. Simon looked concerned. "You did not know, sir?"

"No."

Mr. Simon shook his head. "As you know, the account was in the name of a Swiss concern requiring two signatures of directors."

"When did the withdrawal take place?"

"A week ago. I assure you it was all in order. I expedited the papers myself."

"Yes, I'm sure," said Jay, and handed the file back to Mr. Simon.

Five minutes later he was on a tourist boat on the Zurichzee, the cool breeze whipping at his hair, his back to the jolly tourist passengers, so that they could not see the tears of rage in his eyes.

Whether they were for Angie or himself he did not know.

Heathrow, after Zurich, was metropolitan chaos after provincial order. Too many people, every color of skin, a real crossroads of the world, a smuggler's delight, a baggage handler's paradise, not nicknamed Thiefrow for no good reason. The English take-or-leave-it attitude was well in evidence, from the moment he asked the taxi driver for a quote to Hammersmith and was told twelve pounds. He took it, and waited for the tail he thought he had spotted at the barrier. This was a Chinese man, slightly built and heavily spectacled, but Jay knew neither fact meant anything. Probably plain glass and black belt.

What else was a Chinese taxi driver with an expensive blow-wave hairdo, and clean, pressed clothes and no telltale creases at the crotch, doing, holding a placard saying, "Mr. Tomkins, Central London"? All that meant, if he was right, was that there were two of them: the taxi driver and the pseudo-customer. Jay felt slightly aggrieved. Whoever was running the surveillance plainly thought he was some kind of idiot not to see something as obvious as that. He glanced quickly through the rear window and saw that the Chinese taxi driver (who ever heard of a *Chinese* taxi driver?) and his passenger were in a battered, but probably souped-up, Ford Cortina marked "Taxi" a hundred yards behind. They stayed that way until past the Chiswick traffic circle, coming into the Hammersmith overpass.

"Change of plan." Jay leaned forward. "Take the left lane and head for Paddington Station."

"Jesus, guv!" The driver twisted the wheel. "You left it a bit late. I was on the white line there!"

"Well done!" Jay leaned back and watched the Ford go helplessly on, up the overpass. There was nothing else the Chinese driver could do, and Jay gave him a one-fingered salute as he passed by. There was no way of turning around on the overpass. Even the cowboys of the department (whoever they were) wouldn't risk that.

"You can put your foot down a bit," said Jay. "I'm catching a train. There's a couple of quid in it."

"Now he tells me," said the cabby.

Jay wondered if there would be a backup car. He had not spotted one, but if they were serious there would be one, somewhere. The approach to Paddington Station found the Ford on his tail again. The backup car, wherever it was, had radioed the taxi's position, which meant the Chinese gent or his passenger was running the surveillance. He told the cabby to drop him off at the side of the station. He got out and gave the cabby fifteen pounds. The man didn't say thanks, but drove straight off.

Jay walked briskly into the station and turned right immediately, and waited.

The Ford was there within half a minute. It stopped, and then drove on. Jay knew they would have to drive to the far end of the concourse to get out of the no-parking zone. Not that they would care about that, but they wouldn't want to draw attention to themselves. All of this told Jay it wasn't a snatch squad. Mr. Jones simply wanted to know where he was.

Jay hit the Chinese man with a throat slam as he turned the corner, and the man went down without a sound. He did not move and nobody seemed to have seen the incident, except an old lady with a shopping bag, who stared, transfixed, at the prostrate man. Jay walked quickly across the station and down into the Underground. He got a ticket and ran. Once on the platform, he stood with his back to the wall of the tunnel and took the first train to anywhere, for one short stop. He got out and walked to the surface and found himself in Bayswater. From there, he walked.

Jay was the only white man in the Westbourne Grove whorehouse. The Rasta who ran it smelled heavily of ganja. He greeted Jay's sudden arrival with no surprise. His guess was that Jay was a villain who sometimes had to lie low for a few days. He kept Jay engaged in polite conversation in his sleazy basement room, while giving an almost imperceptible signal to a dwarfish Nigerian gofer to get upstairs and clear the tart out of Jay's room, even if the customer was in mid-orgasm. Jay and he had an agreement that the room was always available. This did not keep the Rasta from letting it out to one of the girls, if it was a particularly busy time. Jay accepted that. Thirty quid a week, fifty-two weeks a year, wasn't much outlay. All he asked from the Rasta in exchange was a shut mouth, and while he paid he got it.

The Rasta passed him a courteous joint and a glass of white wine. "It's good grass, I'm smoking it myself," said the Rasta, his long, coiled strands falling over his face. The weed was strong, and Jay took only a token puff. The wine he drained, and the Rasta replenished it. "I don't carry the hard stuff," he apologized, inhaling a lungful of smoke that would have flattened most users. "The girls steal it, and it makes them so bad-tempered, y'know?"

Jay inhaled a second drag and closed his eyes.

He opened them to find the Rasta, a flamboyant and promiscuous homosexual, looking at him with some sympathy. "Hey, brother, you look as if you've been in a rough old game."

Jay nodded. "You could say that."

"Profitable, I hope to hear?"

"I can pay the rent, if that's what you mean." Jay handed the Rasta two hundred pounds in fifties.

They disappeared into the Rasta's caftan, as if by magic. He relaxed, inhaled his ganja, and grew philosophical. "Rough but profitable? So now, a period of R and R, huh?"

Jay nodded. Rest and recuperation was exactly what it would be. He would hole up here like some old gray rat. He smoked again and felt its potency. He said, "I hope lover-boy changes those sheets up there."

The Rasta smiled. "Oh, he will, mah man. Go you up an' anythin' you want, you let me know. I mean anythin'."

He knew Jay had never asked for women in the few times he had used the room. Or boys. It worried him, but not much. He thought he knew the answer. "Women talk," he opined. "Only one thing worse than women, that's the boys." He drew in a vast and thoughtful pull of smoke. "Why I only has them short-time, never sleep in a bed with them. It's the bed does it. In a bed, you get to rapping. Rap to a rent-boy and next thing the fuzz has you by the balls."

The dwarflike black gofer appeared in the doorway. He grunted and gestured, and Jay realized he was dumb. He put a fiver in the massive hand, and the dwarf led him upstairs, with the Rasta's voice in his ears. "Anythin', brother, just ask."

The room was in the attic, at the very top of the house.

The sheets had been changed and were clean. There was a smell of cheap whore's perfume in the air, but Jay burned a sheet of newspaper, and it was gone. He tapped the dwarf's shoulder and said, "No girls. No boys. No interruption. Right?"

The dwarf nodded. Jay gave him another fiver.

The dwarf's eyes glistened in appreciation. This fiver he would keep. He pointed to the table. There was a loaf of sliced bread, some butter, and a tin of corned beef. A kettle stood on the small electric stove, along with a box of tea bags and a carton of milk. An old TV set stood in the corner. The dwarf gestured, with his thumb up, that it worked. He could have been the manager of the Ritz, Jay thought. He pantomimed thanks, and when the dwarf had gone, he locked the door. Carefully, using his nail file, Jay took away the piece of grubby hardboard screwed over the ancient coal fireplace. He felt up the chimney until he found the ledge.

The Browning was there.

So were the hundred American dollars and the hundred and fifty British pounds.

So was the bottle of malt. If he was in hiding, he would hide in style.

Jay drank half of the Glenlivet before its effects mingled with the potent ganja to produce a weariness verging on collapse. He took off his outer clothes and folded them very carefully over the chair normally used by the underage whores' customers, and, in his undershirt and shorts, lay down on the bed. The Browning he put under the pillow. He had intended to get under the covers, but he lacked the resolve, and anyway, if he had to move fast, the blankets would be in his way.

Jay told his internal clock: four hours only.

Jay told himself: don't dream about Angie. Sleep.

Jay closed his eyes and slept.

He was awake, every nerve screaming, inside an hour, drenched in sweat and panic and staring at the stained floral wallpaper, the bomb blast still resounding in his ears, the stink of burned flesh in his nostrils, in his inner eye the white tweed cap on the grass.

For three days Jay lay holed-up in the attic room.

The Glenlivet was soon finished. He sent out for a bottle of cheap whisky. He drank half of that the first day and half of it the second. He sent the dwarf for a takeout meal each evening and forced himself to eat it. He lay on the bed a lot, and kept the television on all the time, catching the news bulletins on all channels.

There was no story about an English girl being killed by a car bomb near Vence. The English daily newspapers carried no such story, either.

He dispatched the dwarf to Soho for the French newspapers and read *Paris Soir* and *Le Monde* very carefully, column by column. His French was good enough for the task.

Nothing.

Finally he rang the BBC. He was told, "Angie's on leave. I'm not sure when she'll be back. D'you want to leave a message?"

Jay left no message.

He cried, after that call. He had not cried since his mother died.

The dreams came back that night. He forced himself awake, made and drank black coffee, and sat in the armchair until breakfast television began at six o'clock. There was nothing on that, either.

On the fourth day he put on the one clean shirt he'd kept, shaved and washed as best he could in the small, cracked basin, and went out in search of an unvandalized public telephone.

Mr. Jones sounded surprised.

"Ah, there you are, dear boy. I'd been wondering when I'd hear from you."

"I want a meet."

"That sounds like a good idea. When shall I expect you?"

"I'm not coming to the office."

"Why is that?"

"I don't like tails."

"I'm sorry about that," said Mr. Jones equably. "It was for your own good, you know. Where are you, by the way?"

Jay ignored that. He said, "There's a telephone booth in the North End Road. It's a hundred yards down on the left-hand side, coming from Olympia. Be there at eight tonight and the phone will ring. Pick it up and you'll hear where we meet."

Mr. Jones was silent.

"I can hear the wheels," Jay said. "No followers. Just the two of us."

"I say," said Mr. Jones, "is this necessary?"

"Oh, yes," Jay said. "Very."

"You seem somewhat upset. I can rely on your good behavior, can I?"

"Oh, absolutely."

Mr. Jones debated. Jay said, "I'm ringing off now. Yes or no?"

"Yes, obviously." Mr. Jones sounded weary. "I'm worried about you, you know."

"Good," said Jay. "That makes two of us. And remember. No tails."

Mr. Jones sounded offended. "Naturally."

Bloody old liar, Jay thought, putting down the receiver.

Jay could not see the tail on Mr. Jones but he knew the tail had to be there. They would probably be a little cleverer this time. He took the taxi right up to the telephone booth and asked the cabby to stop. Mr. Jones looked bewildered but found his way out of the booth and into the cab with only one glance down the road toward Olympia. That told Jay where the backup car was. There were probably two, or even three. To do Mr. Jones's job you had to be very cunning or very brave, and Mr. Jones, Jay would lay money, never crossed the street against the lights.

To the cabby he said, "Queensway Ice Rink."

The cabby nodded. Two faggots meeting for a bit of nooky, was plainly his thought. Next stop the toilets. He closed his glass partition and drove on.

"Why are we going there?" Mr. Jones asked. Jay was pleased to see that for once he looked flustered.

"We have to talk, and by Queensway we'll have said all there is to say."

Mr. Jones pursed his lips. He was fast recovering his composure.

"I don't know why we can't have a nice talk in the office, or even in some quiet restaurant. I haven't had dinner yet."

Jay said, "Then let me take away your appetite. You owe me thirty-six grand."

"Ah, yes. I heard you'd inquired. Terribly sorry."

"Stick your sorry. If I don't get it I'm going to the papers. With full disclosures."

"My dear boy, we'd just stop anything like that."

"You have a week."

"You sent names? Places? People?"

"The whole enchilada."

"You couldn't tell me who?" he asked. "Which paper or magazine?" Mr. Jones leaned forward, peering into Jay's face in the darkness. "No, naturally not." He mused. "Look here, I'll tell you the facts of the matter. We have a new assistant secretary who is absolutely outraged at some of our activities and has called a halt on everything. We had to do it. We're calling in all our accounts, everywhere."

Jay laughed. Mr. Jones had his nerve.

"Money talks, bullshit walks," he said.

Mr. Jones looked pained. "It's only a matter of time before we get him around to our way of thinking. Then you get your money."

"You have a week," Jay said.

Mr. Jones made no reply. It was raining, and the lights of the shops of Notting Hill Gate were bouncing back off the wet pavements. Mr. Jones started to glance out the rear window but stopped himself.

"The surveillance is behind us, about two vehicles back," Jay said. "Don't worry. I'm only here to get my act clear."

"In what way, dear boy?"

"I'm out. I'm finished. My cover's blown."

Mr. Jones pursed his lips. "With the boyos, to be sure. Not necessarily everywhere."

"The boyos are enough."

Mr. Jones said academically, "They probably think you're dead."

"Oh, how?"

"The body in the car. It was a man."

"What?"

"Don't ask how. The French press will release the story tomorrow. If you're sensible."

"What are you talking about?"

"The French owed us a favor. They were very cooperative, when we explained."

Jay sat, thinking. "What about Angie?"

"An automobile accident. Just outside Cannes. That's released at the same time."

Jay said nothing.

"Her body home, a decent burial, her friends and colleagues there, all that," Mr. Jones added.

"No," Jay said savagely. "Bury her out there."

"That could be tricky, dear boy."

"She has . . . had . . . no parents. And I'd be expected—I can't face any funeral."

Mr. Jones clucked sympathetically. "I'd no idea you were quite so involved with the dear girl."

Jay blew his nose. "You've no idea what goes on in people's heads. Unless they're bent."

Mr. Jones looked hurt. He took off his glasses and polished them on his handkerchief. "If I did all this, arranged the funeral, persuaded the French to play ball—and it won't be easy—can I rely on your behaving sensibly?"

Jay stared at him. "I've just told you, I'm out. I'm finished." He put his hands where Mr. Jones could see them, in the flickering light from the street. "Look at those. They won't keep still. I'm dreaming about the bomb blast every night, I'm waking up in a sweat every two hours, I'm burned out, washed up, fucked up, finished, finito!" The cabby looked around, and Jay realized that he was shouting. He kept on shouting. "You have seven days to get my money. If you don't, I blow everything."

Mr. Jones said, "That would really be most unwise."

"Just try me, that's all."

"How," Mr. Jones asked, "will I get in touch?"

"You won't," said Jay. "I'll call you." He tapped on the window and said to the cabby, "I'm getting out now. My friend will pay."

Mr. Jones frowned. "This is very silly."

"If those guys follow me," Jay said, "I won't karate-chop them, I'll blast them to buggery."

"Which people are you talking about?"

"Tell them. I'll shoot them. I mean it."

Jay got out of the taxi, and so did Mr. Jones. They were in Queensway. Jay ran down the crowded street, very fast, and ducked into a shop doorway. A British Telecom van pulled up at the curb where Mr. Jones stood, blinking forlornly in the rain. Mr. Jones leaned inside the passenger window and spoke. After a moment the British Telecom van drew away into the traffic. Mr. Jones hailed a cab and followed it.

Jay walked all the way to Westbourne Grove, doubling back a couple of times to see if he had a tail. He didn't.

In the attic room, he broke open a bottle of scotch and slowly drank half of it. He watched television (some British imitation of *Dallas*), lying on the bed, and then he closed his eyes. "Angie," he said aloud, "I loved you, darling, after my fashion. You were the best, the loveliest, the most loving thing that ever happened to me. Wherever you are, forgive me. I'll never forgive myself."

He was still sitting, staring at nothing, long after the mindless soap had ended.

In his sleep, the dreams came again, worse than ever.

Jay became very careless.

He knew it but he didn't care.

First, he took the dollars and converted them into pounds, in Cook's in Regent Street, affecting an American accent. The counter clerk didn't even look at him. He took a taxi to Barney's Betting Shop, in Holborn. It wasn't exactly a regular haunt, but it could be a place they might watch. However, he saw nobody he thought looked likely. He lost a hundred pounds in an afternoon, backing long-priced losers. At the end of the afternoon, Barney came to the grille himself and asked him if he was all right.

He said he was, and Barney nodded, unconvinced.

Jay left, after the last race, and bought a bottle of whisky. He walked to his office, and surprised Vi, who was shocked to see him unkempt and unshaven, his clothes baggy and unpressed. Vi gave him a list of callers. A Mr. Jones had telephoned three times and a man had come in person, asking if she'd seen him. Vi told him no, which was true.

"My office free?"

She gave him the key. "Is something wrong?"

"No. Nothing."

He knew she was looking at the bottle, wrapped in brown paper, in his hand. "Medicine for all ills," he said.

Vi grimaced slightly. "Will you need any letters? It's nearly time to go home."

"No letters. Nothing. Just a couple of calls. I can dial direct. Leave me a line when you go. I can let myself out. I promise not to steal the typewriter."

Vi hesitated. "I really shouldn't."

"Go on, break the rules."

She looked at him again. "Are you really all right?"

"No, but I won't do anything silly."

Vi nodded. "All right then. Look after yourself."

Jay went into the office, locked the door, opened the whisky, and drank a measure, slowly. When Vi had gone, he took out the small dictation machine in the desk drawer and, leaning back in his chair, recounted the details of Angie's death and the events that had led up to it. He put the tape cassette in a padded envelope taken from one of the drawers and addressed it to a friend, a writer on the *New York Times*. He had known the man slightly for years and felt he could trust him. He telephoned the man in New York, found him at his desk, and told him that he should expect a tape but not to open it or listen to it until Jay told him to. The man agreed. Jay left the office, locked it, switched out all the lights, walked out, and hailed a taxi, still carrying the whisky, wrapped in brown paper. The taxi took him to Atlantic Parcels, which charged him twenty-five pounds, English, and promised to deliver the package in New York the following day.

He took the taxi back to the brothel in Westbourne Grove, ignored the dwarf's mimed offer to get him food, found his way upstairs to the squalid room, and fell, fully clothed, on the bed.

He slept for two hours and, as usual, wakened in a sweat, screaming inside. He sat up in the bed until dawn, drinking the last of the whisky.

The next day followed the same pattern.

Jay rose, neglected to shave, threw some water over his face, went out, walked to the nearest bookie's shop, and backed a few losers. He took the tube out to the dog track at Wimbledon and went through the card without backing a winner. The third day found him betting the last of his money with Barney, in Holborn. When he had bought, with the last silver coins, raked together from his pocket, a final half-bottle of Scotch, he went back to the brothel, drank it, and slept until dawn, without waking once.

That morning found the Rasta looking in, as if casually, the dwarf worried-looking but sympathetic, in the background.

"Morning, man, how you this day?" The Rasta was on the weed, even this early. He offered Jay a drag, but Jay refused.

"Tell you one thing, man," the Rasta continued politely, "I never interfere in anybody's business, but I got to worrying about you. Five days you been in a bad way. You look a hell of a mess, brother. Is the law right behind you?" He phrased the question courteously. "I has to ask, because if they be, they come here maybe, and that I don't need, catch my drift?"

Jay said, "Did somebody ask about me?"

The Rasta shook his head, possibly a mite too quickly.

Jay said, "I think someone did."

The Rasta sighed. "Looked like fuzz, smelled like fuzz. I didden know you, naturally."

"When?"

"Last night."

All Jay had was what he stood up in. A jacket, trousers. The Browning in his inside pocket. "Is there a way out they won't see me from the street?"

The Rasta looked upset at such a reflection on his professionalism. "Of course there's a way out, man. It's over the roof. The dwarf will show you." He extended his hand. "Blessings, brother."

The dwarf took Jay, very nimbly, over the roof, Jay finding it none too easy to keep up with him, and down, through another house, into another street. The dwarf nodded dumbly to Jay's thanks, and seemed sad to see him go.

Jay walked the London streets all that day, without food or drink, feeling convalescent, but somewhat better. For he had not dreamed the night before and his hands had stopped shaking.

He had no money, no future, but he felt a sensation that was new, or one, anyway, he had not felt for many a year, since he was a boy in fact, since the day his mother died. He felt this was exactly what he deserved.

S·E·V·E·N

MARTY SAT AT THE REAR of the small viewing theater and looked at the back of Jack Virgo's head. The bald part of it gleamed, under the thinning hair, and his thick neck went straight down, in a tube, to his square, beefy shoulders. He seemed oddly unfamiliar to her, which was strange, because she had been away from his authority, or anyway his presence, for much longer periods in the past, in Nicaragua and in Grenada, and had felt him, all the time, at her shoulder, had imagined his reaction, usually discouraging, to whatever it was she happened to be doing. Now, in some indefinable way, he seemed a stranger. Perhaps it was his clothes, the too-tight suit, the leather trouser belt with a buckle, the button-down shirt and plain tie, the gray fedora hat. Nobody in London seemed to wear a hat, unless he was in the City. Sitting heavily, in her room at Chelsea Cloisters, earlier that day, Jack Virgo, back in London again, had not been pleased.

"You're telling me this guy is doubtful? Why didn't you call transatlantic and cancel?"

Marty hadn't been able to answer that. Or not in any way Jack Virgo would accept. "It's not that simple, Jack. Jones wants to lay the whole case in front of you, himself. He's putting on a show for us this afternoon."

"A show? What kinda show?"

"He wants you to see some film of this man, and he'll give you his personal assessment of his suitability."

133

"That's nice of him. I thought all I had to do was meet the guy, talk to him, say yes or no to him."

"That was the plan, but . . ."

"Now, I hear buts already? What's the real problem, Marty?"

Marty did something she could not explain, even to herself. She went to bat for Jay. "I think he's right, but then I don't know exactly what the job is, do I? So I can't be the best judge."

"It's need to know, Marty." Jack Virgo was gruff, but not heated. It was the nearest he ever got to an apology. "You don't need to know. Not yet."

Marty had nodded, looking more irritated than she felt. "That's your decision, Jack, and I accept it. But since I don't know, I can't either write this guy off or take him on board. As I say, only you can do that."

Jack Virgo had shifted irritably and downed his Southern Comfort in a swallow. Replenishing it deftly, just as he liked it, with plenty of ice, Marty added, "You are running this operation, Jack, not me. So run it."

Virgo made a dent in the drink and then said academically, "On the telephone you said he was the man. If he isn't, why not?"

Marty looked at the bridge of Virgo's large bulbous nose, as her anti-interrogation instructors had taught her. "There's been a hiccup, that's all."

"What kinda hiccup?"

"He took a girlfriend to France for a few days. There was an accident. The girl was killed. In a crash or something. I don't know the details, that's all Jones told me."

Virgo asked. "An auto accident? Anything suspicious about it?"

"Jones didn't say there was."

Marty had her own feelings about that. Virgo himself had taught her to sniff at anything unexpected, anything at all, large or small. Now, Virgo was sniffing.

"I don't like accidents where people get killed. Not around me or any guy I'm thinking of using, in a very delicate operation." Virgo finished his drink. She poured him another.

"My own reaction exactly," Marty said, making the measure of alcohol larger. She knew it would take a lot more than three drinks to affect Jack Virgo. She gave him the drink and sat, deep in the low chair, legs apart. If Jack Virgo recognized it as a sexual diversion, which it was, he ignored it.

"So, you say, forget this guy? You say it's all been a waste of time, find somebody else?"

"No, I'm not saying that, Jack. The troubling factor, according to Jones, he's been on the sauce since the accident."

"Jesus H. Christ!" Virgo shook his head wonderingly. "The guy's a lush? Now you tell me he's a lush?"

"Booze might be the natural reaction. Wouldn't you say?"

Virgo's scalp shone as he shook it negatively. "Mechanics don't have reactions. That's why they're mechanics."

"He'd been living with this girl a while, according to Jones."

"Just the same, it shouldn't throw a mechanic."

Marty had said the words before she knew it. "Jack, just because no woman on God's earth means a thing to you, and is only good for screwing, doesn't mean everybody else feels the same way."

Jack Virgo looked hurt and offended. "This is personal talk, Marty. It's business we're discussing here, right? Let's keep the personal stuff out of it." His expression said clearly what he thought: women, all they ever think about is somebody loving them or not loving them; what has that to do with the price of apples?

Marty said, in a more neutral voice, "Anyway, he did a job over in Belfast. Did it well, according to Jones."

"He did?" Jack Virgo looked brighter.

"Of course, it was before the accident."

Marty felt she had to say that, if only to protect herself. She had no idea what Mr. Jones was proposing to show Jack Virgo— probably the stuff he had shown her—or what Jones might say, in view of the latest developments: the dead girl, the car accident, the drinking, all of which he had only hinted at on the telephone that morning.

Marty wondered about the drinking. It *was* a reasonable reaction. Any man might do it, especially if he loved the girl. Yet, as Jack Virgo had said, mechanics didn't love people, they killed them.

So, sitting behind Jack Virgo in a viewing theater in Curzon Street, later that day, Marty wondered why she had set Jack up,

why she had steered him into thinking nothing was wrong with
Jay. For herself, there was a tiny, niggling reservation. Professionally, the hair on the back of my neck says no. Privately, my pubic
hair says yes. Marty didn't like that; it was all wrong. Yet, she *had*
set Jack Virgo up, hadn't she, and there he sat, in front of her, his
powerful body tensing with every moment that passed, into what
she knew must be a deeper, blacker indignation.

He hadn't said anything yet, of course.

That would come when the lights went up. Which did not
promise to be for some time yet.

Mr. Jones had come to the end of the footage about Jay that
Marty had seen in her first session earlier in the week. Now he was
showing some new footage, and it was dynamite. Marty stirred, as
it became clear what the shots added up to: Jay's unsuitability for
the job. The new film clips were very recent indeed, and showed
Jay going into a low-life betting shop, and coming out again,
tearing up his betting ticket. Jay, at the Wimbledon greyhound
track, looking hungover and ill, losing more money. Jay, looking
even more desperate, leaving a sleazy-looking house in Westbourne Grove, unshaven, head down, a sleepwalker. Finally, Jay
on the Thames Embankment, lying on a seat, covered in newspapers. This time he seemed more cheerful. He got up briskly,
folded the newspapers, and walked off in the direction of Tower
Bridge, as if taking an early-morning constitutional. None of this
footage was accompanied by any kind of comment by Mr. Jones.
The film was grainy and had obviously just been processed. The
clips had been hastily put together and plainly represented the
last word on Jay.

To say that Marty felt shocked was an understatement.

To say that Jack Virgo was angry was one also.

Virgo swung around in his chair the instant the lights went
up. He stared long and hard at Marty, but said nothing. The
anger that had been there, in the reddening pillar of his neck, exploded as he turned to Mr. Jones.

"You're trying to sell me this bum? He's on the skids, he's a
lush, he's the worst gambler I ever saw." Jack Virgo's voice was
heavily loaded with sarcasm. "And you think he's right for what I
have in mind?"

Mr. Jones turned politely, the eyes behind his spectacles
blinking in the soft light of the viewing room. "Well, of course,

neither I nor HMG, nor, indeed, anybody—even Marty here, I suspect—knows exactly what you have in mind, Mr. Virgo. Let us, as you might say, get that straight, shall we?"

"Mr. Jones," said Jack Virgo, "your British hypocrisy kills me."

"Oh, I do hope not," replied Mr. Jones equably. "I let you see all that footage because I don't want to sell you a pig in a poke. The dear boy has been through a very trying time."

"I heard, I heard, tough shit!" Jack Virgo was still extremely affronted, and he glanced around at Marty again, as if to try to ascertain her real feelings. She looked steadily at the bridge of his nose. It was all she wanted to see of Jack Virgo at that moment. Virgo turned to Mr. Jones. "I'm worried, my friend, I have to tell you, I'm very very worried."

In the Company, men turned pale at such words from Jack Virgo. Mr. Jones merely smiled his polite English smile and said, "If you notice, in the last clip, he seemed much more cheerful? As if he'd got it all out of his system?"

"Tell me more," Virgo said, without enthusiasm.

"Well, after that, he walked back to his flat, made himself some breakfast, and, presumably, went to bed. As far as I know, he's in the flat now." Mr. Jones made a steeple with his fingers. "You see, he knows we know where he is, and he doesn't care. That means he's done his penance for the girl, and, in my view, he's ready to go back to work."

Jack Virgo looked doubtful. "You really believe that?"

"Yes, I do."

"Well," Virgo grumbled, "he's your guy, but if he was mine I'd be calling for his psychological scenario." He looked up. "Do you have it?"

"Nothing so un-English as that, I'm afraid." Mr. Jones was apologetic. "As long as he functions, that's all we care about. Do you do things differently?"

Jack Virgo looked to Marty to share his astonishment. "We have a hundred pages on every agent in the Company! You mean you have nothing?"

Mr. Jones said stiffly, "His record is in the folder on your knee."

"Jesus H. Christ," said Jack Virgo, in a low, amazed voice. "You haven't the slightest idea, psychologically speaking, why this guy does what he does, what his break point could be, noth-ing?"

"His reasons?" Mr. Jones unsteepled his fingers, somewhat pained by Virgo's remarks. "No need to agonize over that. The dear boy's a patriot."

"If I believed that," Jack Virgo said, "then it would really worry me." He lit a cigar in defiance of the prominent "No Smoking" notice. Virgo turned to Marty. "Give me your opin-ion—what do you really think?"

Mr. Jones rose hastily to his feet. "If you'll excuse me. I'll just thank the operator, back in a minute." And he was gone, leaving them sitting in the half-light of the little viewing theater.

"All right," grated Virgo. "I'm waiting."

Marty let the silence lengthen. When she spoke, she tried hard to strike a neutral tone. The words she would say to Jack Virgo had to contain no element he would not expect to find there, like a hint of admiration or of sexual curiosity, even of compassion, all of which she had in some measure. She had never spoken to the man, but she felt she knew him, something akin to that special feeling a woman has for a man she has slept with, and which never leaves her.

Marty tried to give Jack Virgo the kind of assessment he would accept. "I've seen three other guys. That is, I've seen them on film and I've seen their dossiers. This one is undoubtedly the most intelligent, most likely to have everything you say you need." She paused, as Jack Virgo's eyes never left her face, and hers never left the bridge of his nose. "I'm not trying to sell you any bill of goods on him. I don't like this toot he's been on any more than you do, but maybe I understand it better."

Jack Virgo said ironically, "Because you're a woman?"

"Because I'm a woman."

Virgo was silent and brooding for a long moment, and then he said, "You know what Al Capone used to do with his hoods? When he felt one was burned out, he used to put a blonde in the guy's way. If the guy didn't respond like instantly, y'know what Capone used to say?"

"No idea," said Marty.

"If a guy don't fall for a dame, he's through."

"And that meant?"

"He failed the test." Virgo ran his index finger across his throat.

Marty laughed. "Are you telling me to go find out?"

Jack Virgo said nothing to that. He opened the dossier and read its spare contents once more. "No psychological scenario. Jesus." He closed the file and looked at Marty again, his eyes trying to find hers. When they made love, she never met his eyes, which, she knew, searched for hers all the time.

Marty was suddenly filled with a savage resentment toward Jack Virgo. Who did he think he was, giving her this assignment, sending her over to London all on her own, expecting her to make the choice he seemed none too anxious to make himself? He was even talking about Al Capone, for Chrissake! He always treated her like a whore, didn't he? Was he saying, go and be one? The resentment turned to a cold rage, but her voice sounded ordinary in her own ears as she said, "If you want to see him, let Mr. Jones set up a meeting, why don't you?"

"I don't want to see him."

"Then what do you want, Jack?"

Virgo grinned lazily. It was a smile she recognized from their sex together, just before he reached for her, but this time he didn't reach. He said, "I want you to go see him. I want you to come back and tell me, do we go with him or not?"

Marty felt that if she looked at him another instant she would probably claw his face with her long red nails. She stood and picked up her sling bag.

"If that's what you want."

"That's what I want, baby."

"Where will I find him?"

"Mr. Jones will know."

"Where will I find *you*?"

"That's where you'll find me." He handed her a card with a telephone number written on it. "Whenever you are through. No hurry. Take your time. Make sure. All right?"

Jack Virgo's eyes glittered in the half-light.

Marty found a bleak smile, from somewhere. She heard herself say, "All right."

Then she walked out of the viewing theater.

* * *

Jay was sitting in a Victorian pub near Paddington Station, where Mr. Jones had told her he would be. He had shaved and put on a clean shirt, and he looked tired around the eyes, but otherwise relaxed. A pint of beer, half drunk, stood in front of him. The place was full of overweight young men in colored shirts and leather jackets, but it was not a gay pub. The young men were hetero all right. Muttered comments and low admiring whistles greeted her as she stood looking for Jay.

"Hey, what about *that*?"

"I could give *you* one, darlin'."

Marty didn't mind the young men. They were merely paying ritual homage. Her Bruce Oldfield wasn't something they would see every day in a place like this. She walked across to the alcove, slid into it, and faced Jay.

"Good evening."

His eyes widened a little in surprise, and then he smiled.

Jay's teeth were good, she noticed, and his mouth was full and promised much, but it was the blue eyes that held her. There was something in the eyes, in that first moment, that told her that if she went to bed with this man it would not end there, it would become more than an adventure. Marty felt a *frisson* of something like fear. It was a thing she rarely experienced with men, except for Jack Virgo, and with Jack it was, anyway nowadays, more what he represented than what he was. With this man, it was the man himself.

"I'll have a scotch," she said, looking into his eyes, not at the bridge of his nose. "On the rocks."

Jay called the order to a passing barman. Then he said, "Jones told me to expect somebody, but not a woman."

Marty smiled into his smile. "Are you offended?"

"Not at all. Delighted."

He looked as if he might be. His gaze was appreciative, and soon he started to seem less tired around the eyes. Marty knew that she was the reason. She sipped her drink and wondered how to start the business side of the conversation, now that they had gotten over the animal-to-animal thing. That, anyway, could wait, would have to wait, despite Jack Virgo's ultimatum. She would do things her way, not his. Anything she did she would do because the situation required it, or because she wanted to, or both.

"You're a Company lady, I gather?"

"Yes, I am. Did Mr. Jones tell you any more?"

"Not much. He said you had a proposition and I told him to go screw himself."

Marty laughed. "Then why are you here?"

Jay did not smile. "Jones owes me money, and he suggested I wouldn't smell it, ever, unless I talked to you. So here I am."

"You don't sound very enthusiastic."

"I'm not. I'm just being polite. No offense meant, but I'm through with the game. I've been in it too long and I want out."

Jay was still looking at her steadily, and the look went through her. He's very dangerous, she thought. No fool, either. I don't need to find out if he's right, I can see he is. She said, "I can understand that. You've had a bad time, I believe."

Jay nodded. "I expect Jones told you. It was all my fault. If I wasn't mixed up in this shitty business it would never have happened. But it did and somebody I loved is dead."

The blue eyes softened, for just a moment, and in that moment Marty felt her first flicker of doubt. If Jay was so hurt he was going to carry the guilt, without being able to handle it, then he had to be out, no hard feelings, no personal feelings, just out.

So she asked the question directly, but with sympathy, as if she were just a woman, any woman, inquiring about another woman. "Can you live with the fact that she's gone?"

"I don't know. It's been less than a week."

It was frank enough and told her exactly nothing.

Again she asked an innocent-seeming question. "Are you wanting out because you don't enjoy it anymore?"

The blue eyes regarded her. "Who said I enjoyed it?"

"Most people who do it do."

"You'd know, would you?"

"Yes." Marty wondered what he thought she was, some kind of gofer? "We've mounted a few special operations in our time."

"You have the authority to talk to me?" Jay asked sharply.

"To sound you out and report, yes. Not the final word. You know how it works."

"Yes, and as I told you, I want no part of it."

"If you keep saying that, I'm likely to believe you."

"I hope you will." He smiled, to take the sting out. "Look, if you have any more to say to me, I'll listen, but I'm only here because Jones asked me politely, promising me the money he owes me, at some point convenient to him, if I hear you out. As this place isn't bugged and the noise level is too high for most devices to work, I think it's safe to talk. Go ahead, proposition me, I'll say no, then I can find you a cab and you can go back to the Dorchester or whatever."

"Chelsea Cloisters, actually," replied Marty, on impulse. "And I propose you take me there, to talk, after we've had a quiet dinner somewhere very discreet. I'm starving and I hate to talk business on an empty stomach."

Marty saw the flicker of surprise in the blue eyes and was glad of it. He didn't expect that, she thought, adding: nor did I. It was strictly off-the-cuff. Or was it? Had she bathed and sprayed herself with the Saint Laurent, and put on the Bruce Oldfield, simply to, as he put it, proposition a mechanic?

There was a long silence from across the table. Then Jay said, "I know a place. We can walk to it. The food is Greek and we won't meet anybody we know. Our watchers will have to wait outside. It's too small for them to get in unnoticed."

Marty laughed. "You think we have watchers on us?"

"Nobody in the pub, but they'll be around. Jones would never allow you to walk around London, looking like you do, without some kind of protection." His face was deadpan. "You might get raped."

"Promises," Marty said, finishing her drink and getting to her feet. She was surprised to feel moist, excited and a little fluttery. It was a combination of feelings she hadn't experienced in a very long time. "Do we go?"

The boys at the bar made one or two remarks as they left, of which she heard, "Cor, I fancy that, what an arse on her." Marty was used to American manners, which, on the whole, were polite in a public place. This was something else. The English proletariat, like the tough young men at the bar (known to the Brits as yobs), had no reservations about expressing their sexual opinions out loud.

Jay hesitated as their voices reached his ears, but he walked with her to the door. At the door, he said, "Wait outside—I've forgotten something."

Marty did not wait outside. She stayed in the pub and watched.

Jay walked back to the yobs. He tapped the biggest one on the shoulder and spoke to him in a low, conversational tone. Marty did not hear the words. The yob looked surprised, then angry, then he swung his fist.

Jay's two fingers hit him in the eyes, and he fell to the floor, writhing and clawing at his face. Jay looked at the others and spoke again, softly, almost encouragingly, but none of them moved. They just stared at their writhing comrade on the pub floor. Jay turned and walked to the door. He took her arm and then they were in the street. It was still light and they walked in a leisurely fashion up Praed Street, toward the Edgware Road.

It had all taken about fifteen seconds.

The Greek restaurant was very small, as Jay had said it would be, but not cramped. The proprietor recognized Jay and gave them a table in the corner alcove, with the merest lift of an eyebrow to congratulate Jay on this lady, who must, since the table was to be a quiet one, be married, or in some way risky. Jay ordered without consulting her, or looking at the menu: taramasalata, lamb baked in tinfoil, mixed salad, a bottle of retsina.

"Peasant cooking but quite good," he predicted. It was. Before they ate, he also said, "I'm glad you hate business with food. It's a primitive idea."

Marty, remembering many Company breakfasts, smiled. "It's the best recipe for indigestion there is."

So they talked about families.

He told her his father had been a war hero, she told him her father had been in the Seabees but no hero, unless you thought making airstrips on lava atolls was heroic, as maybe it was, in a way. She told him about business college and then working for the government. He told her about the British Army, but nothing that revealed much. All the stories he told were against himself. It was the British way of doing things, she realized. This man, and a whole class like him (it was obviously a class thing, she couldn't imagine the pub yobs telling stories against themselves), felt confident enough to relate how they had made complete fools of themselves, and could laugh about it. Not many Americans, certainly not Jack Virgo, could do that. Jack Virgo's stories all cast himself as the hero, in or out of the Company. Jay's list of lunatic misadventures, by himself and with his fellow cadets at Sandhurst, and later in his line regiment, were told with gusto. They mostly involved manic drinking, discreet wenching that always went wrong, and instant and exemplary punishment for all concerned at the end of it.

Marty detected, though, a strong sense of irony at the foolishness of it all, and said, "You don't seem to have ever taken anything very seriously."

"In the English middle class, to take anything seriously, especially oneself, is a crime deserving of capital punishment."

Marty laughed. "My stories sounded very dull to you, I suppose."

"Not at all, very interesting. It's not every evening I have dinner with a girl whose father was a garage mechanic turned Seabee, who herself started out as a typist, and is now an executive of the Company." He did not smile. "I realize," he said, "that I'm talking to a very exceptional young lady. I must be very, very careful."

"I think it's time we got that taxi."

As she said it, she felt that rare *frisson* she'd experienced the first time she saw him. Girl, she reprimanded herself, do for God's sake stop fancying the talent.

Marty wakened to find that Jay had gotten out of bed. She could hear him rooting around in the small kitchen, opening the door of the refrigerator, running water into a kettle. She looked at the watch she had not taken off her wrist in the excitement of the previous evening. It was an expensive Seiko bought for her by Jack Virgo, on a freebie in Taiwan. The hands showed eight o'clock. Outside, the morning traffic had begun, a distant hum she had grown used to in the few nights she had spent in the apartment, always, until now, alone.

Marty had not slept with anybody except Jack Virgo for over a year. There had been a young Company agent in Grenada, but that had been strictly a one-night stand, agreed and understood on both sides, without a word being said. Adequate and no more, and over. Was this to be the same? Marty moved her naked body around under the covers and discovered she wanted Jay again. Well, why wouldn't she, he had taken her only once, and that quickly, as if he felt obliged to do it, and while she had responded, it was not the kind of lovemaking she liked, which was long and

slow and had both pain and pleasure in it, and had talk and whis-
pers and sometimes mirrors and movies somewhere, and usually
bound men to her sexually, if not emotionally, almost at once. Jay
had not allowed her to use any of these arts.

This man had, anyway, satisfied her, which was surprising,
since there had been virtually no foreplay. She had simply gone
into the bedroom, taken off her dress, and called out to Jay to
bring in his drink. She had smiled at him and said, "Well, you
expected this, don't tell me you didn't."

He did not tell her he didn't.

He didn't say anything.

He just removed his clothes, and took her.

Then he turned over on his side and went to sleep.

It had all been over in a matter of minutes, and seemingly it
was all there was. No word had been exchanged, of love or lust,
and yet she had come with him. After that Jay had slept solidly
for an hour. She knew that, because she timed him by her watch.
She debated waking him, with fingers or tongue, but decided
against it. At the end of the hour, he had turned, and still asleep,
muttered the name, "Angie." Then he had turned his back again,
and slept on. She had fallen asleep then, and now it was morning,
but early, and she wanted him.

It would, she knew, be easy enough to make him want her.
She knew how. Sensation was what Marty understood, sensation
and success. Well, with Jay there had been some sensation, that
was true, but had she succeeded in learning anything about him
except that he was polite and professional in sexual matters? She
doubted it.

Jay walked into the bedroom, carrying a large mug of coffee
for her and one of tea for himself. That was the good news. The
bad news was that he had put on his shirt and slacks, socks and
shoes, and looked as if he had shaved. Marty was conscious of the
sleep in her eyes and mouth and the moist warmth between her
legs. She said, accepting the coffee, "You're up bright and early."

Jay sat on a chair and sipped his tea. My God, she thought, he
has shaved. Probably used one of my cheap disposable razors. She
began to feel more than a little whorish, sitting there in her na-
kedness. She said acidly, "Did you have a shower?"

Jay nodded. "Just a quick one. I tried to be quiet. I hope I
didn't wake you."

Men, she thought. He washed me off him the first chance he got.

She sipped her coffee and said, "There's no law against getting back into bed, even if you have washed and shaved. Or is there, over here in England, and I've never heard of it?"

He smiled. "There's no law, but it's rarely done."

Stop fooling around, she reprimanded herself, you're here to make a final decision on this man. Marty realized that he'd meant her to be naked and at a disadvantage. Nonetheless, she persisted. "Did you enjoy it?"

"What?" The blue eyes opened, mockingly she thought.

"Me."

His face was deadpan. "In England, we always say thank you."

"Is that all, thank you?"

"Sometimes we say thank you very much."

"And sometimes you say no thank you very much, as you just did?"

Jay inclined his head. "That, too. But I thought we were here to talk business, and we haven't, have we?

Marty made a point of looking at her watch. Her breasts were entirely exposed now, and while Jay was looking at them that was all he was doing. "At eight-fifteen in the morning?"

Jay said, "Well, we have to eat breakfast, don't we? If you want to have a shower and dress, I'll cook bacon and eggs."

Marty said crossly, "No bacon."

"All right. I'll scramble half a dozen eggs and make some toast. I'm pretty good at that."

Marty got out of bed, naked, and stood in front of him. "Is that all you're good at?"

He studied her, as if she were a specimen. "No, but it's all I feel like doing at the moment."

"Can I do anything to change that?"

"A lot of things, but I'd rather you didn't."

Marty laughed. She reached for a silk wrap. "All right. Go and scramble the eggs. I'll be ten minutes." Then she swept past him—getting very close—into the bathroom. He did not reach out to her. He simply said, "How do you like your eggs, sloppy or firm?"

"I like everything firm," Marty replied tartly and went into the bathroom. The cold spray hit her hard. Her intelligence had to take over sometime, and now was as good a time as any. She felt an anger, and an admiration, for the way he had put her down, allied with a determination to make him beg sometime. Slowly she turned the spray to warm and then to hot and soaped herself all over. She wrapped herself in a huge towel and hugged herself dry. The sexual want had slowed down by the time she slipped the silk wrap back on, but it was plainly still simmering, or else she would have put on street clothes. Marty ran a comb through her black hair, so expertly cut it needed nothing more. Then she thrust her feet into some mules and went into the kitchen.

Jay was just dishing up the scrambled eggs. They were not firm but sloppy, as she really liked them. He had made toast and more coffee. Marty ate the eggs and drank the coffee with relish. Jay offered her a cigarette, which she refused (she smoked only under pressure), and lit one himself without asking permission. In the Company, these days, almost nobody smoked except the very old guys, or the powerful ones, like Jack Virgo.

Thinking of Jack Virgo, she excused herself and went into the bedroom and made a short telephone call. When she got back Jay was pouring himself another cup of coffee. His hair shone and his skin tone seemed better and the shadow had gone from under his eyes. The power of sex and sleep, she thought.

"You made your mind up yet?" Jay asked casually.

"Yes. I think you're right for the job we have in mind."

He grimaced. "But you can't tell me what it is?"

"Sorry."

Jay crushed the cigarette in a tray. He uses things, she thought: women, cigarettes. He said, "I won't be taking the job, I've told you that, but if you can't tell me anything about it, who can?"

"A man called Jack Virgo. He'll be here in twenty minutes."

Jay nodded his head. "I've heard of him."

"Most people have," Marty said neutrally.

Jay smiled. "The word is he's a grade-A bastard."

"He's a lot worse than that."

Jack Virgo arrived within fifteen minutes.

It was like him, Marty thought, to come early. A ploy, unexpected, wrong-footing, pure Jack Virgo. It was well Jay had gone out, to buy cigarettes. Marty met Virgo in the corridor as he came out of the elevator.

"Good morning, Jack." She offered her face to be kissed.

Jack Virgo looked at her expressionlessly, standing there in her loose silk wrap, the apartment door half open behind her.

Then he slapped her, hard, across the face.

Shocked, Marty put her hand where he had struck.

"What was that for?"

"You know what it was for." Virgo moved past her to the door, as if nothing had happened. "What do you say? Yes or no?"

Marty said, "Make up your own mind, and fuck you!"

Virgo said, in the same voice, "Did you ask him? Is he in?"

Marty's eyes watered, not only from the hurt of the blow but from the unfairness of it. "Ask him yourself, you shit."

Virgo went into the apartment, and she followed him.

"Where is he?" Virgo sat down, without taking off his topcoat.

"Out buying cigarettes."

"Will he be back?"

"Why wouldn't he be?"

"He might have had everything he wanted from you."

Marty said, "Well, he passed Al Capone's test anyway, if that's of any interest to you."

Virgo did not react. "I sometimes wish I had Al working for the Company. We could do with a few people with balls."

"Some people used to have them." Marty's cheek burned, and she still felt dizzy from the blow. "Then they lost them and took to hitting women."

"I haven't lost them," Virgo said neutrally. "Or I wouldn't be here, would I? I wouldn't be thinking of using that psychopath who has just spent the night in your bed. I wouldn't be thinking of the whole goddam thing, would I?"

"I don't know." Marty looked blindly out of the window. "I never know what you're thinking."

"Glad to hear it," replied Virgo, looking at his watch. "How does he get back in the building?"

"I gave him my keys."

"Very trusting."

"He may be a mechanic, but he's no fool."

"If he's a mechanic, that's just what he is." She could feel his eyes on the back of her neck. "So you say go, right?"

Marty said nothing. She could not bring herself to reply.

One day she would repay Jack Virgo for all the insults and humiliations. One day, it would happen.

Jay opened the door noiselessly. He had entered the apartment so quietly neither of them had heard him. One moment, there were only two people in the room. A moment later, three. It was uncanny, really, but, she knew, part of the training. It was said actors found opening doors on stage the most difficult of all things to learn. Operatives, too, always had trouble with doors, with locks, bolts, handles. No two doors, she'd been told, are ever exactly alike. To Jay, obviously, they all had one thing in common. He opened them without noise.

He stood there, looked at her, seemed to note her tension, nodded, then turned to the sitting Virgo, who watched the performance without moving, except that Marty thought he had turned a shade paler than usual. Like Marty, he knew that had Jay been coming for them, they would have both been dead.

Marty thought, with some satisfaction: if that doesn't impress Jack Virgo, nothing will.

Virgo recovered quickly, but he did not get up. He nodded his head. "Sit down, please. Make yourself at home. But I guess you already have, huh?" This was said with a man-to-man smile that nauseated Marty. "I believe it's Jay?"

Jay did not respond; he did not appear to like Jack Virgo on sight, and he did not sit down.

Virgo didn't show any annoyance. He could live with what people thought about him. "You know me, what I do?"

Jay looked at Marty. She blinked her eyelids once. He said, "Marty told me. I'd heard of you."

Virgo grunted. "First, I'm sorry to hear about your recent trouble." When Jay said nothing Virgo added, "The girl." When Jay still didn't reply, Virgo went on, quickly, "I don't know what I'd do in your place. Maybe give up the game. I understand you've been thinking about that, am I right?"

Too soon, Marty thought, typical Virgo, straight at it.

Jay sat down, before he replied, in one of the old-fashioned chintz-covered armchairs. "It would take a lot of money to interest me, Mr. Virgo. I'm only listening to you because Mr. Jones bent my arm. That doesn't mean I'm going to be interested in a single thing you say."

"Naturally." Jack Virgo smiled the awful smile that he smiled around once a week, usually at somebody else's discomfiture. "I hope to make you interested."

Jay lit a cigarette and said nothing.

Marty was pleased with him. It was nice to see Jack Virgo struggling.

Into the silence, Virgo said, "Of course, we would pay somewhat more than the going rate for the job."

"Cash in advance, or I don't play." Jay looked bored. "I've been burned once."

Virgo nodded. He was happier with the nuts and bolts. "I was thinking of a very large amount."

"You'd better be. I don't want the job. Why don't you use one of your own people?"

Jack Virgo sighed, but Marty knew how angry he was by the way his whole body tensed. Virgo was used to people disliking him but not to people treating him as if he were of no account, people telling him, as Jay was, to stuff it before he even got to the pitch. "I can't use my own people," Jack Virgo said at last, "because the job is in the U.S. and I need an outsider."

Jay laughed, without mirth. "You want me to do something you won't put out to your own people? You must have me down for a very trusting guy, Mr. Virgo."

"No," Jack Virgo replied. "Just for a smart one, because frankly, I think you'll walk this job. It will only take four, five days of your time. It'll be worth fifty thousand dollars."

"In cash, up front?" Jay's voice was calm.

"Half up front. Half on delivery."

Jack Virgo swallowed; he was hurting, Marty could see that, he had realized that Jay genuinely didn't want the job, it wasn't a come-on. The price said that Jack Virgo had decided, there and then, that Jay was right, that she was right. Marty breathed in relief. If anything went wrong now, it was Jack Virgo's hash.

"That's a nice piece of change, Mr. Virgo."

Jay was sitting, musing, as if Jack Virgo had said five thousand dollars. Marty knew mechanics who would do a job for five grand and do it well. A sense of excitement and curiosity boiled up inside her. What *was* the job? For that kind of money it had to be very big indeed.

What Company fund, Marty wondered, was such a large sum to come from? Covert operations were usually very badly financed. As Jack Virgo often said, to anybody who would listen, you could always find money in the Company for some new handgun somebody was developing in Japan (because you could *see* a gun, goddammit), but try getting money to stymie some quite important KGB ploy that hadn't yet happened, but that good intelligence said soon would happen in, say São Paulo, like the taking-out of some very good political friend of the U.S. of A. For that, for protection for a true friend, for getting there first, what money was there? Fuck-all is what there was.

So, fifty thousand dollars for the one job?

She could not think what it might be.

One thing was certain. Jack Virgo would not tell her unless he decided she needed to know.

Virgo, who still wore his topcoat, was mopping his face with a handkerchief. "All I can say is, the job's not far outside New York City, it's a little public but the method is up to you, the exact location is up to you, you case the job yourself, you make the decisions, it's all yours, A to Z."

Jay looked surprised at that and Marty guessed why. All mechanics ever knew of most jobs was when. Not the name even. Generally, somebody fingered the hit and handed them the weapon. They didn't know any more about it than that. From his still expression, she guessed that had been Jay's experience, too. The mechanic might put it all together later, if the story got in the papers or on radio or television, but that was all. She began to feel a certain unease, mixed with excitement. She had never, personally, known Jack Virgo, or any Company boss, to use outside help when the help planned the hit. Company agents, yes, but not free lances.

"What makes you think I'd want all that responsibility, if I came in?" Jay asked. Nothing about him had changed, his voice was still level and crisp and disinterested, but Marty had slept with him and she thought she recognized a sudden look in his eyes, a tilt of his head. Jay was intrigued, possibly even interested, and trying hard not to show it.

If Virgo saw the interest, he too showed nothing. "Jay—may I

call you that?—I accept your probable negative answer. My reason for giving you full responsibility is because I can see, and
know from my briefing, that you are not the ordinary guy in your
particular sphere of operation." Virgo wiped his face with the
handkerchief again. To Marty, the gesture showed how hard he
was trying.

Jay said icily, "What briefing was that, Mr. Virgo?"

Virgo held up his hand in protest and smiled an ingratiating
smile that cost him a lot. "Nothing that could harm you, blow
cover, embarrass, nothing like that, I give you my word."

"Don't," said Jay coldly, "talk such bullshit, please."

The color drained from Jack Virgo's face. Marty wondered
how Virgo would take *that* remark. Virgo took it. He didn't try
the smile but said, "Okay, I had to hear a lot about you. But it's
all safe with me."

"I hope that's true."

The way Jay said the words made Marty's spine tingle.

Virgo, though, was off and running, the words adding up to
the sort of sales pitch that Marty had seen him use so often before,
in Company conferences, or briefing sessions. He leaned forward.
"Jay, we're both pros, all right? You know and I know that I had
to run some sort of detailed scenario on you before I went ahead,
right?" Virgo waited, but when Jay did not nod or otherwise respond, he pressed on, "Not that I learned a hell of a lot. You Brits
don't seem to bother keeping records, and who knows, maybe
that's wise, but I tell you what impressed me most, one fact that
stood out, when your Mr. Jones said it." Virgo paused, for effect.
"The fact that you are a patriot."

Jay said nothing.

Virgo's voice dropped so low that it seemed almost a seduc-
tion, which, Marty reflected, it was, only not as honest as her own
attempt. At least she had enjoyed it. Jack Virgo was hating every
single minute of it.

"Look, Jay, I admire any guy who does unpleasant things because he believes in the necessity of doing them. In your country,
what do you have? The empire gone, right? A whole bunch of
people glad of it, glad to see the Great go out of Britain, right?
Trots, Commies, a whole bunch of militants wanting the country
to go down, I mean really like desiring it, working for it every
minute of every day of their lives, right? Plus a whole scad of lib-

erals and media guys and like that, innocents abroad every one of them, voting the same ticket." Virgo paused, tried a smile. "A lot of these people, I grant you, are very sincere. They are also living in a dream world. Not just this country, but in Europe generally, am I right? They think they can have a nice little game of footsie with the big brown bear. They've never even seen the bear close up, but they think his murderous instincts are wildly exaggerated, that he's really a very nice vegetarian bear who's no danger to anybody. They just don't believe he has a lot of friends in this jungle called the world, hyenas and jackals and like that, living right among them as they lead their nice, protected, liberal lives.

Jay said nothing. Virgo leaned forward again.

"But *they* aren't our enemies, Jay. Our enemies are the pros on the other side, the organizers of the bear's long-term plans, and the guys who carry out those plans. To give aid, succor, training, to terrorists. To take over a union or a country. To take over a political party. To eliminate anybody who might stand in the way of the long-term plan, which is well known and openly declared, right? Europe first. Then South America. Then they have it all. To do it, nothing is too small. A guy running a union vote here, one who can start a strike there, a liberal lady TV producer who might be useful sometime." Virgo smiled and shook his head.

"But we aren't concerned about them, are we, Jay? We are after the big fish, the guys who run the hyenas and the jackals. If anybody means us harm, they get help from the good ole bear. But you and I *know*—because we struggle with the ole bear, on a day-to-day basis, and we know his ways, right?—that it's our business to see his friends the jackals and hyenas don't eat us alive before he gets here. Because, if he can, if he ever can, he's coming, there's no doubt about that, right?" Virgo's eyes glittered. "And the ole bear has some friends in high places, right? People who don't even know they're his friends, people who just think and act, like, fashionably, right?" He leaned back. "I mean, really big people that don't know shit, politically, that can put our great countries at risk, am I right, Jay?"

Jay still said nothing.

Virgo's voice dropped even lower. "Your country. My country. What's the difference? It's the same war. You're a patriot? So am I. We're in the same army. Simple as that."

There was a long silence.

Virgo leaned back in the chair. Marty hadn't seen Jack Virgo put himself out so much since he spent an hour talking a Company committee out of allowing the media into Grenada. He hadn't won that battle alone; he'd had plenty of support. A lot of people were beginning to see things his way these days.

"I'll get some coffee." Marty moved toward the kitchen. Neither of the men said anything, or even looked at her. We are the invisible ones, she thought. In the Company there were more male chauvinist shits per square mile than anywhere outside the Kremlin.

In the kitchen, she made strong, fresh coffee. She overheard Jay say, "I think you are going to have to tell me a little more, Mr. Virgo," and Virgo reply, "Delighted, so long as I can take that as a mark of interest. I'm not going to name names or places, naturally, for the moment."

"Naturally," Jay said, with that offhand English irony.

Marty ran cold water over a cloth and held it against her cheek, for a long time. Her face was still flushed, but it did not seem to be swelling too much. Jack Virgo, she thought, I hate you. One day. One day. She picked up the tray and took it into the living room.

Jay had gone.

"What happened?" Marty asked.

"He left." Virgo stood up and removed his topcoat. He threw it in the chair and said, in a low, disgusted voice, "These Brits, they think we're the original country cousins. Would you believe that guy, just sitting there, giving me a hard time?"

"He might have said goodbye." Marty didn't know why she said that, except that she meant it.

Jack Virgo looked pleased. "A guy doesn't trouble to say goodbye to a whore." He took a cup from the tray and poured himself a measure of black coffee.

Marty felt the words more sharply than the burning shock of the blow to her cheek. Jack Virgo had called her a lot of things in the past, but never whore.

"It was all your idea, all that talk about Al Capone. What did you expect?"

"With you, baby, I expected what happened, is all."

He sipped his coffee, then took out a cigar and lit it. He drew in the smoke and expelled it in a gray stream. "That guy is right. For what we want, he is so right."

"I'm glad I did something you approved of," said Marty, feeling hurt and hatred mix, in a steady cocktail. "You don't think he's burned out?"

Virgo drew on the cigar. "Nearly. Not quite."

"Will he say yes, do you think?"

"With that type guy," Jack Virgo mused, "who knows? Not right away, which is why you have to stay here and convince him."

"I do?"

"You surely do, baby, because I can't. I have to catch the evening flight home today."

Marty said coldly, "So, you want him, and I get him for you?"

"That," said Jack Virgo, "is the size of it."

"What if he still says no?"

Virgo grinned, a crooked, lopsided grin. "He didn't say no last night, did he? He'll go away and think about you, baby, and then he'll be back just like all the other suckers, just like me."

Marty said, "Well, at least he gets into the action, unlike some people, who get their rocks off watching it."

Virgo gazed at her steadily for a moment. He finished his coffee, and then the look that she recognized came onto his face, only there seemed more hate in it than usual, and a minute later, on the bed, he was inside her and she was raking his back with her nails, meaning to hurt, and succeeding, but not halting his possession of her, only adding to the force of it. Jack Virgo was more aroused than she had known him to be in a long time, but as he thrust into her he whispered, "Whore, whore."

And Marty thought, you used to love me once. She almost said, but didn't, Why do you have to use me like this, why?

To come, she had to think of Jay.

E·I·G·H·T

THE OLD MAN LIVED at Hove, in one of the 1930s apartment blocks, just off the seafront, with about fifty other senior citizens for company, some still in twos, many, like himself, alone. Driving down the deserted divided highway from London (the summer visitors had long gone), Jay had wondered why, apart from the money, he was bothering to make the journey at all. No good could come of any meeting with the old man. Why should this time be any different? The old man's voice, on the other end of the line, hadn't sounded exactly welcoming. "Why are you ringin' from a box? They cut yer phone orf or somethin'?"

Jay could not very well tell him his own telephone was almost certainly tapped. So all he said was, "See you about four o'clock, all right?" And rang off.

Now he was committed, and that was that. Not that he had any real choice. The four hundred pounds that he'd kept in his current account would not last long. After it went, it would have to be a job, any kind he could get. Jobs, one that Jay could actually do, were not exactly growing on the trees of Green Park, where he had walked after he'd left Marty and Virgo, trying to make up his mind what to do next, whether to take on the American operation or not. If Virgo's job was worth fifty thousand dollars, one thing was certain: it was iffy in some way. It was very open, Virgo had hinted; lots of people might see him, remember him. That was anything but a plus. On the other hand, it was in another country and he had freedom to do it his way.

156

Jay drove the Jensen at a steady fifty. He had taken an Advanced Motorist's Test, years ago, but since his conviction he never speeded unless he had to. The empty road unfurled before him, and he felt the old anticipation: driving down to Brighton, always a favorite family place, when he was a boy. The old man had driven a prewar Railton in those days. He'd bought it as a young officer—the family money had gone with the family house, into the government's tax maw. Jay had heard the old place was a social security office now. He passed a large lorry barreling along at forty-five, bloody things were road hazards, and he wondered what was wrong with Virgo's offer, something had to be.

The money. Quite simply, the money was too much.

With fifty grand, Jay reflected, he could kiss it all goodbye: Mr. Jones, the Zurich account even, about which he was now having very strong doubts. They had been reinforced by his unannounced visit to Mr. Jones, made after his stroll around Green Park.

Mr. Jones should have been surprised at his turning up out of the blue like that. He didn't seem to be, and that told Jay he'd had watchers on his tail all the way from Chelsea Cloisters. Jay hadn't seen them, but there had probably been several. Certainly not the Chinese man, who would still be in the hospital. Jay smiled sourly to himself. Who did he think he was kidding? Jones had the big battalions, and as the old man was always fond of saying, God was on the side of the big battalions. His father quoted Napoleon, Wellington, and Julius Caesar at almost no prompting at all. He seemed to think they were the only people worth quoting on matters military or civil. Mr. Jones, on the other hand, would, no doubt, prefer Machiavelli.

"Dear boy, how nice of you to drop by like this." Mr. Jones had almost taken Jay's hand, but not quite, finding instead something to do with a file. He had waved Jay to a seat, and asked on his telephone for tea.

The tea had come surprisingly quickly, brought by one of the heavies, which again made Jay sure Mr. Jones had expected him. It was still the hot, perfumed liquid Jay disliked, so he didn't drink it. This was the first time he had ever been in Mr. Jones's office and not made the ritual gesture. So what? He hated the piss, and he wasn't here to be nice and cooperative. On the contrary.

"When do I get my money?"

Mr. Jones had looked at him as if he had farted in church.

"Now, you know I'm doing my best. I thought I explained that."

"You explained it. I just don't believe you."

Mr. Jones sipped his tea. "Dear boy, it's this new man we've had foisted on us. Very, very regimental." Mr. Jones sighed and peered at him, somewhat like a secretary bird, over the rim of his cup. "I thought you might be happy to fill in the waiting period till he comes around by talking to our transatlantic friends. How did that go, by the way?"

"You know bloody well how it went," Jay said wearily.

"Well, yes, in broad outline, I admit." Mr. Jones's formidable molars crunched on a digestive biscuit. "Not in detail. I gathered from our Company friend that you'd gone away to think about it. Have you done that?"

Jay said, "I've done that, and something about it smells. Anyway, my deal with you was that I'd listen to the proposition, and my money would be on the way. I've listened. Where's the money?"

Mr. Jones looked at Jay sadly. "Only a few days ago, you were sleeping on the Embankment." He smiled; some of the biscuit had lodged in his teeth. "Well, for one night, anyway. A penance, I imagine?" Mr. Jones was smarter than he looked. "The whole episode, the drinking and betting and the night on the hard bench, it was all a sackcloth-and-ashes thing, I take it, and now it's over? We can get down to business, what?"

"No, we cannot get down to business, unless you give me some definite news of my money!" Jay replied, feeling very uncomfortable that Mr. Jones had put his finger on things so adroitly. It had indeed been a penance. The truth was that he was trying very hard to forget Angie's face, her voice, her body. It had been only a very short time, an unforgivably short time to be trying to do that, but Jay had been forced to forget the faces of good friends overnight in his time, men he'd fought with in the freezing deserts of the Radfan. Angie was harder to forget, a lot harder. He'd almost cried when he collected her clothes and gave them to the Oxfam people. He'd given everything. He hadn't even kept a photograph.

Mr. Jones was still talking about the money. "I can't give an exact date, dear boy, but at a guess, an educated guess, I'd say six months, perhaps less, but I like to be conservative in these matters."

"Six months?" Jay stared at him. "How am I to live that long on no money?"

"Well, it's the best I can do. As I say, it might take less." Mr. Jones didn't look as if he believed that. "I'm afraid I can't offer you anything at the moment, because, as you so pithily put it on the telephone from Paris, you are getting a mite too well known. Anyway, here in London." He coughed. "It would probably be no bad thing for you to be out of the way for a while, what?"

"I'd only be in the States, even if I take the job—which I won't—for a week."

Jay knew it had been a slip to say anything at all about taking the job, but once the words were out he could not reclaim them. Mr. Jones put down his teacup and looked a little more cheerful. He said, "If you do take the job, and the decision is entirely up to you, you'll have enough ready cash to take a long holiday somewhere afterward, while you wait for me to arrange the Zurich money, as it were."

"Screw the as it were!" Jay said. "That money's mine and I want it. Otherwise I let my reporter friend print the story. I sent him the tapes last week."

Mr. Jones nodded regretfully. "I know you did. Naturally, we intercepted them." He spread his hands. "Well, we had to. Anyway, the *Times* would never have printed it. They know the underground war goes on, but it isn't news. If it had been news, somebody would have told the story a long time ago."

"No, they wouldn't," Jay said. "You'd have stopped them like you stopped me."

Mr. Jones did not seem to hear his remark.

"How did you get on with Jack Virgo?" he asked.

"I thought he was a typical Company boss."

"Typical in what way?"

"Very gung-ho. Very 'Let's go, Geronimo!' "

Mr. Jones looked pleased. "I like that. 'Let's go, Geronimo.' Very apt, I must say."

"Tell whoever is holding things up I said it, and maybe he'll release my money," said Jay sourly.

"Wouldn't dare tell him that," reprimanded Mr. Jones. "He loves the American cousins." He steepled his fingers. "Some of them, I must say, are very lovable."

Jay knew he meant Marty and said nothing, but Mr. Jones was unstoppable. "So very forward, the American women. So very, how to say, demanding. In all ways, I have no doubt." The boiled eyes looked at him through the thick lenses. "Of course, some of them are very smart, too. Often they can be more ruthless than the men, wouldn't you say?"

"No idea," said Jay shortly. "I came here to talk about my money, and I might as well have stayed home and washed my neck."

"What a curious expression," said Mr. Jones. "I wonder who thinks up such phrases. An old music-hall derivative, probably, yes." He leaned forward. "Why don't you think about Virgo's offer most carefully, dear boy? It would fill the bill beautifully for you, y'know?"

Jay stood up. "Not a chance, and I want my money in six weeks. If it's not there I talk to your idiot of a minister myself. Face to face."

Mr. Jones looked very disapproving. "You know you can't do that, dear boy. Not the thing."

"Even so, I give you my word. Six weeks."

As Jay was closing the door, he heard Mr. Jones's last words, uttered in a tired whisper: "But the dear girl is still at Chelsea Cloisters, waiting for your answer, y'know? Such a very charming—"

Jay had slammed the door on that, hard.

He had walked past the heavies at the elevator, gotten into the Jensen, and driven south, out of London. On the way, he had telephoned the old man.

He was putting some physical distance between Marty and himself.

It was the only way.

Jay wondered about what she had done, the straight sexual invitation he had half expected from the moment he had set eyes on her. He didn't know then, but knew now, that she was Virgo's woman; otherwise why would Virgo strike her across the face? He had not seen the blow, but the red welt was there all right. Jay had an uncomfortable feeling she had planned their encounter to end in bed before she even saw him. Of course, she had seen him before, on the Brecon Beacons; she was the woman in the jeep. Marty had been there to look him over. Obviously, she had liked what she saw. Jay slowed the Jensen down for the suburban streets that would take him to Brighton's seafront. The sex itself had surprised him. He had not thought that he would be ready for any woman, so soon after Angie.

The truth was that afterward he had felt sickeningly disloyal to Angie, to the memory of her.

Well, it wouldn't happen again.

Yet, the memory lingered. The woman's body, subtly perfumed, the whole look of her: somewhat decadent, ready for anything at all, unsurprisable, waiting to be shown something new, some sex trick she'd never seen before. So he had just taken her, as if she'd been a girl in a brothel, ignoring all the frills he guessed were there, waiting to seduce and snare him. He'd performed the act quickly and turned his back. Two could play at that game.

For whatever reason, the sex could hardly have been because she loved him.

Jay slowed at a crossing to allow several of Brighton's army of old-age pensioners to cross the road. One of them in tweeds and cap, ex-army written all over him, saluted Jay politely with an ash stick. Jay smiled and drove on.

The sun dappled the dome of Brighton's Pavilion. He had deliberately driven through the Old Town. He used to love the shops, the old lanes, the sand and the sea and the senior citizens. In the old man's more prosperous days, they had used the Hove apartment as a family holiday home, kept it all year. Now the old man lived in it alone, or rather, as he put it, camped out in the bloody place. He would, he had declared to Jay, have much preferred the south of France, all that sun on his old bones, but Jay did not believe it. The old man would be lost without his daily *Times* and its contents, most of which he found bloody shameful.

The old man lived in the past.

Well, who wouldn't, in his place?

The past had been good to him.

The past, Jay thought, as he parked the Jensen in the lot at the back of the apartments, had meant courage and medals and comrades and friends and marriage and a child and a career. It had meant respect and a fair bit of money, mostly spent, one way and another, but surely there was some left? The old man had talked about a big insurance policy maturing on his seventieth birthday. By Jay's reckoning, that was two months ago.

He felt bad about putting the bite on the old man (face it, that was what he was doing), but, after all, he was the only son and he'd never asked for much, just the usual extras necessary when you were a second looey in a line regiment, nothing big. The old man had always gone on a bit about the gambling debts and so on, and of course they'd never been close since the old school had kicked him out, but any port was better than Mr. Bloody Virgo and his dangerously overpriced offers.

The old man could be perfectly bloody if he wanted to, Jay reflected, walking into the building, but at least all that happened was that you ended up chastened, not lying stiff in some morgue. Jay took the lift to the third floor and knocked on the door.

The old man opened it at once, as if he'd been standing on the other side.

"Oh, it's you?" The old man's tone made it seem Jay was a surprise visitor. The gray hair, sparse now, and clipped gray mustache were the same. There were pouches under the eyes, but the old man looked quite chipper in his brown houndstooth jacket, cream shirt, and regimental tie. Better, in fact, than Jay could recall him looking for some time. Neater, brighter. At least he wasn't exactly going to seed, down here among the senior citizens.

"Well, come in, come in, don't stand out there!"

Jay went in, feeling about nine years old. He extended his hand, but the old man didn't seem to notice.

"Fancy a snifter?" The old man had consulted his watch and seen from it that the sun was somewhere near the yardarm. In fact, it shone golden into the room, which looked quite tidy, considering the old man was living on his own. "I'm having whisky. You?"

"Same please."

Jay always found it hard to say "Dad," so he didn't say anything.

The old man had been away a lot of the time when Jay was a boy. Or Jay had, at school. Then Jay had gone into the army himself. They hardly knew one another, really. His mother's idealized wartime photograph stood on the sideboard, a beautiful mahogany relic, rescued from some temporary officers' mess at the end of the war. Jay tried to remember his mother but couldn't. He never could except in the odd dream. Then he saw her very clearly, but on waking he could not remember her face.

The old man splashed a tablespoonful of soda into both glasses and handed Jay his drink.

"Well, here's to us."

"Cheers."

"I hate that word, y'know."

"Which word?"

" 'Cheers.' Damn people say it instead of 'thank you' these days."

"It's just a new, democratic form, that's all."

"What's undemocratic about 'thank you'?"

"It needs a 'sir,' or a 'madam.' Or a name. 'Cheers' doesn't."

"Sir or madam?" The old man stared into his drink. "You'll go a long way before you hear anybody say that these days. Or go to a decent hotel, and then it's some Italian or Spaniard or somebody. Did I tell you about the time I was in the Ritz with Willy?" Willy was a titled friend of the old man's. They'd served in the same regiment. He was, in fact, a genuine lord, but hardly ever used the title. "This bloody waiter fellow, Italian or something, said to old Willy, 'A little more rice puddin', Lord?' " The old man shook his head in silent mirth. "God, we laughed, I tell you." He shook his head again, a long regretful shake this time, like a sad gun dog just out of the water. "Old Willy's gone, y'know?"

"No, I didn't."

"Well, you wouldn't, would you, don't read the *Times,* don't keep in touch. Six months ago. Seventy-nine. Decent innings." The old man finished his whisky. "No pain much. Big plus, that."

"Yes," said Jay. "I suppose it is."

"Well, sit down," said his father. "Staying for dinner, aren't you?"

Jay, who had expected to stay at least overnight (he always carried a toilet kit in the Jensen), said, surprised, "Yes, well, fine, thanks." And he sat down.

The old man said, "How's the job going?"

"The job?"

"That paint company, or whatever it was? Obviously all right, judging by your motor car." To Jay's raised eyebrows, he said, "Saw you drive it in. How much does a car like that cost?"

"New, about ten thousand, I suppose. I got it secondhand for four."

"Good God! I haven't bought a car for fourteen years." The old man always told him this story. "Still got the Mini, y'know, does me to run about the town, and one or two slightly longer trips."

"I thought you hated driving on motorways."

"Well, I keep off 'em. It's the eyes." The old man sighed. "I drove a racing car, y'know, once, just before the war. Did I ever tell you that?"

Only a thousand times. Jay shook his head.

The old man got him another drink and told him the story. It was still a good story. Then he looked at his watch.

Jay said, "Are you going somewhere? Is this a bad time to come?"

"No, no," said his father hurriedly. "Just thought we might eat out, what? This place gets a bit like bachelor quarters after a week. Some little place in the Lanes?"

"Do we book a table?" Jay stood.

The old man waved him back into his seat. "No, no. I did that. Decent little place."

"I thought you hated restaurants."

"Used to. Now I like the company. People. All that."

"Of course," Jay said.

He wondered at what point he should mention the money. If the old man could come across with a thousand or so, or even a few hundred, it would be something. It would buy time. Jay cursed himself for throwing away the cash reserve he'd kept in Westbourne Grove, but of course it had been part of what Mr. Jones had called the penance. Never mind. He'd talk to the old man after dinner, over a brandy perhaps.

That would be the thing to do.

The restaurant in the Lanes was small and obviously not cheap. To Jay's surprise, his father was recognized by the head-waiter, awarded his rank, and guided to a table, set, again to Jay's surprise, for three. They ordered gin and tonics and the old man coughed and said, "Look here, I invited a friend, a lady actually. Thought you might like to meet her, what?"

Jay could not hide his surprise. "Did you have this dinner arranged? I wouldn't have imposed."

"Not at all, not at all," said the old man enigmatically. "Have to meet her sometime, won't you?"

"Will I?"

"Well, she's more than just a friend, actually." The old man coughed, in rather an embarrassed fashion. "Y'know, old boy, you get damn tired of your own company. After your mother died, I had a lot of girlfriends, well, one does, never thought to marry any of 'em." He grinned. "Some of 'em married already, what?"

Jay thought: like father, like son. He also thought: If the old man is taking his lady friend to places like this, he must be spending a fair bit of money. More than his army pension, anyway. He said, "Who is she, a local or what?"

"Aren't any locals in Brighton." The old man swallowed a mouthful of gin and tonic. "No, she's a widow, most of the women here are. Her husband was a businessman, left her pretty well off." The old man's drink was going down quickly, the only sign that he was in any way apprehensive. "She's only fifty-two, y'know, she could have her pick, but she seems to quite like my company, so there it is."

Jay said, surprised, "You're not thinking of marrying her or anything, are you?"

"I could do a lot worse."

"You are serious?"

"Of course I'm serious. Trouble is, I'm seventy. But don't tell her that. She thinks I'm sixty-three."

"Won't she find out, if you marry her?"

"I expect so, but it won't matter then, will it?"

The old man looked slightly irritated, and moved the conversation onto another topic. "You doing any work for the government these days?"

"Now and again."

Jay had never told him any details. All he had ever said was that sometimes he went on reserve duty, that he was in a special section of the Army Reserve. He felt his father did not quite believe his story. He didn't want the old man to be totally unprepared if anything happened to him. Of course, Mr. Jones would make sure that if anything ever did happen, it would be declared an accident. Like poor Angie. Mr. Jones had sent him a clipping from a French newspaper to say that the remains of an English tourist, Miss Angela Browne, so tragically burned to death in a car accident near Vence, had been buried in the churchyard of St. Michel's, in the town. The memory was almost too much. He found himself fighting the absurd urge to get away, to sit on the promenade, maybe, and just think about her. He remained very still, and the moment passed.

His father was looking at him curiously.

"You all right, are you?"

"Rather warm in here." Jay knew he was sweating. "I'm still in the Reserve, go off to camp once a year and so on."

The old man brooded, staring into his gin and tonic. "Reserve? What could any Reserve do, if our Soviet comrades decided to have a go? Nothing that would stop 'em, in any conventional war. Far too many of 'em, what with their East German tank regiments, and all the rest of their people."

The old man's eyes brightened; this was the sort of shop talk he liked and understood. "Don't let anybody tell you the Soviet Army is democratic, by the way. Officers in wonderful warm greatcoats with fur collars, gauntlet gloves, high boots, troops in rough serge blouse affairs, with a blanket slung around them. Stalin let them loose in Berlin, all restrictions off, rape and looting, if not encouraged, certainly not stopped. In a way I don't blame 'em after what the Germans did to them." He sighed. "Still, all we did was put 'no fraternization' orders out. Nobody took any notice of 'em after the first few weeks. If you wanted to impose it you'd have to arrest the entire British Army." He ate a cheese straw, and looked at his watch. "Glad you're doing something, somebody has to, but the essential thing is to keep the Yanks in with us. If they go, I'm afraid it's a case of 'Hands up, Tommy!' "

Jay said academically, "We have our own nuclear weapon."

The old man brooded a little more. "For how long? Anyway, my point is, we must forget the conventional alternative. NATO can't live with 'em in conventional weapons, tank for tank, aircraft for aircraft, man for man. They outnumber us ten to one, across the board. Of course, as I say, they hope never to have to use any of that." His sharp eye was on the door of the restaurant. "They'll hope to do it with terrorism, sedition, infiltration, puppet governments sympathetic to them. Of course they can't do it if we wise up, as our Yankee cousins say, and try to stymie them."

"I suppose that's true," said Jay.

"You bet your life," said his father, rising gallantly to greet a small, attractive woman in a neat black dress, with very expensive jewelry pinned to it. She had gray eyes and darkish hair that had gray highlights, a miracle of the hairdresser's art. There was also a face lift in there somewhere.

The lady, introduced to Jay as Catherine, with no surname, sat down, ritually apologized for her lateness, and said, "It's so nice to meet you. Your father's always talking about you."

"Is he?" Jay was astonished.

"Yes, he's very fond of you, you know."

"No, I didn't know." The old man was glaring, so Jay turned it into a laugh. "He's never forgiven me for being chucked out of school."

"Of course he has," said Catherine. "He just doesn't bother to say these things." She pressed his father's hand. "Has he been boring you with his war talk?"

"Not boring me, no," said Jay.

"Well, it is a very bloodcurdling scenario, if you want to believe it." Catherine consulted her menu and made a dieter's choice: prawns, veal, vegetables. "Your father thinks Armageddon is due around 1995. I don't know why he's fixed on that particular year."

"Because the Yanks will have gone home by then," interposed the old man. "Unless some people show more sense than they have until now. And it won't be Armageddon. It'll be a walkover." The old man ordered tomato soup and steak. "Anyway, that's only an old soldier's opinion."

"Look, darling," said Catherine briskly, "the country's changed. We're a third-rate power these days, a bit like Italy—"

"Italy?" the old man shouted in anguish, then dropped his voice. It was, after all, an Italian restaurant. "Better than that, surely?"

"There are only two powers who matter," said Catherine, sipping her Beaujolais. "And those are the superpowers. We're in the middle. It's no good backing one or the other, and we shouldn't try. We should just declare this country a neutral zone. Why not? The confrontation theory won't work. The two sides just go on upping the ante." Catherine speared a prawn delicately. Her table manners were very exact. "One day, one of them will do something silly and we'll all go up in smoke." She smiled, showing small, well-cared-for teeth. "You know, I quite admire our woolly-hatted peace people. At least they do something, don't you think?"

Jay said politely, "The problem isn't a moral one. It's about politics and power, isn't it?" He saw that her eyes were quite candid and gray and that nothing anybody said was going to affect her, and he thought: My God, the old man's met his match and he doesn't even know it.

She said, "The young people don't remember the War, as your father does. He remembers Hitler, all that. The young don't know Hitler was just across the Channel in 1940. He's real to your father but hardly at all to me, or, I suppose, to you."

The old man said, "Of course he doesn't remember Hitler. He wasn't born until the War. The thing is, the bloody fellow got there because we appeased him, gave in to him. The Socialists were pacifists then, just as they are now, most of 'em. A lot of the Tories, as well." The old man attacked his steak with vigor. "The case is exactly the same. There's an aggressor. Tell him to keep off. Simple enough. He's kept off since 'forty-five. Just continue to keep the old guard up, what?"

"Darling," said Catherine, "the Soviet tanks aren't going to turn up in Brighton tonight, so I propose we forget them. Let's enjoy our lovely dinner, shall we?" She gazed at Jay a moment. "Your father did say what line you were in, but I've forgotten, I'm sorry."

"Paint," said Jay.

The old man looked disbelieving, but said nothing.

"Paint?" echoed Catherine politely.

"That sticky stuff," said Jay.

"And will you be staying a while?"

"No," Jay said. "Unfortunately, I have an appointment first thing tomorrow morning. I just came down on impulse really. Felt like a drive. We used to come here a lot, as a family, when I was a boy."

"Really?" Catherine looked interested. "You never told me that, Toby darling."

The old man kept his eyes on his steak. "Long time ago, that. Didn't think you'd be interested."

"My dear, I know you were married before. I think it's very nice of Jay to come down." She smiled at Jay. "You should do it more often. We'd be absolutely delighted to see you, anytime at all. Toby, do eat more slowly. You'll get your indigestion, you know."

"Nonsense," said the old man, but he didn't seem to mind the reprimand, quite the contrary.

Jay applied himself to his own food, which was excellent, and the evening passed in almost civilized fashion, full of small talk about the motor tour of the south of France they were planning for the spring, before the hordes of tourists arrived, and about the price the apartment would bring if the old man decided to sell. Of course, that hadn't been decided yet, Catherine said. They had lots of little details to work out and absolutely nothing was finalized, but, well, her home in Hove was much too large for one person, although two, with the live-in housekeeper, filled it quite nicely.

Jay declined the old man's none too enthusiastic offer of a bed (the old boy, he thought incredulously, had sex in mind), made his promise to come and see them again, very soon, and escaped, quite early.

Driving the first miles toward London, Jay found he had the grin on his face that he'd been repressing all evening. The old man was starting all over again, at his age, and here he was feeling sorry for himself. The old man's last surreptitious words echoed in his ear: "Splendid woman, what? And don't let anybody tell you sex is over at sixty. It's better because it's just sex. No romantic nonsense or worrying about families or faithfulness or the future. All you have to do is enjoy yourselves, what?" He patted Jay's shoulder through the car window. "Come down again, soon."

Jay had nodded and driven away. He had never once mentioned the money. The rate the old man was going, he needed it more than Jay did.

He switched on the car radio, and thinking of the whole episode, he laughed out loud. What had he been looking for, the old man's money or his affection? Surely not his affection, not after all these years? He was still smiling, but rather wryly, at his own idiocy and expectations as he drove through the night-quiet streets of Hammersmith.

The flat was, of course, cold and empty, and there was no milk in the refrigerator—he always forgot food when he was on his own—so he took his coffee black and went to bed, pulling the quilt over him. There was a faint scent of Angie on it, or in the place somewhere, despite his hoovering and dusting and polishing of everything; carpets, dressing table, mirrors. Nothing seemed to take the scent of her away. Maybe he was imagining it.

When he awakened, the birds were singing in the trees in the street outside, and he was in the middle of one of the dreams. This one was the replay of the Lisbon operation. Jay had booked on a pleasure-boat and gone ashore with the passengers, and laughingly excused himself as too tipsy to drink any more of the port everybody was imbibing, buying it by the bottle, it was so cheap. He had gone to the bar (why was it always a bar?) and there a young, well-dressed Portuguese man met him. The man had a Fiat with a loaded Russian automatic (of a kind he'd never seen before) waiting in the glove compartment.

Together, they had driven to a house in the suburbs. A middle-aged, untidy man, who seemed to be alone in the place, had answered their knock at once, in his shirt and trousers, a man who had led a rough life, by the look of him. All his eyes had registered was surprise as Jay took the automatic out of his pocket and shot him twice in the head. The middle-aged man had fallen back into the hallway, his body blocking the door. The young, well-dressed Portuguese man had pushed his body inside and closed the door.

By that time, Jay was in the passenger seat of the car and the Russian automatic was back in the glove compartment. The other man had gotten in wordlessly, and without exchanging a glance, they had driven back to the bar, and Jay had left the Fiat and rejoined the other passengers from the ship, apologizing for his absence. "Too much of a good thing—I was about to throw up!" They laughed, happy holidaymakers all. He had been away from them for twenty minutes.

An hour later they were back on the boat.

Two days after that he was back in London, bronzed and fit from his break in the sun, and apparently none the worse. Cherry had joked that she'd come with him on one of his paint-selling trips if she could get a tan like that. They had tried to make love that night. It hadn't worked. It wasn't working, regularly, by that time.

That was the least of it.

He hadn't known then that he would wake up, dream-haunted, years later, staring at the bedroom wall, every item remembered with awful clarity: the bluish bullet wound, the blood, so much of it, so sticky, the surprise in the man's tough, world-worn face—who was he, why was the deed done? He hadn't known then that these nightmares, these sweats, these horrors, would happen, four, five years later.

Sometimes it was that particular hit. Sometimes it was another. They had only one thing in common. They were crystal-clear.

Jay peeled off his sweat-soaked pajamas and took a shower. He made himself some coffee and waited for breakfast television. He felt nothing, no hope, no regret.

Nothing.

For the next five days, Jay holed up in the flat.

He left it only to buy bread and milk and cheese, and a few frozen meals at the corner shop. His stock of alcohol was low, and he bought a couple of bottles of red wine and one of scotch. He lay in bed late, most mornings, after watching a lot of early television. He shuffled around the place in a dressing gown and pajamas, and didn't bother to shave. He ate plastic food, heating it in the oven for the statutory twenty minutes, or he had just bread and cheese. He answered no telephone calls, and most days there were at least two, one in the morning at around ten (Mr. Jones just arriving in the office?) and another at four in the afternoon (Mr. Jones having his afternoon tea?). He carefully assessed how much money it was taking him to live like this, and worked out that if he could stand it, he could survive at this level for at least five or six weeks.

Long enough for Marty to go back to the States.

Long enough for Virgo's offer to go away.

The dreams came and went. He had one particularly bad one, the fifth night, living the Belfast experience all over again, and wakened to the inner certainty that the boyos knew where he lived and would come for him one night. They had got Angie, after all, and how had they found out about the cottage except by tailing them? The flat was, very probably, not safe. London itself was not safe. He shouldn't be in it. Jay put a chair against the outside door each night, and slept with the Beretta under his pillow.

By the sixth morning, he knew one thing for sure.

If he stayed here, he was a sitting duck.

A feeling of unease, between his shoulder blades, when he went down to the shops, to get the morning papers and buy some more provisions alerted him to the dark, Irish look of a couple of men who didn't seem exactly right in the workingmen's clothes they were wearing. He saw them first in the newspaper shop, and again, later, outside the flat, sitting in an old van. Of course, it could be nothing, but in Jay's business you lived on paranoia, it was the thing that kept you alive.

Jay found himself sweating, back in the flat.

It was possible he was wrong.

Of course it was.

What had he to go on?

Enough.

He had to get out of London, away from the U.K. altogether. First he had to leave the flat. Nobody had come for him, but if someone did, it was finito. Unless Mr. Jones had watchers on him. If he did, that could quite possibly be the only reason he was still alive.

The white cap, the last image remaining from the dream, stayed bright in his mind. It was a very clear and exact symbol. It was a death sentence, then as now.

The point was: did he want to live?

Jay sat a very long time, thinking about that.

Would Angie want him to just sit holed-up like this? Would it help if somebody got to him, here or elsewhere, on some quiet side street, or in the flat? Would his death bring Angie back?

Jay drank a large scotch, took a hot shower, shaved for the first time in the five long, aimless days, put on his dark suit and his Burberry, and packed a small bag. He took some shirts and socks and nothing else, except the Beretta, in a shoulder holster under his left armpit.

He rang Marty. No reply from her room, the operator said.

Jay called Mr. Jones.

For some absurd reason it was reassuring to hear his nasal, pedantic voice. Not so absurd really, come to think of it. Mr. Jones was better insurance than anybody or anything. Anyway, Jay reflected wryly, in the short term. He made an appointment to see Mr. Jones in half an hour.

Jay got to the point at once, before Mr. Jones could send for tea or coffee, pleased with the wincing pain this clearly gave Mr. Jones.

"I think a couple of the boyos are on my tail. I can't go back to the flat. I'm thinking seriously of getting out of the country. What I'm asking for is enough money to run, to stay away for, maybe, six months, until the heat's off."

Mr. Jones steepled his fingers. "What makes you think the boyos are on to you?"

"They found me in France, didn't they?" Jay asked coldly. "There's a leak in your organization somewhere." As Mr. Jones looked hurt, he added, "Probably in Belfast. Haven't you heard there's no such thing as security in Northern Ireland, everything gets out?"

Mr. Jones sighed. "I'm sorry about all that, if it's true."

"I don't want your sorrow. I want some of the money you owe me. A few thousand would do."

"Difficult, I'd say. Can you tell me where you want to go?"

"I have a friend in South Africa. He's in BOSS."

"What's his name? I might know him."

"Never mind his name. What about the money?"

"If he's such a good friend, couldn't you go anyway?"

"I can't just turn up there penniless, can I?"

Mr. Jones debated. "Why South Africa? It's very unfashionable these days, isn't it? I mean, the Americans are talking about stronger sanctions, and we're even getting a bit short of patience with them ourselves."

Mr. Jones made the Afrikaners sound like fourth-formers who hadn't cleaned their muddy soccer boots.

"I don't give a shit about their politics," Jay said, "although we were bloody glad of their naval bases, I notice, in the Falklands. The silly buggers think we're still their friends. The only friends the Foreign Office has in southern Africa are murderous black Marxists. They're only sorry they haven't any more lumps of Africa to give away."

Mr. Jones's eyes gleamed. "Yes, the liberal gents who run the FO aren't exactly my cup of tea, either. I suppose you could go to live with the Voortrekkers. Might suit you."

"I'm not going because I want to," exploded Jay. "I'm going because if I stay in London, I'm dead."

"Yes," said Mr. Jones pensively, "I suppose there is that."

"You bet your arse there is," said Jay. "So what about my money? Make it five thou, I could manage on that, pick up something when I get there."

There was a long silence. Jay could almost hear him thinking.

The answer turned out to be what he expected.

"I'm terribly sorry, dear boy. I'd do it if I could, but as I say, this new Minister would never stand for it. Isn't there any other way you can raise the cash?"

"Would I be here if there was?"

"What about your splendid motor car?"

"It belongs to the bank. I'm two months behind on the payments."

"Oh, I see. What a pity."

Jay sat, defeated, and listened to the traffic along Whitehall. He had tried, but what the hell, he had lost. He had expected nothing else. He said, "So you aren't prepared to help. Thanks a bunch."

Mr. Jones looked hurt. "Of course I'm prepared to help. Didn't I put that very excellent offer your way? From the cousins?" He shook his head. "I take it you're absolutely not interested?"

Jay said, "I'm not up to any job at the moment. My nerves are shot and I'm all screwed up."

"From what Jack Virgo told me—and, I must stress, I know no details—it's something you could do very easily." He paused, and let the bait settle. "Then, I suppose, once you'd got that money, you could go where you like, even South Africa, what?"

Jay sat and looked at him in total silence for almost a minute. Then he said, "If Marty is still in London, I'd better see her."

Mr. Jones smiled.

"You see, you do want to live. Congratulations, dear boy."

* * *

An hour later, in Marty's bed, Jay knew that was true.

He felt like a shit, but it was true.

Marty had answered Mr. Jones's call, made before his very eyes. Mr. Jones had used a signal. He rang twice, with a thirty-second interval. Marty answered the second time. Yes, he had heard her voice say, of course, we have a lot to talk about, send him over, I'll give him tea.

Instead, she had given him sex.

And he had taken it, without any feeling of affection, just as pure sex. As pure sex it had turned out to be most impressive.

Marty had been waiting, dressed in a silk sheathlike dress that showed her figure. There were china teacups on the small table and even a teapot. There were small iced cakes and little plates and knives. "I got them all from Harrods, I'm taking them home, they're stylish, aren't they?"

"I've already had tea with Mr. Jones," Jay lied.

"Oh? Then is there anything else I can give you?"

In answer, he had put his hand gently on her breast.

There was nothing under the Harrods dress.

Two minutes later they were in the bed, and this time Marty was the dictating partner. Not only in the small actions, some of them new to Jay, who thought himself experienced, but in the fact that she talked, all the time, whispered sweet obscenities in his ear, but not shamefacedly, looking directly into his eyes as she did it. He began to react to her sensuality. She was enjoying it all as much as he was, on a purely sexual level. Whether she was lying on her back or touching her toes, her pleasure and enthusiasm surprised him, but there was a decadence that drove him to heights of sexuality that he'd never experienced with any of his women before. Marty made Angie, who had been an enthusiastic lover, seem, in memory, quite inexperienced, and Cherry positively dull. This, he thought, coming to orgasm for the third time in an hour, was like making it with some skilled Japanese courtesan; all they needed was the hot baths and the flower arrangements. When he finally became detumescent, she switched on a hard-porn video, and they lay watching it, smoking a joint she'd lit and drinking from a bottle of retsina ("I saw you liked it"), and then they imitated one of the positions the screen performers had used, and did it all again.

Jay said afterward, "Did you notice the man didn't have a

real erection? In porno movies they never do." He drew on his joint. "Who taught you to screw like this?"

Marty laughed. "Nobody. It's just a talent. Why, do you object?"

Jay lay back in the pleasant bedroom, with the late-afternoon sun dappling the walls, his head slightly hazy from the pot.

The frenzied running away, the betting, the hideout in Westbourne Grove, the Irishmen outside the flat, even Mr. Jones, all seemed unreal, faraway. He had used this girl, lying sated beside him, her eyes closed, but not asleep. He had started by hating her—why not, she was another instrument, pushing him to do something he didn't want to do—but what the hell, she was probably being pushed along by other, more powerful people, Virgo, for instance.

What did it matter?

Angie was dead and there was no bringing her back.

What did anything matter?

"When do we fly to New York?" he asked.

N·I·N·E

"Politics by assassination isn't new," said Jack Virgo, lying, with his shoes off, on the bed in Marty's room in the St. Regis Hotel. "It's been happening since Julius Caesar and before that." He lit his cigar. As usual he was talkative after sex. The sex, this time, had not been the full-blooded thing. Marty found Jack Virgo oddly repulsive that evening. After all, she had lain with Jay only twelve hours before. Jack had asked no more of her than fellatio. It was something he liked, more, she sometimes thought, than the act itself. She had skillfully pleasured him, and he had acquiesced. How long had she been sleeping with Jack Virgo, for God's sake? Years and years, it seemed like all her life. And now, since she had been with Jay, all she wanted was him. It was frightening, but it was fact. It was also something that Virgo must never know.

Jack Virgo was pontificating. "Forget ancient history, look at our own time. Fourteen Japanese cabinet ministers were assassinated in the thirties, three of them prime ministers. The First World War started because an unknown prince was murdered by anarchists in Sarajevo. Dollfuss was murdered by Hitler's Brownshirts, in Vienna. In a way, that started the Second World War, or anyway it prepared the way for it. Mussolini murdered Matteotti, his rival, some say by forcing castor oil down his throat. Sadat was killed, only the other year, and he was a guy who slept with a revolver under his pillow every night of his adult life. He was expecting it, see, but not the way it came. Nor was Roehm, Hitler's rival. He got it at a homosexual orgy. Jack Kennedy got his because his brother Robert was giving the Mob a hard time, and the Pope very nearly got his courtesy of the KGB, because he was a very big pain in the ass to the Politburo over Poland. Who can be bigger than a president and a pope, for Chrissake? They make the whole goddam business respectable. If they can get it, anybody can get it. The hit man's a necessity of political life in our time."

He smiled sourly. "Without him, how would the politicians go on ruling us so peacefully? The hit man removes the irritant, the guy who can't be removed any other way, by bribery, intimidation, sweet talk, or nooky. A guy like that, he's too good to live anyway." Jack Virgo grinned.

Marty was irritated. In these post-sex seminars, she never knew whether Jack Virgo was joking or not. Probably half and half. Whichever way, he was enjoying himself, all this talk. He didn't seem curious about Jay and her. He hadn't asked details of how she had persuaded Jay to take the job. She had simply told him that Jay needed the money. Jack Virgo had nodded, as if he had expected nothing else. "Gelt, that's all mechanics ever think about."

He had told her to relay to Jay the news that the big day was tomorrow, and to get a good night's sleep. Then he had added he'd drop by the hotel for a last checkup. Marty told him, accepting his call in the bar of the St. Regis, "I think you're going to have to talk to Jay about his money. He isn't going to do anything until you do."

Jack Virgo exploded. "Doesn't he trust us?"

"No," Marty replied. "Why don't you talk to him? He's here."

"I don't want to do that," Jack Virgo countered. "I don't have the money—well, not all of it."

"You'd better get it, or he'll be on the first flight back for London tomorrow morning."

"All right, I'll come over."

"Where are you, in New York City?" Marty asked, surprised.

"I'm at the Pierre."

"That's pretty public."

"See you in a half hour. I'll ask for your room." Jack Virgo put the telephone down. He never said goodbye, on or off the telephone.

Marty returned to Jay, sitting sipping his scotch and branch water, in the bar of the St. Regis. "He's coming over. I'm going to take a shower, and change. I'll call you in your room, right?"

Jay looked at her, hard. "He'd better be bringing my money."

"I'm sure he is." She had no idea if Jack Virgo would bring the money or not. Virgo knew that Jay had stood still for Mr. Jones's holding on to money due him, and she wondered if Jack Virgo might try the same tactic. He would be unwise if he did, she thought, looking at Jay's grim face.

She sat and picked up her drink in her right hand and let the other fall into his crotch, under the table. "Cheer up, lover. We'll get the money."

She felt Jay grow erect. God, feeling up men in bars, she was beginning to act like the natural whore Jack Virgo said she was. The thought crossed her mind that if Jack could get himself to think of her that way, he could also feel he owed her nothing.

"Come up to my room?" Jay asked.

It was all she could do to say no, but she said it.

"Then take your hand away and let me enjoy my drink."

Marty laughed. This man made great love to her, and he also made her laugh. Jack Virgo had never made her laugh in his life.

Virgo had made her listen, however. Anything she knew, everything she knew, about the underground war, Virgo had taught her. He had taught her the way the Company worked. The all-purpose excuse, for example. What you said was: operational necessity. For instance, you know it is necessary to terminate (with extreme prejudice) some Soviet agent or fellow traveler, so you do it. You then plead operational necessity. If you ask permission first, the desk man will always find reasons to say no, and your enemy does his work, and melts into the dark. Jack Virgo was famous for not asking permission of anybody and getting away with it. "Marty, you can get away with a hell of a lot in the Company, if you plead operational necessity."

Was Jay's job something like that? She had asked Jack Virgo the question. "Tell me, Jack, is this another of your famous operational necessities? Are you going to come clean, go to the very top, as soon as it's over, and say, events were pressing, I had no alternative but to take this guy out?"

Jack Virgo had lit his cigar and squinted at her along it. He wore only an undershirt. Jack was probably the only man in the Company who wore an undershirt. "Marty, you sound like you disapprove of this out-take."

"I can't disapprove, since I don't know who it is you're taking out." Marty poured herself a glass of white wine and seltzer, the dieter's drink. "If I did, then I might have an opinion."

Jack Virgo waved his cigar. "You're against it, in principle?"

Marty retorted. "I'm against it because you haven't cleared it with anybody at all, as far as I can see."

Jack Virgo smiled, like a shark. "Some very important people are behind it. Unofficially."

"Company people? Very top brass?"

"The very top."

"But not the director or anybody like that?"

"Not quite the director."

"But his close associates?"

"Let's say, some of his close associates."

Marty didn't know why, but she didn't believe him. He's doing this one alone, she thought. He has to be. When Jay goes in on the job, he goes in alone, too, because there's no backstop, nobody to bail him out if anything goes haywire.

The idea caused a tremor to run through her body and end between her legs. Am I going entirely off the wall? she thought. This guy is a mechanic. If Jack Virgo had the faintest idea of how I really feel about him, he'd have me back in Langley before I could take my pantyhose off.

The idea made her smile, a smile that was not unnoticed by Jack Virgo. He shifted on the bed, his shriveled and sated member stirring with the movement. "What's so funny? You think it's all some big joke?"

Marty wiped the grin. "I just feel you're in above your head, and I don't want to be with you when you sink."

"I'm not going to sink, baby." Jack Virgo pointed the cigar at her. "Nor are you."

"Thanks very much, but when do you think you can tell me some more?"

"The job's tomorrow. I'll brief you both then. I have to get back to the Pierre in fifteen minutes. I'll come over for coffee, here to your room, at eleven tomorrow morning. When it happens

I want to be seen in the bar at the Pierre, and I want you there with me."

"What about Jay?"

"What about him?"

"After the hit, what does he do?"

"He finds his way back here, that's what he does."

So, Marty thought, no backup, none at all.

"Somebody has to be there, outside, with a car, to get him away."

"Who?"

Marty didn't know why she said the next words. "Well, me."

Jack Virgo looked at her in silence for a long moment.

"Why you?"

"Because you don't seem to have anybody else."

Jack Virgo frowned dangerously, but she pressed, "Jack, you don't, do you? This is a one-man operation all down the line, right?"

"Right, but like I say, I have friends in high places."

"Who won't want to know if it goes wrong."

Jack Virgo shut up like a clam. "Never mind all that. Just do as I say. Be in the Pierre tomorrow evening, sitting having a drink with me and one or two of the boys, when the job is being done."

"Where is the job?"

Jack Virgo frowned again.

"Jack, where is it? I have to know that much."

Jack Virgo drew deeply on the cigar, in a disgusted fashion that said: women. "All right, all right, it's a hotel. Atlantic City."

"Atlantic City?" She stared at him. "You expect an English guy like Jay to find his way back to New York, to this hotel, after a hit, all on his own?"

"Why not? I expect he's done it before."

Marty said slowly, "Of course he hasn't done it before. He's always had backup, that's standard."

She stood and poured herself another glass of white wine, forgetting the seltzer this time, and she did something she had never done before—she defied Jack Virgo. "I'm sorry, I can't do it. I'm not letting any guy walk into some hotel in Atlantic City, do a job, and try to walk out, without having anywhere to go, no car waiting, no cover at all. It's crazy to expect anybody to do it."

"If he can't do it, he's the wrong guy."

Marty said quickly, recognizing the note of desperation in her voice, "He won't do it unless he has backup. He isn't a fool. If you put it to him as you've put it to me, he'll say no."

"Even if I wave a sackful of dollars in his face?"

"Even then."

"You seem to be pretty sure about that."

Marty controlled her voice. "He's not one of the psychopaths we normally use on these jobs." Marty talked on, a mite too fast, she knew, but she couldn't help it. "Because he's a Brit and nobody knows him does not mean you don't need to provide him with cover. What if it goes wrong and he's picked up? He could break wide open and talk. He has your name and he has mine."

"He won't talk, he's not the sort." Jack Virgo smiled his shark's smile, but she could see the thought troubled him. "You seem to know this guy pretty good."

"You threw me into bed with him, Jack, it was your idea, and the fact you did that tells me how important this operation is to you, because you've never done that before!" Marty felt a sudden cold anger. "If you had top-level backing, you'd have gotten some honeypot from the Company list who'd go to bed with him for a thousand dollars!"

Jack Virgo did not reply. He just looked at her.

Marty took a deep breath. "Why me, why use me?"

Jack Virgo smiled. "Because you're the best there is."

"In bed?"

"Where else?"

"You're a shit, Jack."

"I know it."

"You have nobody, but nobody, in this thing with you, do you?"

"Yes, I do." In truth, he probably had, she thought, until it went wrong.

"All right. I've gone along with you on this, but I've slept with him and I don't know where that leaves our relationship."

"I didn't know we had a relationship," said Jack Virgo brutally. "I thought we just screwed."

"If that's all it's ever meant to you."

"It's all it's ever meant to either one of us, baby."

Not true, she wanted to scream at him, not true and you know it isn't true, there was a lot of tenderness in it, once, love even, on my side. You taught me everything I know, Jack, you changed my life, I'd have been a superior typist at Langley but for you, that's what I would have been. Are you telling me all the years of waiting for the telephone to ring, of broken dates and burned dinners and lies about your wife and the kids I never had (never wanted really, but what the hell), are you really telling me all that was because we just screwed?

Marty said none of that.

"All right, Jack, if that's what you think, then that's fine, but I'm not going to put my head on the block just because you say so. I'm going to be there myself, as backup for Jay, or it's all off, as far as I'm concerned."

There, she thought, it's said and he can make of it what he likes.

Jack Virgo was a long time making anything of it.

Finally, he stood up and pulled on his clothes. He went across to the basin and splashed cold water across his face. All the time, he was thinking hard. She knew it, from the way he seemed, mentally, to have gone out of the room. He toweled his face and slipped on his coat. Then he turned to her.

"He certainly got to you, in the sack. Am I right?"

"No," she lied coldly. "The sack isn't what we're talking about here. We're talking about safety, yours and mine. I do the backup, or I'm out. You decide."

Jack Virgo grinned the crooked grin, which, she knew, meant he was hurt. Well, let him be hurt, she was hurt. This was a guy she had once thought might marry her. Yes, sloppy fool that she'd been, once she'd even thought that.

"You know what the Earl of Stafford said to his favorite daughter?" Jack Virgo stood, his hand on the doorknob, ready to go.

"No, and I don't give a shit."

He said, "When I sell you, my dear, I will be indeed hard pressed."

"Well, hooray for the Earl of Stafford, whoever he was."

Jack Virgo looked at her, his eyes, somewhere very deep down, signaling hurt. She felt nothing.

"You got it. You back him up. I'll arrange for a car. See you here tomorrow at eleven."

The door closed, and Marty was alone.

She went into the bathroom, took off her dress, and showered. She sprayed herself with Saint Laurent and put on another dress and nothing else, except a pair of shoes. Then she picked up the telephone and called Jay, in his room.

Marty had slept with thirty men, one or two whose names she could not recall, but Jay was something different. He was, for one thing, her first Englishman. She had always expected Englishmen to be courteous and thoughtful, and in the words of Eartha Kitt's famous song, to need time. Jay didn't need time. He took her the moment he discovered that she was wearing only the dress and the Saint Laurent, standing up, against the dresser, and she encouraged him, with small cries, and even then, she came. It surprised her, or it should have.

Normally, she was in charge of the sex, but this man did not give her time to use any of her techniques, he simply took her and then talked to her as if nothing had happened, as if, in fact, what had happened did not matter. Probably the fact that he was very strong and held her so firmly that she could not object or change the sexual tempo, to gain mastery of the situation, unnerved her. Something did. She felt helpless and obedient (if only for the duration of the act) and actually wanted to please him, not just to appear to please.

This reaction was new and puzzled her; it had puzzled her from the first. This man has ambition for none of the things Jack Virgo wants, Marty thought. That makes him stronger than Jack. There's nothing he wants, he's done it all, he's past ambition, drink, drugs, or possibly even women, in any deep emotional way. She didn't care, he took her urgently, and seemed to mean it, and that was as much as any woman, or anyway any woman like her, could expect.

It was enough. Leave love out. Take the rest.

It had been enough with Jack Virgo for years and years.

It was enough with Jay, now.

It had to be. It was all there was.

After the sex, Jay called room service, and they drank the champagne and ate the club sandwiches, sitting on the bed, like a picnic. Jay didn't ask any questions about Jack Virgo, and she didn't, for the moment, tell him any answers.

"You make love like a twenty-year-old, do you know that?" she said, still surprised, and amused.

"You don't seem to mind." He was smiling.

"I could, but no, I don't."

"Well, we had the trimmings the other night." He looked at his watch. "Are we going to watch television?"

Marty laughed outright. "You aren't serious?"

Jay said, "Oh, but I am. Nobody can possibly go back to London without a report on the latest episode of *Dallas.*"

"Who says you're going back to London?" Marty asked.

"If I don't get the money, I'm on the next flight."

Marty felt a pang right through her body, which had felt enough pangs in the last half hour; but this was sharper than sex, a sense of loss. Looking at Jay, who had found a quiz show of total banality and was laughing aloud at it, she knew she felt a kind of fever which, if not love, could well be sex, and what was the difference anyway? Something, anything, was better than the nothing she had been feeling, for a very long time, with Jack Virgo. If Jay was like all the rest, and she had to accept he probably was, then she would at least enjoy him while she could. He had a good body, and she liked that. He didn't give a shit. She liked that. He hated Jack Virgo's guts. She liked that even better.

"Do you know," Jay was asking her, still watching the game show on television, "that the television pros call these things *reward* shows? Rather like rewarding a monkey for doing a trick."

Marty got off the bed and crossed the room, still wearing her dress—he hadn't even taken it off during the sex, simply lifted it to her armpits, crushing it more than a little in the process—and switched off the set. "You've had your ration. That's enough."

Jay chewed on his sandwich. "All right, what do we talk about instead?"

"The job. Tomorrow."

He was silent, but still and watchful.

"Jack talked to me. He's coming over tomorrow, to brief you."

"What time?"

"Eleven in the morning."

Jay shrugged. "Will he be bringing the money?"

"I told him to, or to forget it."

Jay leaned over her on the bed and kissed her. "That was smart of you. Where's the job?"

"I can't tell you. Jack will do that."

"Fair enough. Who'll be my backup?"

"I will."

"Who else?"

"Nobody else. Just me."

Jay looked at her with his deep blue eyes for what seemed a very long time.

"Just you?"

"Just me."

"Where are the other members of this great organization of yours?"

"There won't be any." Marty added quickly, "This is all very hush-hush."

Jay remarked calmly, "Usually the Company uses too many people. Usually they throw people at a problem, they fall over each other's feet there are so many of them."

"Not this time," Marty said lightly. "Jack will tell you why tomorrow, if you ask him, I guess."

Jay shifted his weight on the bed. He set the champagne glass down on the bedside table. "I never ask questions about any job. Never ever."

Marty said, "That's very professional of you."

"I don't want to know, or I start to think why. Was it right, or fair? That's not my concern. Other people make those decisions, and I have to trust their decisions are made for all the right reasons or I'd be working for the other side."

Marty said, curious, "You really do believe in what you're doing? I wondered."

"Yes, or I wouldn't do it, couldn't do it. I don't believe that my employers always get it right. They're human and fallible. Look at Jones. So, it's best I know as little as possible." He paused. "I like the weapon in my hand at the last possible moment, and I like to have a team of people who know less about me than I know about them. That's how I like things."

Marty took a deep breath. "It may be a little different tomorrow, but I'm not exactly a virgin in these matters, am I?"

"Not in any sense, I don't suppose," he said. Then he smiled.

As Marty held her arms and all of her open to him, she was filled with a sense of rightness, and was grateful he didn't ask any more questions, because she didn't know any of the answers. She had a feeling of unease about the whole operation, but she'd had that since the very beginning. One thing she knew for certain. She would protect this man as best she could.

Marty held his body to hers and, resisting his demands, slowed him down and began to bind him to her sexually, with tongue and lips and breasts, and words and wetness. Only this time, she was not working for Jack Virgo or for the Company but for herself.

Jack Virgo sat in Marty's room as if it were his own. The maid had been in and straightened the bed Marty had deliberately crumpled. She had stayed the whole night in Jay's room, and the morning had come bright and brash. Jay had ordered more champagne with orange juice and they'd had Buck's Fizz, with lox and scrambled eggs. The best breakfast in the world, said Jay.

Sated and aching pleasantly, Marty had come back to her suite, showered, and put on a demure black dress with a large white collar. It should have reassured Jack Virgo, but of course it didn't. He came bursting in, fifteen minutes early, and called for coffee before he sat down. He did not kiss her or say any friendly word. He simply put down on the bed a very expensive crocodile briefcase and gave her a hard look. "You seem very cheerful this morning?"

"I slept very well."

"I'm glad to hear it. I lay awake most of the night."

"Why, are you worried, Jack?" She could not keep the irony out of the words.

Virgo sat in a chair, across the room from her, and stared at the bedroom, visible through the door. "And how is our friend?"

"He sounded fine when I called him. He'll be along in a few minutes."

"When you called him. I like it." The shark's smile came and went. "Did you tell him anything about the job?" He paused, then added dryly, "When you called him, that is?"

"No, I didn't."

"Nothing about backup?"

Marty looked at the bridge of Jack Virgo's nose. "Nothing."

"You haven't changed your mind?"

"No, I haven't."

Jack Virgo said, "If anything goes wrong, you're on your own, remember that. You and him, just the two of you. I'm out of it, I was never in it, it's your operation, not mine."

Marty felt the blood leave her face. "I don't even know what the operation's about. How could it be mine?"

Jack Virgo said, "It's yours if you go on it, baby."

"And if I don't go?"

"It's his. All of it."

"If I don't go, he won't."

"You have talked to him?" Jack Virgo smiled a smile he didn't mean. "After all? You lie very nicely, baby."

"You taught me, Jack."

"So I did."

"I told him I'd be going, Jack."

"And what did he say?"

Marty said icily, "He seemed happy."

"Why shouldn't he be happy? He's getting laid by a wonderful piece of ass, and he's got a lot of money coming his way for an easy hit. I'd be happy in his place, the President of the United States would be happy in his place."

"You've left me with no alternative, Jack. I have to go."

"You wouldn't be in it, baby, unless you wanted to be."

It was true enough, but the whole situation was Jack Virgo's doing, just the same. Against all that she knew of him, Marty tried for honesty. "Jack, you knew what was going on between Jay and me. It suits your book, as of now. Tell me to stop, tell me to get on a plane south, and I'll go, right now. I won't even wait for him, I'll pack my bag and be gone in five minutes. If the present arrangement pisses you off so much, then maybe you think more of me than you say? Just make up your mind what you want. Do I go, or do I stay?"

"What do you want me to tell you? Go back to Langley? Forget him? Forget the job?" Virgo's voice dropped a full octave, into the lower, would-be-sincere bass she associated with persuasive arguments in Company committees, or even from the days when he had still felt it necessary to placate her, talk her around, when he still felt, perhaps, some guilt at the situation between them. That particular tone she called his come-on voice. He was using it now, on her, and she deserved better. She had tried to be honest, tried to build bridges, and what did she get?

She got shit.

"Look, baby. If you want to go, go. But . . ." Now came the *but*, already. "I have to tell you this job matters. If you feel he won't do it without you, then I don't know. I have to leave the choice to you."

"I have no choice at all."

Jack Virgo came across, took her hand, pressed it, and kissed her on the lips. "I won't forget this, baby."

At that moment the door opened, and Jay stood there. Marty could have sworn she had locked it, but maybe she hadn't. Jack Virgo did not let her go. He kissed her on the lips, again. He cupped her left breast in his hand and squeezed very hard. She bit her lip to stop herself from crying out.

Virgo said, over his shoulder, "Come in, you aren't interrupting anything important."

Marty was conscious of Jay's eyes, looking questioningly into hers, but she avoided them and moved quickly away from Jack to the table and poured coffee. She was surprised to find her hands were trembling.

"Here, let me."

Jay took the coffeepot from her and did not look up until he had finished pouring the coffee. Marty sat down in a chair and tried to compose herself. It wasn't easy with Jack Virgo standing there in the middle of the room, the shark's smile on his mouth and his eyes cold and dead.

These men could easily kill for me, she thought, yet they'll work together because the work is more important than I am. The Company instructors on her operational courses had taught her (along with weapon-handling and ambush tactics and anti-terrorist ploys and all the rest of the curriculum) that nothing mattered: not feelings or friendships or even their lives. All that mattered was the success of the operation, whatever it was.

For the first time in her life, Marty did not believe that.

Jay sipped his coffee and sat down, across from Virgo.

"Before you waste time briefing me, where's the money?"

Jack Virgo's face worked, with what Marty recognized as acute distaste, but he said, in a level voice, "In the case, on the bed. It's all there, twenty-five grand. The other half when you're done. Count it, if you like."

Jay opened the case and quickly leafed through the bundles of used notes. He nodded. "Now we can talk."

Jack Virgo said, "There's a car in the street. It's a Caddy. Plenty of speed, well maintained. Who's driving?"

Marty looked at Jay. "I am. I know the roads."

"Fine, fine." Virgo took out a cigar. "There's a weapon and ammo in the glove compartment. When the job's done, leave the automobile in any parking lot in the city." He was looking at Marty. "Then give me the ticket."

"Is it bulletproof or anything?" Marty asked.

"No, just the regular model. There are insurance papers in the glove compartment."

"Is it a Company auto?" she pressed.

Jack Virgo smiled. "Yes and no. Anyway, that's academic. The job's a breeze."

"Glad to hear it." Jay didn't sound glad, Marty thought, he sounded grim, and he was looking at Jack Virgo with the same cool animosity he'd shown since he came into the room. "If it's easy as all that, why do I rate Marty as backup?"

Jack Virgo fielded the question as if he'd rehearsed the answer, which he probably had. "Because we're paying you a long way over the odds, for what is a simple operation. High visibility I grant you. Recognition factor higher than usual I also grant you."

"Does that remark mean I'm to be in the company of the hit, at any time?"

"Yes, I'm afraid it probably does. It depends how you want to play it. I told you, certain decisions are up to you. That is one of them."

Jack Virgo waited. Marty waited. If Jay was going to leave, he would leave now.

"I don't like that," he said at last, quite evenly. "Not one little bit."

"When the time comes, it may not be necessary." Jack Virgo leaned forward, a thin sheen of moisture across his forehead. "It'll be up to you."

Jay said, "Also, you didn't say high recognition factor. At any time."

Jay's voice was neutral. Marty thought: he isn't thrown. She breathed in, sharply, but neither of the men looked at her. They were locked, two stags.

"No, I didn't," said Jack Virgo. "But you'll be back here to collect the second half of your money, and away on the next flight, inside of two hours. Unless something goes wrong, and there's no reason why it should, you'll be in London, or wherever you want to go, within twenty-four hours." Jack Virgo tried a smile. "With your money in your hot little hand."

Jay looked long at him. Virgo stared back innocently. "What happens to this money while I'm doing the job?"

"You wanted the money." Virgo shrugged. "Put it in the hotel safe. In a deposit box. Wherever you like."

"You have to be joking," said Jay icily.

"Then take it with you. Or I could hold it for you." Virgo looked pensively at the crocodile case. "I wouldn't like you to lose it."

"I won't lose it." Jay picked up the case and handed it to Marty. "You'll look after it for me, won't you?"

Marty glanced at Virgo. His face was stone.

"Of course. It'll be fine in the Caddy with me. It won't go anywhere."

"I sincerely hope not." Jay turned back to Virgo. A suspicion of a smile crossed his lips. "All right, let's hear it, very, very slowly."

Not looking at Marty, not looking at Jay, or at the crocodile case containing the twenty-five thousand dollars in used notes, Jack Virgo began to talk.

T·E·N

Marty parked the Caddy at the rear of the hotel. She had intended putting it in the hotel parking lot, but Jay had said no. "If we have to run, we don't need any guy who's seen our faces."

Marty peered along the street. "It's restricted parking here. If you take more than an hour, I may have to cruise around."

Jay felt his nerves tighten. "Then cruise around, but don't attract attention." He debated. "Tell you what. This has to take an hour. Go eat something. Come back then."

"Is that wise?"

"Better than being noticed."

"All right. I'll park somewhere along this street, or I'll just cruise."

"Be where you can see me if I'm standing on this corner. Even if you have to park the Caddy a block away."

"Right," she said. "Good luck." Crisp, businesslike, no darling or anything like that. Jay did not reply.

He took the .22 Beretta out of the glove compartment and slipped it into his coat. He had asked Virgo for it, specifically. It was single-shot, but held sixteen rounds. It was so small and neat it hardly made a bulge in his inside pocket. Jay knew it as the best small gun in the world, and he felt a little better about the operation. Not much, but some. "If I'm not back here in an hour, hang around. This could take time."

Jay opened the door and got out. The cold breeze coming off the Atlantic cut through his thin suit. Atlantic City was to him vividly reminiscent of Blackpool, with its large hotels and the Boardwalk and the Steel Pier and the general air of new paint covering old seediness, and vulgarity and money and possibly danger.

Jay closed the door of the Caddy and did not look back. He walked, head down, toward the front of the large new hotel. This was a Mob town, and that was another thing he didn't like about it. He still had a very strong feeling that Jack Virgo had not told him everything, but so what? If it all went well, he'd be in South Africa in two days, knocking on some door in Joburg, asking for his old friend Brandt. He walked on, feeling tight, no nerves. So it was all to end here, this was to be the last one, as the job in the German pissoir, only three years before, had been the first?

It would mean goodbye to Marty, but he'd always known that.

Marty's life was here, she was a Company operative with most of her career still in front of her, and she had going whatever she had going with Virgo. She wouldn't leave all that, and anyway, how would he cope with a woman in his new life? He had to disappear, for at least a year, maybe two. Later he had to surface long enough to try to extort his Zurich money from Mr. Jones. Then he had to disappear again, this time for good.

He would miss her.

The sex was sensational, better than he'd ever known. But Jay knew that the sex was an extra, a perk, something to hold him to the job, and that had, on balance, to mean the idea was really Virgo's. It was, however, just possible it was Marty's own choice. He could not know, and, in the last analysis, it did not matter.

Jay, hunched up against the chill breeze, turned abruptly into the hotel entrance, walking quickly, not looking up. Doormen were inclined to remember people, even with the traffic they'd see in a place like this. Inside, it was almost dark, in the manner of American hotels. A long reception desk stood to the right, as Jack Virgo had told him it would. There was a high bustle of gamblers in the foyer, men and women, dressed in what passed for evening clothes here. A lot of perfume and cologne was in the air, and people seemed to be hurrying, in large crowds, in and out of the elevators.

The dining rooms were upstairs, Virgo had said, overlooking the ocean. Best not to get up there, keep everything on ground level, Jack Virgo had advised. Jay wondered how he was to do that. He had memorized the entire layout of the place, but it was all much more spacious than he had expected. This was a hotel with a large betting clientele. The gaming rooms were on ground level, and he could hear the clang of a hundred one-armed bandits.

Jay slowed his pace. A man in a maroon tux that did not go with his face took a step toward him. "Can I help you, sir?" he asked, but Jay just shook his head and kept walking. God, the place was alive with security and all kinds of greeters and housemen. He began to feel cold, and sharp, and angry.

Where *was* the bloody bar?

Then he saw it, at the far end of the reception area.

Inside, it was darker than the foyer, so dark he could hardly see the line of drinkers at the bar.

Walking toward it, trying to adjust to the dark, he saw a face he recognized, from the photograph Jack Virgo had shown him. What the hell, this place was crawling with security, it had to be in and out, it meant speed. He bumped, deliberately, into a man standing talking to two women, a few yards from the bar. The man's drink jogged but did not spill.

"Terribly sorry," Jay said. "My fault, entirely."

"I *say*!" said the man, who had red hair and a ferrety face and was small-boned and loudly dressed, as Jack Virgo had said he would be. "Terribly, terribly sorry! You British, bud?"

"Guilty." Jay smiled.

The man, whose name Jay had been told was Begby, took his arm. He seemed rather drunk. "I like the Brits. The Falklands. That was some show, huh?"

"I'm glad to hear you're a friend," Jay said, looking quickly at the two women and smiling. Inside, he cursed. Women, they never forget a man's face, any man's. "I'm sorry I spilled your drink—may I make up for it? What are you drinking, ladies?"

The women looked at each other. One was a brunette, one a blonde; they both wore too much makeup and their dresses were new but not expensive. Neither wore a wedding band. Girls on the town, divorcées probably, he thought, and Begby was the best they could do.

"Hey, my drink wasn't spilled," Begby protested.

"A new round coming up." Jay vainly signaled the bartender.

"Buddy, you're a gennelman," said Begby, his arm going around Jay's shoulder and his alcoholic, tobacco-ridden breath into Jay's face. The women smiled fixedly, their bright eyes assessing Jay. He was ten years younger than either of them. They relaxed and looked cheered and told him what they drank.

It was easy as that, and as dangerous.

"My name's Begby, call me Al," said Begby. "The girls are Mandy and Cheryl."

"Hi, Al," replied Jay. "I'm Smitty. Hi, Mandy and Cheryl." He called their order to a passing waitress and indicated seats at a corner table. It was a time for dark corners. This was all too public. It seemed every job he did got more public.

When they were all seated, the drinks in front of them, Jay said, "I'm in computers."

Begby said, "I work for Uncle Sam."

Jay waved his glass. "That sounds fine."

"Till payday it's fine," replied Begby sourly.

Cheryl and Mandy looked serious at this information, glancing doubtfully at each other and into their drinks. Jay recalled that Americans were always serious about money, whether it was one dollar or a million, it was the way the country ran, it was the way the Brits used to be in Victorian times. Everybody had to look after himself. The girls were not happy to hear that Begby wasn't very well paid, working for the government. It boded ill for the evening, possibly.

Begby blinked, suddenly conscious of his mishap. "Hey, listen, girls, I may not be rolling, from what Uncle Sam pays me, but I got a coupla things going, don't worry, I'll be picking up the tab for the drinks all right."

Jay said, "You and me both, Al. I insist."

Cheryl and Mandy looked reassured.

Jay considered Begby, in the noisy gloom of the bar. The lived-in face did not go with the expensive sport clothes, the blazer, the designer silk shirt, the gold medallion on the scrawny neck. Begby had red hair, but he did not look, like most red-haired people, brave. He looked washed-up, over the hill, cheapo. Jay wondered why he was worth all the effort, money, and sweat that Virgo had put into him. Of course, he worked for the government, and that could mean access to all kinds of information which, if delivered to unfriendly people, could be valuable. After all, Fuchs had looked like nothing and he'd given the atom bomb away. Jay put speculation from his mind. He was here to do a job, not to figure out the who and why of it.

The women were a safety net—nobody would look twice at two sets of partners—but also a complication. They would, sooner or later, have to be got rid of. The problem was, they had seen his face and they would know him in a thousand.

Jay sipped his drink and smiled at Cheryl and Mandy, who smiled back their we-love-ya synthetic smiles, and he thought: Yes, they have to be got rid of but it's going to take time. Sex was in the air for Begby, and it would be difficult to separate him from it. His hand lay on Cheryl's knee in a proprietorial fashion that went with his next question.

"Hey, Smitty—you mind I call you Smitty?—whaddya think of these two girls, huh? Don't you think we're the lucky guys, having these two beautiful ladies with us tonight, huh?"

Jay raised his glass to Cheryl and Mandy. "I certainly do."

Begby said, "You think I know these ladies well, huh, Smitty?"

Jay nodded. "Very well, I'd say, Al."

"Then you'd say wrong, ole buddy." Begby's thyroid eyes bulged, as if Jay might not believe him. "Only met them tonight, thirty minutes ago, to be exact. That right, girls?"

"That's right," said Mandy crossly. She was the brunette.

"We was waiting for our two friends but they never showed," explained Cheryl. She was the blonde.

Begby looked anxious. "Hey, you ain't expecting any fellas?"

Mandy smiled at Jay. "Not now. Too late. It was only, like, a loose arrangement, y'know."

"Hey, am I glad to hear that," said Begby.

"We're free as air," Cheryl said, nonetheless removing Begby's moist hand from her dress. "Also, I think I'm getting hungry."

"Hey, you girls wanta eat this early?" asked Begby in a solicitous voice, glancing quickly at Jay. "I thought we might hoist a few first."

"It's just," said Mandy, "we're both on diets. But we saved our appetites for dinner." She paused meaningfully. "The restaurants in this hotel are great."

Begby sighed. "Girls, you get dinner, but later, huh?"

It was a decision that Jay could see hurt him. Plainly, he was not one to spend valuable drinking time eating. Jay said, "Look, why don't I order sandwiches, for now?" Before they could answer, he had waved to the waitress and ordered. "Where you girls from?" he asked.

He was not going to sit in a well-lit restaurant with Cheryl and Mandy if it could be avoided. But Cheryl was answering his question. "We're staying in the hotel. We go back home early tomorrow morning, to New York City, that is."

Jay breathed in. With any luck the girls would be away from the hotel before anybody asked questions about Begby. Anyway, it was all academic. He might have to abort the operation, if no opening showed itself, or if he couldn't get rid of the girls. Begby seemed glad to hear that the girls were staying in the hotel. Presumably he considered it a major saving on his weekend budget.

"Hey, isn't that great, I'm booked in too." He winked at Jay. "You as well, Smitty?"

Jay shook his head. "Not yet, but maybe I should. I hadn't thought to stop over." He looked at Mandy. She looked back, with interest. He thought: I wonder what *that* would be like? He said, "Look, I'll go make inquiries at the desk, back in a minute."

"Hey, no hurry, Smitty—" began Begby, but Jay laid his hand on Begby's shoulder and pressed and said, "No time like the present, Al."

He smiled at Mandy and walked out of the bar. He did not book any room at the reservations desk, but made his way out into the street and walked swiftly around to the back of the hotel. The wind off the Atlantic was colder now, and he shivered. He looked around but could see no sign of the Caddy. He stood in the dark and waited. After what seemed a very long time, but was only four minutes, the long black limo turned the corner and he recognized Marty at the wheel.

Four minutes. She would have to do better than that.

The Caddy stopped. Marty opened a door.

Jay got in. "It's difficult. I may not be able to do anything until midnight or later. Can you be back here at exactly one o'clock, and I mean exactly? If I can't do it by then I'll abort."

Marty looked serious. "Jack won't like that."

"Then screw him." Jay felt his anger rising. "This is all too public. The guy's got two women with him, both of them have been staring at me for half an hour, two cocktail waitresses have looked me full in the face at least twice—what does Virgo think he's doing, setting me up or something?"

"No," Marty answered slowly driving the Caddy around the block. "It can't be that. Why would he do that?"

"It's hairy," said Jay. "Not only the women, there's the guy himself. He's a drinker, he's loud, he makes people notice him. I'm earning my money here. If I do it."

Marty tapped the crocodile case on the seat. "The cash? You don't want to give it back?"

"Be here at one," Jay said. "Be parked if you can, but be here."

Jay started to get out of the Caddy. Then he paused. "There's something odd about this guy, he's a nobody, he's a cheapskate. Why is he so important? What's he done?"

"You said you never ask."

"I don't, usually."

"All I know," Marty answered, looking straight ahead, "is what Jack told me, which wasn't much. This guy has been peddling state secrets. That's all I know."

"See you here, at one." On a job like this, people, even Marty, were like an audience in the theater. You had to tell them you were going to tell them. Tell them. And tell them you'd told them.

Five minutes later he was back in the bar.

An hour and a half later, Jay was still in the bar, alone with Begby for the first time. Mandy and Cheryl, looking hungry and mutinous, had taken themselves off to the powder room. Begby was drinking steadily, and showing some signs of wear and tear. Jay glanced at his watch: ten-fifteen. Still they had not eaten.

Begby's hand was on Jay's arm, his bulbous eyes staring blearily into Jay's. "Hey, ole buddy, sometime we gotta split up, go our separate ways, y'know? I mean, I take Mandy and you take Cheryl."

"The other way around," Jay said.

"Is it? Whichever." Begby's hand weaved, and his drink would have spilled if there had been any drink in his glass. "The thing is, you go to your room and I go to mine. Each of us with a lady, right?"

Jay thought: wrong. He signaled the cocktail waitress, who had a short skirt, a deep cleavage, and a sour expression. "Same again, please."

"Hey, mister," said the cocktail waitress, "I dunno what you're drinking. Tell me."

Begby told her.

The girl wrote down the order on the pad and went away.

"We should really buy the girls dinner, Al," Jay said.

Begby shook his head. "They had the sandwiches, right? An' me, I shouldn't drink any more booze, Smitty. You didden do me no favor, ole buddy, calling for another round."

Jay almost smiled. For some insane reason, he was beginning to tolerate Begby. It was an astonishing thought, that he could be any kind of spy or traitor. Burgess and MacLean and Philby had been terrible drunks, and they had got away with it for a very long time. Yet, Begby's behavior was classic. Boozing was a way of relieving stress—booze and girls. The drinks arrived. Jay paid for them and put one in Begby's hand.

Begby stared at it unhappily.

"I've had a lot, Smitty."

"Another one won't hurt." Jay did not want Begby in any condition to slink off to a bedroom with one of the girls. If that happened he would definitely have to abort the operation. He would have to get them all out of the bar at some point, possibly try to lose the girls in the gaming rooms.

Begby was talking to him, slowly and ponderously, as one who imparts a close personal secret. "Smitty, I gotta tell you this, it's the God's truth. I get kinda stupid if I have too much alcohol, I get kinda overactive, know what I mean?"

Jay asked dryly, "Overactive sexwise?"

Begby shook his head. "Underactive sexwise. Overactive stupidity-wise."

"How's that again?" asked Jay.

"I tend to go ape, ole buddy. I do stupid things." He stared at Jay as if he might not be believed. "I've always been like that."

Jay raised his glass. "Here's to stupidity. Bottoms up."

"Bottoms up, I like it," replied Begby, and drained his glass.

"Hey, is he ever gonna stop tanking that stuff?" asked Cheryl. Mandy stood next to her. They had both plainly been well powdered and painted in the powder room. The stuff on their faces glinted, like ammunition. Also they had decided on action. "I vote we go eat, if Al ever eats, which I doubt."

Jay had no option, and besides, the way Begby looked, he'd collapse unless he ate. "Ladies, be my guest," Jay said. The girls smiled at that, and within fifteen minutes, by shameless bribery, Jay had them, all four, seated in the Hawaiian restaurant, which was crowded and, fortunately, even darker than the bar. The bribery had consisted of putting two ten-dollar bills into the hand of the maître d', who was already shaking his head as Jay approached, noting the none too expensive ladies and the worse-for-wear Begby in tow. The shake turned to a vigorous nod, and suddenly, a table was, unexpectedly, free. Jay promised to see the maître d' again at the end of the meal, and that effected prompt service, albeit of a kind of food Jay did not care for—traditional large servings of meat, with hot, sweet Polynesian sauces poured over them, and large Polynesian drinks, consisting mainly of Bacardi rum flavored with fruit juices, the tall glasses festooned with fruit and flowers. Cheryl and Mandy loved all this and brightened up considerably. It turned out they were sisters-in-law, although both of them were now divorced. Jay asked if it still counted, the sister-in-law thing, and they both laughed and said indignantly, sure it did, and laughed a lot at everything else Jay said.

Begby ate steadily. Jay hoped the food would sober him, anyway a little.

Mandy's shoeless foot twisted around Jay's leg, under the table. She leaned forward. "Is it true Brits are gentlemen even in bed?"

"No," said Jay promptly. "They're brutes in bed."

"Oh my," replied Mandy. "Am I ever lucky, huh?"

Cheryl said sullenly, "Sounds wonderful. What about buddy-boy here?" Her melancholy gaze indicated Begby, now drinking black coffee. "I think if this guy sees any bed tonight, all he'll do is sleep in it."

Jay paid the bill in cash and looked at his watch. Eleven-fifteen, but in this place, that was early. He said, "I think you've got something there, Cheryl. Why don't I take Al up to his room, let him get an hour's sleep? I come back down, soon as I get him settled. Then I take you girls to the roulette tables, show you how to win a few dollars."

Cheryl said, "Beats hanging around the bar all night."

Mandy added, so only he could hear, "Cheryl and I are very close, Smitty. Sometimes we do everything together, know what I mean?"

Jay looked back at her. "Sounds great to me, but listen, I have to get Al upstairs to his room first, right? Might take a little time, right?"

"Wrong," said Begby, who had heard that. "I ain't goin' up to no friggin' bedroom."

"Just for an hour, baby, sleep it off a little." Cheryl closed a heavily colored eyelid at Jay.

Jay thought, Begby is not the only one in danger here. He laid his hand on Begby's arm. "Al, you'll feel great after an hour's sleep. I'll wake you, I promise, you'll come down to the tables, fresh as a daisy, ready for anything."

"Sure," soothed Mandy. "We'll be down here, waiting for you."

Begby raised a warning forefinger. "Two things. First, I don't go to no friggin' bedroom. If I go to sleep, when I wake up it's morning already." He gazed owlishly at them. "No, sir. I know a way that I get sobered up pretty good, in no time at all."

"And what way is that?" Jay asked.

Begby looked around. A smile of infantile triumph played across his worn features. "Why, I take a swim, is all," he told them. "I take a friggin' swim."

The staircase was blocked by a notice: THE MANAGEMENT REGRETS THE POOL AREA IS NOT IN USE UNTIL MORNING.

Begby regarded it as a personal insult.

"Hey, what's this, no midnight swim? What kinda holiday hotel they call this, Smitty?"

Jay said, "Probably need all their staff in the restaurants and gaming rooms. Anyway, it's a washout."

Mandy and Cheryl laughed, without humor. "Just as well," said Cheryl. "Anyways nobody around. Let's all get back upstairs, huh?"

Mandy nodded in agreement, looking down the dark stairwell to the pool. "This place gives me the creeps. No lights or anything. Let's go back on up, go see if we can win a few dollars, what you say, Smitty?"

But Begby had stepped over the chain that roped off the pool area and was making his way down the stairwell that led to the pool itself. "C'mon," he called, "let's go swim, huh?"

"This guy kills me," said Cheryl, not laughing.

"I'll get him." Jay stepped over the chain and followed Begby down the steps. When he got to the bottom, Begby had disappeared into the gloom. Only the whispering of the water could be heard.

The girls, tittering, followed Jay, stepping very carefully over the chain. It occurred to him that they were both tipsy. Not surprising, the amount of liquor they had taken aboard. Neither of them, though, was as far gone as Begby, whose voice could be heard calling back to them from the darkness, "Hey, c'mon, this is gonna be great!" The voice added, echoing hollowly in the half-dark, "Hey, Smitty ole pal, there must be some lights somewhere. Try to find them. Let's have a little light here!"

With a set smile on his face, Jay looked for a bank of lights. All he could find was a switch serving the stairwell area. The lights for the pool were somewhere else, and he didn't propose finding them. He proposed getting Begby out of there, and as soon as possible. The stairwell lights gave a glint of illumination to the water, and to Begby, who was teetering along the shadows at the side of the pool, his final drink still in his hand. The girls stood at the bottom of the stairwell and stared into the gloom.

Jay called, "Easy, Al!"

Cheryl added, "C'mon, Al, knock it off before you fall in the pool, for Chrissake!"

Begby called back to them, "Not me, folks! Look, no hands!"

Mandy whispered in Jay's ear, "Shall we leave him, go on someplace, all three of us?"

Jay said, "We can't leave him like this. What if he can't swim?"

The words echoed around the gloom of the pool. Begby drew himself up to his full height, which was all of five-seven.

"Hey, Smitty, who says I can't swim? Who says that?"

"Never mind, Al, just come back. Let's get out of here."

But Begby had taken offense. "I can so swim. Who says I can't swim?" He placed his glass, very carefully, on the tiled floor. "I was school diving champion one time!" With that, he staggered abruptly into one of the cubicles that lined the pool.

Mandy called, in wheedling exasperation, "Hey, Smitty, c'mon, let's go, whaddya say?"

Jay thought hard. There was a possibility here. "Look, I can't leave him, but you girls go on back. I'll do what I can with him, sober him up some, or get him to his room. I'll pick you girls up later."

Mandy looked like a girl to whom that, or something like it, had been said a good many times. "We'll wait awhile, in the bar. He could drown, right, if we left him?"

"I wouldn't worry too much if he did," said Cheryl sourly.

Jay walked around the side of the pool. "Come on, Al, let's go."

In reply, Begby came out of the cubicle, very fast, so fast that he seemed to be another shadow in that place of shadows. His pale sluglike body gleamed dully in whatever light there was.

"Jeez!" shrieked Cheryl. "Get a load of that body!"

"Ohmigod," laughed Mandy.

Jay was mute. Begby was naked, and it was not a pretty sight. He hit the dark, glinting water in a tremendous bellyflop, and sank at once. After a moment his head appeared and he called to them, through a mouthful of water, "Hey, c'mon in, the water's fine!"

"No shit," replied Cheryl. "Who needs this?" To Mandy, she added, "That body, did you get a load of that body? That hard up I'm not!"

Mandy took Jay's arm softly. "If I'm not in the bar, I'm in room one thirty-seven. Call me when you get free of this guy, but don't leave it too late, huh? We got an early start in the morning."

"If you're more than an hour, forget it," added Cheryl. "I had too much of this evening already."

"All right, girls." Jay smiled at them in the gloom. "You do understand I can't leave him like this?"

"Sure, sure," said Cheryl. She started back up the stairs. "What a night. The creeps you meet in this world."

Mandy pressed Jay's arm. "See you then, lover." Her face was turned to his. Behind him, Begby shouted incoherently, splashing wildly in the water.

Jay kissed Mandy on the cheek, which was like kissing porcelain, and said, "If I ever get him to bed. If not, be lucky."

"You, too," trilled Mandy.

She followed Cheryl up the stairwell.

For a minute, Jay could hear the complaining voice of Cheryl, and Mandy's placatory noises, and the sharp smack of their heels on the stone steps, and then all was silent, except for the lapping of the water and Begby's voice, as he sang tunelessly to himself. He was splashing around in the six-foot area.

"You coming in, ole buddy?" he called.

Jay hesitated. "Yes. Sure. Why not?"

"Great, great, c'mon in, ole pal," cried Begby. "I'll go in off the top board for you later, show you how I won that school diving competition, huh?"

"No hurry," replied Jay. He went into a cubicle and took off all his clothes. After a moment's hesitation, he left the Beretta in his coat. He was feeling less and less enthusiastic about this whole business. He stepped out of the cubicle, stood beside the pool for a moment, then dived into the water. He swam up the pool, away from Begby. The water was chill, and he was suddenly very sober, and his mind worked. Here, it would have to be here. He had not brought the weapon with him, but maybe there was no need of the weapon.

The water was the weapon.

In a way, it was perfect. The girls would not wonder, if they ever found out about it, how it had happened. They would take it that Jay had run away from trouble. They would understand that; they were girls who had run away from trouble all their lives. Anyway, did it matter? Other people had seen him, he'd been highly recognizable. It was a crap assignment Virgo had given him, a typical Company operation, badly researched, badly set up, too many people, too many eyes, not at all the kind of thing he usually did. Usually it was in and out, fast, knowing very little, talking to nobody, the weapon in his hand at the last possible moment. That was Mr. Jones's way. This fuck-up was possibly not even the Company's way, just Jack Virgo's way. He wanted no more of it. He wanted his money and he wanted to take off. The job would probably be no trouble, except that he had killed nobody with his hands since the paratrooper on the exercise in Germany, all those years before, and he was not looking forward to doing that again.

The water was very cold, and suddenly he was seeing things very clearly.

He should say: screw the money.

He should abort. He really should.

Jay turned toward Begby, the decision half taken, to find that Begby had clambered out of the pool and was more than halfway up the ladder that led to the top board, which jutted out, a thin plank, almost touching the ceiling. Jay called, "Hey, Al, don't go up there, don't jump, don't be a fool!" But he did not call too loud, because he did not want half a dozen hairy security men clodhopping into the place.

Begby, with the acuteness of the very drunk, nonetheless heard him. "That's okay, Smitty ole pal. I used to dive pretty good. Here I go, ole buddy!" Begby was at the top of the ladder and teetering toward the plank. He put a foot on it and walked forward shakily.

"Al," Jay called, "turn back, climb down."

Why am I calling that? he wondered, and his answer was: if he hits the water hard, I'll have to get him out. Or will I? He was still debating that as Begby changed his mind about diving, tried to turn on the plank, lost his balance, and fell. Begby half-hit the edge of the pool in a loud, delayed splash, and in the awful sound, there was another component: the crunch of bone. Jay shouted, and swam rapidly to the end of the pool. The water was already turning red, and Begby's head was split open and pumping brains and blood. Jay took a long, hard look and saw there was nothing he could do, even if he wanted to. He climbed swiftly out of the pool. In the cubicle he wiped himself half-dry, using his shorts as a towel. He donned his clothes, combed his wet hair, and walked out of the echoing, ghostly place.

He did not look back to where he knew Begby would be floating, half in and half out of the water. Nobody challenged him, and he was out of the hotel and into the Caddy at exactly four minutes to one o'clock.

A miracle, he thought. A bloody miracle, timed to the minute, at that.

Marty looked sideways at him. He anticipated her question. "I got wet. Just drive. Not too fast."

Marty drove, not too fast, out of Atlantic City.

E·L·E·V·E·N

JACK VIRGO WAS SMILING his shark's smile. "Hey, morning news-casts carried the story, you see it?"

Marty nodded. Virgo went on, "Tragic accident in hotel pool. Well-known government employee, all that shit. I don't know how your guy did it, but he did it right."

Virgo was grinning, but more in anticipation, Marty thought, than satisfaction. Perhaps he was just looking forward to giving Jay the rest of his money. Maybe it was in the large buff envelope he nursed on his knees.

"He isn't my guy, Jack, he's nobody's guy. He's strictly his own man." Marty felt she had to add that little extra knife. She was very tired, she had slept only three hours, after the long, silent drive back to the city, and the dumping of the Caddy in the parking lot. She handed the ticket to Jack Virgo. "The weapon is in the glove compartment, unfired."

Virgo leaned forward eagerly. "How did he do it. Did he say?"

Marty grimaced. "Don't tell me you haven't contacted the local police."

Virgo nodded. "They think the guy was drunk, fooling around, fell off the top diving board, hit the side of the pool, fin-ito. I'm asking, was your guy up there with him, or what?"

"I don't know," retorted Marty. "Does it matter? If the local police are accepting it happened that way, then the job got done. I thought that was all you cared about."

Virgo pressed. "Didn't he say anything on the drive back?"

"He seemed very mad about something."

"Like what?"

"I don't know," said Marty, who did. Jay hadn't said much on the way back, but he'd said enough. "Maybe Jay didn't care for being conned into doing a high-visibility hit like that. If he'd blasted the guy, made an obvious hit of it, twenty people might have remembered him."

"He said that?"

"Jack, that hotel was crawling with security. Jay has every reason to think you put him at risk. Which you did." Marty could not stop herself asking, although she knew that Jack Virgo would give her no ready answer, "Why did you do that?"

"Reasons." Jack Virgo stone-walled, as she expected him to.

Marty steeled herself: Jay would now take the money and go. That, after all, was the deal. Jay was, almost, out of the game. If she really cared for him, she thought, in a conventional, loving way, she would be glad for him, and wish him well, even if she was never going to see him again. The trouble was, she wasn't a conventional, loving woman and she did want to see him again.

Virgo was asking her a question. "So, lover boy said absolutely nothing about the hit, how he did it? Nothing at all?"

Marty looked steadily at the fleshy bridge of Jack Virgo's nose. "No details."

"If you say so." Virgo looked as if he didn't believe her, which was reasonable enough. Marty had debriefed mechanics before now, and the nearer the debriefing had been to the action, the more the mechanic had wanted to talk.

Not Jay. He had simply said, "Sending me to do that job, in that place, on that poor useless guy, makes me the best-known face in Atlantic City. If anybody puts one and two together and makes three of it." Jay had stared ahead, as they drove through the dark night, once they were clear of the glittering resort. "Tell Virgo I want my money, and I want away, fast."

But all she told Virgo was: "He seemed anxious to move on."

Virgo grinned his shark's grin and looked at his watch. "Not too anxious. You called him fifteen minutes ago."

"He said he'd have coffee first." She couldn't resist it, it was what Jay had said, as she'd roused him from his sleep to tell him

Jack Virgo was in her room wanting to talk. "Let him wait," Jay
had said. "I'm having a shower and coffee first. Just tell him to
have my money ready."

"Coffee?" Virgo looked annoyed. "He could have had coffee
here." He indicated the coffeepot and cups on the side table. "I
tell you, this guy has his nerve. I guess it's the SAS training. Nobody seems able to do it their way, not exactly. The Israelis try,
the rest are nowhere."

At that moment, the door opened without noise and Jay stood
there. He carried the crocodile case in his left hand. Although
Marty knew he'd had only a few hours' sleep, he looked rested. He
had shaved and his golden hair glistened, and in his dark suit and
clean blue shirt he looked like a businessman who worked out and
played a lot of squash. Except for the eyes. The eyes were still the
same startling blue, but this morning they looked very hard indeed. Marty stood up quickly, and gesturing to a seat, asked,
"Jay, coffee?"

"No thanks, I had some." Jay sat, opposite Virgo, and looked
directly into his eyes.

Virgo looked back. He ought to be shaken, Marty thought, the
man coming in the room like that, fast and silent, but he isn't, he's
smiling into Jay's smile and congratulating him. For the first time
in many a month, Marty found herself admiring Jack Virgo.

"Jay, wonderful job, congratulations, you saw the telecast?
No? Well, I have to tell you there's no police curiosity, it's gone
down on their blotter as an accident, congratulations again."
Virgo leaned back, still holding the bulky buff envelope, and
beamed at Jay, as at a favorite pupil. "Wonderful job, and no
weapon used. I'm impressed, very impressed, I have to tell you
that."

Jay nodded at the envelope. "My money in there?"

"Sure is, and it's all yours." Virgo, however, didn't release the
envelope, if anything he held on, in what, to Marty, seemed a
high state of glee. It was unusual to associate Jack Virgo with
such an emotion, but there it was. Marty began to wonder about
the whole operation. Yet it had gone well—what was there to
wonder about?

Jay said icily, "I wonder if you'd like to consider giving me a
sort of clue about this guy Begby. What was he, some kind of
spy?"

Marty saw Jack Virgo stiffen. It was written into a Company man's consciousness that no real names were ever used in the underground war. Virgo had told Jay the man's name, he'd had to, at the briefing. Jay was now free to break the rules, since Virgo had broken them first. Her own Company training was all against it. She felt uneasy. A hotel room like this was safe, of course, but then she'd been told a thousand times that no room was ever absolutely safe. Virgo seemed to be debating Jay's question, giving it serious attention, and at last he answered it, much more fully than Marty expected.

"Albert Sidney Begby was a small-time Soviet contact, in prime need of termination. He had been slipping small but important items of interest to them—he worked in the design office of a large aircraft manufacturer, and had access to confidential items of military hardware—for a very long time."

"A very long time?" Jay repeated the words, slowly. "You've known about him for a very long time?"

"We've known about him for long enough to identify his contacts in the Soviet embassy."

"Then you could have taken him out at any time?"

"Yes, we could have."

Slowly, Jay said, "I'm put into a very public situation to take out a minor informer you've known about for a very long time?" He kept the implacable blue eyes fixed on Virgo. "To do a job that somebody local could have done, possibly in a much more discreet manner?"

Jack Virgo grinned. He was enjoying this. "Correct."

Jay's voice was light but deadly. "All to prove what?"

"That you are the right man."

Marty thought: Oh, God, no. Not even Jack Virgo would pull this one.

But Jack Virgo had. He leaned forward and gently placed the bulky buff envelope in Jay's lap. "There are two packets of money in there. One is the second half of money due, to wit, twenty-five thousand dollars, for the job you did in Atlantic City last night." Virgo shot a glance at Marty; he wanted her to see just how clever he was. "Another hundred thousand dollars is in the second packet. It is payment in full, and in advance, for another, very important job. You get all the money, win or lose, the moment you say yes.

"If you don't, all you have to do is take the smaller packet out of the envelope and go get yourself a flight to wherever you want to go. I won't stop you."

Jay did not move. He said, after a long silence, "A hundred thousand dollars *more*?"

"It's all there." Virgo leaned farther forward, a cigar in his hand, his match flaring. "Do you want to hear the rest?"

No, Marty wanted to cry out, no, don't. She said nothing. The training took over. She waited. Besides, she was insanely curious.

After a moment, Jay said, "You put me at all that risk to see if I was right for this final, important job? Is that what happened?"

Jack Virgo nodded, delighted, exhaling cigar smoke. "Not me. I'd have said go on your record alone. My associates, they had to be sure. I've talked to them this morning. They're sure."

Marty did not know how much of that she believed. Some of it had to be true.

"I'm very much reassured to hear they are sure," Jay was saying. "After I am put into the shittiest operation in some considerable time. For that, I hold you"—Jay's eyes locked with Virgo's,—"personally responsible, however much you talk about having to convince these other people, whoever they are. You pissed me around, Virgo, and I don't like that, I don't like that at all."

Jack Virgo bobbed his head, as if in apology, but Marty knew he had never apologized to anybody in his life. "I'm sorry about that. I'll tell them your feelings, if you decide to bug out. Their reply is likely to be, so what's his beef? He got paid."

Jay sat looking at Virgo.

"Well, so I did, didn't I?"

Jack Virgo flashed a brief glance, triumphantly, at Marty. "Then you want to hear more?"

Marty was convinced that Jay would say no. She was beginning to read him, at least to recognize the obvious signs, and she could see that he was very angry. She knew it from the way he went very still, showed nothing at all. Yet, the other side of his character, the element that made it possible for him to do what he did, to do it at all, was still one that she could not predict. So, again, her Company training took over: be surprised by nothing.

She waited, as Jack Virgo waited, until Jay looked at Jack

Virgo for that very long moment and said, quite casually, "Why not?"

"Why did you say yes?" Marty asked Jay as they boarded the Boston shuttle, at Kennedy. They were booked under the name of Hampton, which Jay, for some reason, seemed to find funny. He did not reply until they were settled into their seats and the skyscrapers of the city were falling away beneath them.

"Did you expect me to say no?" Jay's tone was quizzical. "Or did you hope I'd say no?"

"I tried to have no feelings about it one way or the other." Marty pulled her camel-hair coat around her. It was fall, cool and clear, the best time of the year. New England promised to be a blaze of color. If only they were going there as lovers, it would be perfect. As it was, she wondered if they would get out of the new operation alive. That thought gave everything the new, sharp edge of danger: the weather, the images of white cloud and blue sky, and the body of the man sitting next to her. The danger, the love of it, could get to be a drug, her Company counselors had warned, don't get to enjoy it too much.

Marty said, "I didn't want you to say yes, because I knew, if Jack Virgo had gone to all that trouble, using that poor guy Begby as a try-out, then the follow-up had to be a lulu." That had to be true anyway. "There's probably still time to say no," she added, secure in the knowledge that this man would never say no, once he had said yes. "Jack Virgo would probably can me, at the least, for saying it, but I don't think you've realized exactly what you might be facing here."

"What I'm facing," said Jay quietly, "is a job that doesn't look a lot more difficult, if Virgo's briefing is on the nose, than some I've done before." He ordered a drink for them both from the flight attendant. "It's no use being angry with Virgo, or Jones. Those guys are desk guys; they've forgotten, if they ever knew, what it's like in the field. They're talent users." He smiled. "I thought you were one, too."

"I'm trying to be one." She smiled, to take the sting out. "Jack thinks I have what it takes."

"You've been his woman a long time. He should know."

It was just a statement. There was no comment in it.

"I haven't been, exactly, his woman for a while," Marty said quickly, and, she thought, untruthfully. Jack regarded her as his woman. "Besides, he never lets his personal feelings get in the way of the job."

Jay took the vodka and sodas from the attendant, and passed one to her. Even the alcohol tasted sharper on this day, she thought, holding it on her tongue.

Jay said, "Virgo's a Company man through and through, everything for the flag? All right. It's just that I keep wondering, and perhaps you can tell me why I'm wondering, how it is Virgo seems to have no real backup." He paused, then said, in his neutral voice, "Except you, of course."

Marty answered, very carefully, "I thought Jack explained all that at the hotel. Don't worry—he'll have people around to get you away after this job is over. He said so."

"But nobody there, up front?" Jay mused, as if to himself.

"Except me, of course," said Marty, smiling. "Anyway, I don't think we should talk on the plane, do you?"

"Probably not. But I didn't answer your question. You asked why I took the job on. The answer's a very simple one."

Marty waited. He was going to say: so that they could be together, depending on each other in the most desperate situations, bonded in the kind of trust that soldiers in action have for each other. This man, trained to trust nobody, seemed, at that moment, prepared to trust her. Jay had asked few questions as Virgo had outlined the job, leaving out the identity of the man in the big house; leaving out reasons why; leaving out everything, except the precise details of how and where, and repeating those details over and over again, so that Jay—and Marty—could not forget them. Watching Jay memorize everything Jack Virgo said, and repeat it back word-perfect, hardly glancing at the maps and photographs Jack passed across to him, Marty had thought: he's taking this job partly because I'm involved in it. If it had been anybody else, anybody strange or new, he would have said no. He trusted her, and now, at last, he was going to say it.

"I took this job," Jay said slowly, "because I don't think Mr. Jones is ever going to pay me what he owes me. I called him, but he was out. I called him again, twice more. He was still out. Finally, I got him. He waffled on a bit, but I got the message. There will be no money, anyway not soon. As far as he's concerned, I'm a liability. I'm blown in the United Kingdom, and after Atlantic City, I'm probably blown in the U.S." Jay paused, weighing his words. "I know that fifty thousand dollars is a nice piece of change, but a hundred and fifty thousand dollars is a hell of a lot nicer. A hundred and fifty gives me a decent shot in Voortrekker land." Jay paused again, as if thinking it all through for the first time. "So, you see, I had absolutely no option. I had to say yes, something your charming friend Virgo probably knew all the time."

Not a word, Marty thought, about how much he'll hate flying off to all that South African sun without me. Not a word about how reassured he was to have her there with him on this last mission, on which, if he had told it truly, what remained of his future depended. He didn't see her as a woman, was that it? She was just some Company honeypot, still Jack Virgo's girl, no matter what had happened between them, the danger they'd shared, the beds they'd shared.

"Just that?" Marty asked hollowly. "Nothing else?"

He reached out a hand and took hers. It went through her like an electric shock. "You, too, of course. Once I knew you were in on it." He grinned. "It absolutely decided me, having you along."

"It did?" Marty turned to him, and he nodded, gazing directly into her eyes. She gripped his hand and turned, so he would not see her face, to look out of the window, at the phenomenally sharp blue of the stratosphere.

He had said it, whether he meant it or not.

Emotion flooded through her, and she turned back to him to say something she had never said to any man, not even Jack Virgo in the best days, but as the words formed on her lips she saw that he had leaned back in his seat, and closed his eyes.

Jay slept all the way to Boston.

The Mustang was waiting in the parking lot at Boston's Logan Airport, as Virgo had said it would be. Marty got behind the wheel, and Jay opened the glove compartment. It contained a .35 British army-issue Browning. Jay looked at it with sudden reserve. "It's single-action, and why British?"

Marty drove out of the airport. The traffic was light, and she knew her way. "Does that trouble you?"

"Yes, it does, a bit."

"Why?"

"It could tie in with me, a bit too neatly. Browning .35s can't be all that common in the States."

"How many rounds does it hold?"

"Twenty. It's a machine pistol but very compact. My objection is it's British Army issue."

"It was that or a bigger job altogether. It seems right for the job, though."

Jay debated a moment. "Yes. I suppose so." He didn't sound convinced.

"Is there anything else there?" Marty asked.

Jay picked up a long white envelope. "It has 'M' on it, so I take it it's for you."

"Open it and read what it says."

Jay ripped open the envelope. "There's a map of how to get to the place, which I guess you already know." He added, "And we are booked in at the Hi-Way Motel for tonight. There's a map here, tells us where to find it."

"Nothing else?"

"No." Jay crumpled the paper.

"Burn it, please," said Marty.

Jay did that, and crushed the ashes in the ashtray.

"Why book in at a motel?" he asked. "People who run motels look at their customers."

"You heard what Jack said. We have to wait for his call. We have to be sure the guy is in the house. Jack has to have someplace to call us. So the motel makes sense."

Jay mused, "On the plane you said it was over with you and Virgo. How do you feel about him now?"

Marty said, "I think sometimes that I hate him."

There was a long silence.

"Then why stick with him?"

"Because I've been doing it a long time and I guess I don't know how to stop." Marty looked at the road in front of them that led to the biggest hit, according to Jack Virgo, that anybody in the Company had ever, but ever, put into operation. Virgo had not told her who the hit was. Marty had waited for Virgo to show his faith in her, and tell her, even if he didn't tell Jay. He had not told her.

Marty's fingers tightened on the wheel. Would Jack let her go into this thing blind, as if she were some secretary who didn't have to be told shit? She had waited, in that hotel room, for Virgo to make some excuse and get rid of Jay, if only for a few minutes, so that he could confide the details to her. As the only controller of operations there was, she was entitled to that much.

It hadn't happened.

Reserve judgment, Marty told herself. Wait and see. There's still time.

"Something the matter, some problem?" Jay was looking at her curiously.

Marty kept her eyes on the road. "Just thinking, that's all."

"About Virgo?"

This was getting too close. She was beginning to know Jay, his moods and ways, his very personal, human signals. Just as obviously, Jay was getting to know hers. Marty smiled. "I was wondering if this motel has a large bed."

Jay laughed. "There's always the floor." He put the Browning and the ammo into the crocodile case, along with the money. He was carrying $150,000; it had to be some kind of first. Marty said, "What about the money? You were stupid not to leave it in some bank vault, or somewhere in the city."

"I'd have been stupid if I had." Jay locked the case and put the slim golden key in his pocket. "It would have meant going back into the city after the job. No thanks."

"Do you want to leave it at the motel? It will have a safe."

Jay lit a cigarette. "We'll see."

"You're nervous. You only smoke when you're nervous."

He smiled at her. "Or when I'm bored."

Marty put her free hand on his knee. Everything was sharp, every word, emotion, action. He took her hand from his knee and gave it back to her.

Marty laughed rather wildly, as if she were on something, which she wasn't, and drove on, through the riotous and oddly sharp reds and browns and yellows of the New England fall.

The Hi-Way Motel had a large bed.

Jay ordered a fifth of scotch with ice and soda from room service. He tipped the boy, who suffered from acne, a dollar, and they sipped their drinks lying on the bed. Jay kicked off his shoes and said, "Why don't we just pretend we're here on a dirty week-end?"

She looked at him. "Is that how you see it between us?"

Jay mused, "Not getting broody or anything, old girl?"

She laughed, as she guessed he intended her to.

"When I went to the Company I was nineteen. When I was given a job in Jack Virgo's division I was twenty-three. Now I'm thirty-five. I could be excused for being a little broody."

Marty took a swallow of her scotch. Jack Virgo didn't trust her, he told her nothing, he let her, no, he encouraged her, to sleep with Jay. This man, lying on the bed, drinking his scotch, he didn't expect anything of her, he didn't offer anything either, but at least he was honest.

Jack Virgo would have laughed at the word.

Marty looked at her watch. Virgo would not call for two hours. There was still a lot of daylight, and by the map directions they were about an hour from the house, by road. "When I met Jack I was twenty-three. I became his girl, I don't know how it happened. It happens everywhere when you're twenty-three and the guy's forty and he knows everything and the whole world's in front of you."

Jay asked quietly, "And what about now? You just go on, do you, as before?"

"Once I could see the point of it all. The job was exciting and new. It was worth doing. I was glad to be part of something bigger than myself." He waited, and she added, "Maybe I just did it for Jack. Now that things are maybe over between us, well, it all just seems such a waste, that's all."

Why am I telling this man all this? Marty wondered, with a sudden sense of panic. If this room was bugged, and it was possible, she could be out of the Company for uttering such words. "Why would you want to hear about my troubles?"

Marty wondered why she felt able to talk this way to Jay. Could it be because he might not survive the operation? Anyway, her private feelings were irrelevant. They had a job to do, and because they were the people they were, they would do it.

Jay said, and he seemed to be serious, "I have one hundred fifty thousand dollars in that case. Why don't we just take it and run?"

Marty laughed. "We wouldn't get out of the airport. This job is too important."

"To Jack Virgo? Or to you?"

"For all I know, to the U.S. of A." Marty was agitated. Surely Jay hadn't meant her to take the suggestion seriously?

Jay yawned. "Once the job's over, would Virgo care if you left with me for South Africa?"

Marty felt hot and slightly delirious. "You don't mean any of this, do you?"

"What would you be giving up?" Jay freshened his glass, and then hers. "You say yourself, you've had enough of it all, or very nearly. Unless you feel there's a big career in the Company ahead of you."

"In the Company? A woman?"

"All right." Jay sipped his scotch. "If this job is so important to Virgo, we do it, and then we go. We tell him we're going, if you like. He's got what he wanted—why would he want to stop us?"

"Because," said Marty, "he's Jack Virgo. I'm his woman, or he thinks I am."

"Only if you want to be."

Marty did not reply, and thought to herself: the man's right. Only if I want to be. Do I want to be? The idea of life without Jack Virgo, without the Company, was unthinkable, yet she thought it. Sooner or later, Jack Virgo would move up, or find himself another, younger woman, or both. That would leave just the Company. It had filled her days and nights for most of her adult life, it had taken the place of friends and family. Was it possible to live without it? Marty had seen other women, very smart women, working in the intelligence-assessment rooms at Langley, or seconded to some other, more exacting task, like her own, grow old in the job, loving men who very often loved (or anyway were married to) other women, but who really loved only the Company. Was she as dedicated as the rest, as dedicated as Jack Virgo? She had always thought so.

Marty dragged on her cigarette and looked at the silent television screen in the cheap room. The boy had courteously switched it on when he brought the drinks, assuming everybody wanted television twenty-four hours a day.

The Company had been her life for a long, long time.

Jack Virgo had been her life.

Was it possible Jay could take their place?

The idea, on the face of it, was ridiculous. Yet, the truth was, she had started to live again. With this man's body in hers, she had felt emotions that she had not experienced for a long, long time. It was possible that he really wanted her to go with him to South Africa, or wherever, once this operation was over. If he did, then the temptation was strong. It came from her loins and not from her logic, but after the hit she would have to decide, in a moment, just like that. There would be no time to deliberate.

Marty put out her cigarette and stood up. She took off all her clothes and then slowly, using all her skills, began to make love to Jay.

It was always possible, she thought, that this was the last time.

When Jack Virgo called, at eight o'clock, Jay and Marty were eating hamburgers and drinking coffee. The lovemaking and the alcohol had made them hungry. Marty was still damp from the shower, and took the call in the nude. When she heard Jack Virgo's voice she felt very naked indeed and gestured to Jay to throw over her wrap. He just grinned and lay on the bed in his shirt and trousers—typically, he had showered first—and gave her the thumbs-down. He stared at her appreciatively, as she turned away from him and tried to concentrate on what Jack Virgo was saying.

He was saying the job was on.

Marty felt her damp skin go very, very cold.

Jack Virgo was using the rough code they had devised at the briefing. "Our friend is home. You should talk to him. He has the usual workload."

That meant the two servants were in the house.

"Nothing extra?" she asked carefully.

"He has a couple of friends who might drop in."

"Two?"

"That's my best information."

Marty willed Virgo to be more specific. "Will they be working inside or outside?"

"I have no information as to that."

Two security men, as well as the two black servants? Of course, the two servants were nothing, but the others? Virgo had said there might be one, now he was talking about two.

"Can you tell me more?"

Marty knew she was breaking security by asking, but what the hell.

Jack Virgo's voice thickened with anger. "Your partner shouldn't have problems." He was telling her that the two men in the house were not as skilled as Jay was at their chosen trade. Jay had to go in there, Marty thought, and Jack Virgo didn't, that was the difference. She grew colder and angrier, and was conscious that Jay had stopped smiling at her naked body and was watching her face very intently.

"I'll tell him all that. Is there anything else?"

Who, for Chrissake, had two security men more or less on tap every time he went to his house in the country? Who was big enough, outside of some Mafia boss, to need it? Plenty of people, she supposed, but none of them likely to be on Jack Virgo's list. He hadn't told her who the hit was at the St. Regis briefing, and he wasn't about to tell her now. Still, she pressed, "Can you give me any more information on the client?"

There was a long silence at the other end of the line.

She could almost smell Jack Virgo's anger.

Yet his voice was calm enough when he answered.

"I regret I can't do that, at this time. However, there is a communication possible for you to use, from the vehicle, after your partner has left you. It is imperative you talk to me at that time. I will make all things clear then." The gravelly voice paused. "That is all I can tell you right now. Good luck."

The line went dead.

Jay threw her the wrap, and she put it on and tied it. Marty wondered how much he had guessed. She sat on the bed and poured more coffee. "It's on. We leave in thirty minutes." She looked at his watch. "An hour after that, you go in."

Jay asked, steadily, "What was all that about?"

"He said you'll be looking at two security people, not one."

"He didn't say where they'll be, in the house?"

Marty smiled. "No. He didn't know, I guess."

"What *else* did he say?"

"Nothing that matters."

"You were asking him, or am I wrong," said Jay lazily, "for the name of this man, in the house?"

Marty took off the wrap and began to put on her clothes. It

meant she didn't have to look directly into Jay's eyes. "I asked him, but he didn't tell me."

"Isn't that unusual? You should know. Even if I don't."

Marty pulled on her slacks and shirt. They had no labels, and her sling bag contained nothing traceable. Jay, she knew, had come to the States with the dark suit and the Burberry and little else. His passport had been false but obviously good, and he had kept it. He was too professional to go in anything but clean. He was very clean indeed, as far as the Company was concerned, if anything went wrong. So was she. This thought did not reassure her.

A feeling of anger, unknown to her on any previous operation, began to flood over her. She tried to suppress it, but it showed in her next words. "Apparently I'm not to know, any more than you are, who it is."

"As soon as it's over we'll know, so why worry?" Jay plainly did not think it too important that Jack Virgo had refused to trust her.

"You don't want to know anything at all, do you?"

Jay shook his head. "Only the fastest way in and the fastest way out."

"I think Jack Virgo told you that, at the briefing."

"Well, I hope he's got it right for once."

Jay did not laugh.

It was dark when they got to the house. The lane along which Marty drove the black Mustang was overgrown and little-used. She had cut the headlights as she turned off the road. As they reached the wire fence that surrounded the house, Marty cut the engine and looked out. The fence was high, around fifteen feet, and Jack Virgo had said sometimes electrified.

Jay got out of the Mustang and looked at it. He said, "Virgo seemed sure it had no current going through it at this hour, right?"

"It's switched on at midnight, automatically," answered Marty.

Jay got out of the car and stood there, still carrying the crocodile case containing the money. In his coat pocket the Browning bulged. He had taken off his Burberry and thrown it onto the seat. Now he tossed the crocodile case to Marty. She caught it neatly, and looked inquiringly at him.

"What's all this?"

Jay grinned. "I can't very well take it in there, can I?" He looked, for a moment, directly into her eyes. "And I have to trust somebody, right?"

Before Marty could answer, Jay walked to the rear of the Mustang and took the rope ladder from the trunk. He stepped quickly toward the fence. He took a nail file from his pocket and threw it at the wire mesh. No sparks flew. He threw the rope ladder over the fence and, when the grapple hooked securely on the other side of the mesh, climbed the fence very quickly, wearing the thick gloves that formed part of the kit that had been left, along with the ladder, in the trunk of the Mustang. One moment Jay was poised atop the fence, the next he had fallen lightly to the the ground on the other side, into the heavy brush. And then he was gone.

Marty listened for sounds of his progress on the other side of the wire, a footfall, a twig breaking, anything. There was nothing, only the hum of faraway traffic on the road.

Jay was inside.

Then, and only then, did Marty put down the crocodile case with the $150,000 inside it and start to search the Mustang for the radio that Jack Virgo, in his coded conversation on the telephone, ninety minutes before, had told her would be there.

T·W·E·L·V·E

THE DOG CAME AT JAY noiselessly, straight out of the night.

The animal did not bark because his mouth was full of Jay's forearm, thrown up instinctively as Jay fell back to protect his throat. The dog was a Doberman, full-grown and fierce, and Jay could feel the teeth, sharp into the flesh of the arm, through the cloth of his coat. In a moment there would be blood, and if he did not move quickly there would be muscle damage. A useless arm would end everything, probably his life. The dog was trained but not well trained, or he would have barked at some point, to alert his master, and he had not done that. Instead, he was now releasing Jay's arm, to try for his throat. Jay twisted his arm away from the dog's jaws, and remembering his SAS training (who had taught him, Nair?), he grabbed hard at both the dog's front legs. He found the left one. The right was groping, trying to find a purchase on Jay's chest, so that the Doberman could reach his throat. Jay knew he had only this one chance, so he grabbed again, and this time he found the right leg. The dog's breath was hot on his face, the sharp teeth only inches away. Jay gave a sudden jerk, pulling the two front legs violently apart. The dog's weak point, the SAS manual said, was the joint between the two front legs and the breastbone. He hoped to God the manual was right. It was.

The Doberman stopped thrusting for his throat. The dog whined, a low keening sound, and tried to move, but could not. Jay pushed the dog's weight from him and reached for the knife

222

he'd bought at a shop on 42nd Street the day before, one of a number of things he'd purchased that only he knew about. He plunged the blade deep, between the front legs of the animal, finding the heart. The throat was no good, the manual said. Dogs had good muscles around the throat. He felt the Doberman convulse and then go absolutely still. Jay rolled away, before the blood came, and cursing soundlessly, he pulled up his sleeve, to find, to his relief, severe bruising and numbness, but no blood. He flexed his fingers. The arm seemed to work.

Jay moved away from the dead animal and knelt under the cover of a tree. The night was moonless and he could see very little except the lights from the house, three hundred yards away. He listened, taking deep, regular breaths, but there was no sound.

Jay wiped the knife on the grass and slid it back into the sheath under his left armpit. He had spent some time secretly donning it, in the toilet, before they left the motel. He was very grateful that he had thought of it. It had come to him, as had one or two other things, as he lay in bed, Marty asleep beside him, in the St. Regis Hotel. He had gone into the Atlantic City farce with nothing but the weapon and his bare hands. This was a much more SAS type of operation, or he was going to make it one. He owed that much to the Regiment, which had taught him everything he knew. It wasn't its fault he didn't really like to work in the traditional SAS unit of four, but on his own. He trusted nobody to cover his back, although in the Regiment he'd often had to. Now he was absolutely alone, and there was a certain reassurance in that.

Jay waited for three or four minutes, but nothing stirred in the darkness. He had stopped trembling, and his arm still worked. No noise came from the house, where every possible light seemed to be on. In a way that was good, because it made the run easier. In another way it was bad, because he might be seen. He strained his eyes for the door to the kitchen garden that Virgo had said would be there, across the wide expanse of lawn that graced the house on three sides. The fourth, the front, was the main drive and door, Virgo had said; the drive had huge iron gates, and, if anybody thought to switch them on, floodlights.

Jay did not like the sound of that much, but if it all went to plan there would be nobody around to want to switch them on, at least until after he had gone. What he could not understand was why Jack Virgo should give him a Browning .35. Of course, it was a super weapon, and he was unlikely to need to reload—no small point. But it would make a lot of noise, especially in a confined space, and all his training was to keep things quiet.

Virgo had not made much of the servants or the security around the house. He had simply told Jay where the target would be found: in his study. He always went there to work after dinner. Virgo took it Jay would do the hit first, and then see. Jay had other ideas. He did not want the job done but the alarm already raised and two security men coming at him from different points of the compass. No indeed. He would get closer, he would smell around a little, and then he would see.

Jay did not trust Jack Virgo, and, more important, he did not trust his planning, not after Atlantic City. That was why he had the knife and various other items on his person, along with ten thousand dollars in big bills tucked into his hip pocket.

A voice came from the blackness.

Jay moved back one pace, into the cover of the brush, and stood still as stone.

No point in moving farther. The man was close now, and coming closer.

"Flash?" called the voice. It was old and querulous and had to belong, Jay thought, to the black manservant.

"Flash, you want your supper, you horrible dog you?"

The figure loomed in the darkness.

He was no more than six feet from Jay.

"Well," said the black man, "then do without!"

The figure turned and trudged back across the lawn. Jay stood and watched for him, picking him up again when the light from the windows of the house fell upon him. He was in shirt sleeves and carried a pail, and looked old. Jay kept watching as he opened a door in the stone wall, using a key and impatient at the delay that caused, and then went inside and closed the door.

There was a woman's voice, faint and high and questioning, and the old man's reply, deep and grumbling. Jay did not listen for the words. They were unimportant.

The important thing was that he now knew the location of the door. He knew his way in.

*　*　*

Jay stood in cover and debated his next move. Virgo had told him the lawn was a problem, but he had added that there was no other approach. Virgo obviously had faith in him to navigate the lawn his own way. Jay wondered about Virgo, as he had wondered ever since the briefing. Virgo had smiled and sweated and sold the whole idea very hard, that this was an operation for a man with Jay's particular expertise, that to throw a CIA team (or any other) at it would raise more problems, particularly noise, than it would solve. That this had to be a one-man operation, in and out, *bang*, just like that. Virgo had leveled his fat forefinger at Jay and said the word *bang* very softly, and smiled.

Jay had not smiled. He had looked at the drawing Jack Virgo pressed on him, giving the layout of the house interior, and memorized it, particularly the approach to the study. The exercise seemed, on Virgo's plan (which included distances from room to room; he must have somehow obtained a design of the original construction of the house), a very simple matter. Across the lawn, first. Then through the gate in the wall, across the kitchen garden, bypassing the servants' quarters, and into the house by the back door. This, Virgo said, was usually shut.

The servants were old, a married couple, and would be unlikely to respond quickly to any noise, and the old manservant was deaf anyway. His wife, who cooked, would be watching television, as she always did at that time of night, her duties over for the day. It was very unlikely, Virgo insisted, that his employer would want the manservant for any reason after dinner. As long as Jay could get into the house itself, without incident, he could write the servants off as any kind of danger factor.

Virgo had smiled reassuringly, still sweating, as he had said it, and Jay was forced to concede, having seen the old manservant, or anyway heard him, looking for the dog, that he did not seem any kind of threat. Jay wondered idly who had been the source of research for Virgo. Some indigent son or nephew of the old servants, no doubt, thinking (not too hard) that he was talking to some newspaper hack interested in the family habits of the man now sitting, if Jack Virgo's research was right, upstairs in his study, working at his papers, a glass of scotch on the desk in front of him.

He could crawl across the lawn, but there was more risk in

doing that than there was in running across, in one go. That was a risk, too, but the SAS way was to do whichever was faster. He bent down and took a handful of moist earth and smeared it across his face. Carefully, he made sure that nothing in his pockets rattled. Then he ran, very fast indeed, across the smooth green lawn, watching the lighted windows as he went.

Jay felt exposed, although he was running flat out, for what seemed a very long time. As he ran, he glanced up and saw, at a window on the first-floor level, the brief, shadowy figure of a man. The man did not look out, and Jay kept running, as if under water, soundlessly, his lungs bursting; and then he reached the stone wall.

Jay crouched down and waited for the pounding in his ears to lessen and for his breathing to return to normal. This took time, but he needed the pause. It was just possible the man at the window had looked out. Jay was almost certain he had not, but the prudent thing to do was wait. After a full three minutes there was no noise from inside the house, and although that didn't definitely mean the man had not seem him, Jay was satisfied.

As he crouched in the dark safety of the wall, Jay wondered where the two security men would be stationed inside the house. His guess would be—and he had not discussed this with Jack Virgo, he had discussed almost nothing with Jack Virgo, he had just listened—that one man was likely to be on the other side of the door, the one that was left open for the servants, possibly sitting facing it. That, anyway, would be where Jay would sit or stand or lounge, in his place.

The second security man might be anywhere, but the probability, if he knew his business, and Jay had to postulate that he did, would be somewhere near his employer's study. In a house this big he should be sitting in a chair in the corridor, reading or just sitting. From time to time, one or the other of the two security men would make a tour of the house. Such a thing was standard security procedure, and if these two were ordinary security men and nothing fancy—and Jack Virgo had insisted they were recruited from a reputable agency, which meant they were almost certainly retired cops—Jay could rely upon their doing everything by the book.

So, how often would they—or one of them, more probably—go on a tour of inspection, checking upstairs doors and windows and bedrooms, nothing too elaborate, just an excuse for a walk? Every two hours or every three hours? How long would these inspections take? Possibly fifteen minutes. Jay debated, waiting and observing the lighted windows. Stay outside the house, making no move until he knew for certain where the two men were. That was the safe way, but it would take time.

No, he would have to go in, and then see.

Of course, there were ways and ways of going in.

Geoffrey Keyes, one of the earliest of the wartime leaders of the Long Range Desert Group, forerunner of the British SAS, had gone blind into a room full of German soldiers off-duty. That had been in the raid on Rommel's HQ in the desert. Some old hand in the room had put the light out and poor old Keyes had been caught standing in the light of the corridor. His example was known about, and sometimes cited, as the brave way but the wrong way. The right way was to open the door and roll a grenade in, then stand well back. The idea, then or in the Falklands or now, was to kill but not to be killed. Even Colonel H at Goose Green was thought by some SAS people to have been a mite over-brave. As one had said to Jay, you can't do a lot when you're dead.

Keyes hadn't got Rommel, either.

And Jay had no grenade.

He sat in the shelter of the stone wall and thought hard. He could dash in and use the Browning at once. The chances were that if he did, the first security man would be surprised and out of the way. The second man, however, would be alerted, and he would, if he knew his business, keep still, pick a vantage point (the banisters that loomed over the downstairs corridor?), and wait for Jay to appear. It was never easy to fight your way upstairs against somebody who knew you were coming, and also, that way, the hit would have time to press some alarm or dial the police number. Noise could work your way. Noise paralyzed the opposition. He could probably rely on the man upstairs, near the study (if he was) not to do anything brilliant. Jay would have to deal with whatever the man did, how he reacted, once he had disposed of the security man downstairs. If he was downstairs.

Jay checked that he had everything he needed.

He decided that in two minutes he would move.

Two minutes to think.

After that it would all be action.

Jay felt tension but not fear. This was no ordinary hit. This was a complex operation, everything about it much more like an army exercise than one of Mr. Jones's straight jobs. This was army, in everything except the ultimate aim. He felt better, thinking of it that way. Jack Virgo might have a lot of faults, but it was unlikely that the Company would want anybody hit as badly as this unless he constituted a real threat to the country itself, and therefore to the Western bloc, including all the Company's allies, including, therefore, the United Kingdom. Jay had not troubled to think about it before, because it was a fruitless exercise. He had to take the job to get the money to run to South Africa. To be safe. Never to have to do anything like this ever again.

Jay savored that thought: this was, indeed, the very last one.

The fact that he was able to do the job at all he owed to Marty.

Marty had given him back his manhood, and with it, his desire to live and to function.

It was as simple as that.

Jay resisted an impulse to scratch his face; the mud was drying out. Better they saw him like that, whoever they were, than get a clear look at him. Too many people, in too many situations, had got clear looks at him by now, starting with Belfast, and ending here, on this damp green lawn.

It was time to go, but still he waited.

Marty?

She would be at the front of the house, on the other side of the iron gates, with the Mustang, ready to drive him to the Boston airport. Perhaps she would even be coming with him.

Did he need that? Probably not, but he desired it. Oh yes, he desired it, all right. After Angie's death, all will to live had left him, and it would have been very easy to succumb, to let the guilt run him, as it had for a while, until he allowed the Irish hit team to find him and dispose of him. Marty had persuaded him that he could function again. She had done that not by encouragement or sympathy but by her sexual skills. Marty had repaired the damage done by Angie's death. Marty had been what he needed when he needed it.

Jay decided that if Marty wanted to go to South Africa with him, then he would welcome it. He had given up on romantic love and all that it meant: trouble, heartache, everything too much. No more. He would settle for sex and companionship. Marty could give him that.

Also, she seemed to love him, or as near to it as anybody like Marty could get. Jay looked at his watch, a cheap digital he'd bought at Kennedy. He'd move off in ten seconds. Love, who needed it? All it did in his kind of life, was screw you up.

The ten seconds were up.

Jay got noiselessly to his feet and very carefully walked toward the door, hugging the wall. If he had brought the rope ladder he could have attempted to climb the wall. Virgo had said no to that, partly because of the noise the grapple would make and partly because the wall had been plastered smooth on both sides and there would be nothing for the grapple to hook onto. Also, the wall was overlooked by the lighted windows. Jay had almost asked Virgo what kind of man would have this sort of extra-tight security, but it was not his business to ask. One thing was sure. The man who owned the house must value his life very highly or he must live in considerable fear of losing it. Probably both.

Jay reached the door set in the wall and tried it, very gently.

It was, as he expected, locked.

It was also of wood and could probably be kicked in by somebody who did not care about noise. Jay had to get through it silently. He took from his coat pocket the plain tube of solvent that Jack Virgo had left in the Mustang. Then he put on his thick gloves. If this stuff dissolved metal it would certainly do his skin no good. Very carefully, he removed the cap from the tube, placed the nozzle into the keyhole of the heavy, old-fashioned lock, and squeezed, holding his breath, as Jack Virgo had said he should. Then he stepped back, staying in the cover of the wall, and waited. There was no sound as the solvent did its work. Jack Virgo had told him this was one of the latest gimmicks from the Company scientists. Jay had heard of such solvents but had never used one before.

After three minutes by the cheap digital, Jay took from his pocket a piece of rough rag and a six-inch file, also left by Virgo in the trunk of the Mustang, and carefully prodded and scraped at the lock. The metal came away in small, puttylike lumps, surrounded by a wet seepage of solvent. He pressed the small lumps into the rough cloth, doubled it over, and cast it away.

Then he tried the door handle, still wearing the gloves, very gently.

It opened without a sound.

Jay took off the heavy gloves and threw them away into the night.

Then he closed the door behind him and stepped into the small kitchen garden that ran all the way to the house. He stood in the garden and took stock.

It was all as Jack Virgo had said it would be.

With one exception: the black servants had not pulled their blinds. A shaft of light fell onto the rows of late vegetables and on the stone path that led to the door of the house. The noise of a television set percolated into the night.

Jay stooped down and crawled on his hands and knees past the window. A lot safer than going past in a crouch, where balance could so easily go wrong. The television set was turned up loud, and that was just as well, in view of what he intended to do next.

When he had passed the window, Jay stood and walked quickly to the house door and tapped on it.

A voice inside said, "What now?"

Jay, in a passable imitation of the black manservant, growled, "Open the door, man. I got this tray here."

The door opened at once.

A red, meaty middle-aged face stared out of the brightness at Jay. In his hand the man held a *New York Post*. Jay hit him hard, in the neck, with a karate chop.

The man fell forward without noise, and Jay caught him. He was out, but still breathing. Jay bore him inside and put him into a chair. The man had a large belly, and his sleeves were rolled to the elbow. A vulgar, expensive watch was strapped on his hairy wrist. He did not look rich. He looked like an ex-cop who was earning more money now than he'd ever earned in his life, pulling security for some moneyed guy. Jay knew he should dispose of him totally, if he went by the SAS book. But here he was running his own show, and he made the rules. The guard's face was a pale shade of yellow. He did not look as if he would come to for a long time. Just in case, Jay took the long-barreled Magnum .44 from his shoulder holster and threw it into the soft soil of the vegetable patch, where it fell without a sound. He closed the outside door, locked it so that the servants could not get in, or the guard, if he recovered, out. Then he looped the coil of rope from his pocket around the man's wrists and ankles.

Mercy was fine, but it had to be sensible mercy.

Jay walked through the kitchen, with the huge, ancient stove by which the ex-cop had been sitting. The servants' quarters had been built on, so Jack Virgo had told him. Jay took the stairs to the second floor, one at a time, placing his feet very carefully at the extreme edge of each stair. If a stair creaked, it creaked in the middle.

Jay came out onto the landing. He was now fifteen paces from the library door. It stood along a richly carpeted corridor. A grandmother clock ticked softly. There was no sound except that of a man's low voice, coming from behind the library door. Speaking on the telephone? Or dictating into a machine? Jay could not know which.

There was no security man anywhere to be seen.

Perhaps the man had gone on a tour of inspection. Always possible, and the most probable thing to assume, because a small Windsor chair next to the library door contained a rumpled newspaper and a pack of cigarettes, open, and one crushed cigarette, in a tray.

He listened just the same.

Nothing at all.

Jay walked, very slowly, along the corridor, past the oil portraits and the softly ticking grandmother clock, toward the door of the library. He reached the door and put his ear to the jamb. From inside, a deep voice droned, without pause. The man was dictating letters.

Jay took the Browning from the coat pocket. The shot would alert the other security man, of course, but by that time Jay would be out of the library and walking swiftly along the corridor toward the front door and out into the night. After that, there would be but a hundred yards to go, down the drive to the iron gates where Marty would be waiting with the Mustang.

Jay turned the brass knob of the door, very gently. Virgo had said that he did not know whether the door would be locked or not, but why would anybody bolt a library door? Virgo was right. Jay opened the door with his left hand and stepped inside, the Browning in his right.

The man at the desk spun around in his chair.

Jay held the revolver in both hands now, leveled directly at the man.

The man said, "What the hell?" The color left his face. He stayed in shock for the statutory five seconds before he showed any kind of reaction at all.

Still, Jay did not fire.

He knew the man.

Not personally, of course not, but he knew him. The Irish face, famous for its little-boy pugnacity, was a media event in itself. The man's refusal to accept that he did not belong to a dynasty that gave him the highest office by right was a fact that Jay, and the rest of the world, knew very well indeed, from the newsreel and television screens. The brothers, of course, were legend, living or dead.

This man carried their stamp, he was of the clan.

Jay saw it all quite clearly now. Jack Virgo had not told Marty who the hit was to be because he had been afraid that she would not go along with it, probably certain that she would not. He had expected that Jay would have to. By the time Jay got to the library, Jack Virgo had reasoned, he would have eliminated at least one of the guards, the one downstairs or the one outside the library door. Virgo must have known a man was normally stationed outside the door, known or guessed.

The fatal five seconds had long gone by. The man said, in an unexpectedly firm voice, "Don't do it. If it's money, I can arrange that. If it's any other reason, it's pointless."

Jay kept the Browning aimed straight at the man's head, legs braced, both hands gripping the weapon, unwavering.

The man said, "For God's sake, be sensible. What will it accomplish?"

Jay was astonished at the man's clarity of diction.

He was astonished at the man's calm.

Then he thought: this man has been through this before; he has anticipated this scene many times. Nothing about it is new to him.

Jay looked at the man and the man looked steadily back at

him for another five seconds. Then Jay turned, very swiftly, and stepped out of the library. He closed the door, looked quickly along the corridor, saw nothing, and ran along it to the stairs that would bring him to the downstairs hall and to the front door.

He took the steps down to the hall two at a time.

As he did so the hall light went out, and a bullet went past his head into the wall. Jay cursed: the second security man. Jay hugged the banister rail and fired blind into the darkness. As he did so, the front door was pulled open and a bulky figure in a dark suit ran out of the hall into the night. Jay jumped the last five steps and ran across the hall to the open front door in time to see the security man running toward an automobile parked in the drive. The man had given up subterfuge for speed and was obviously bent on flight rather than fight.

The headlights of the car came on in a blinding glare. There was a sudden, devastating burst of submachine-gun fire, and the bulky man in the dark suit crumpled to the ground.

Jay fired the Browning twice at the flare of the submachine-gun. After he did so, far too late, his finger froze on the trigger.

Marty took the blast of the Browning full in the chest. She spun around, her hair a dark cascade in the piercing headlights of the Mustang, and fell, jerkily, like a puppet, in a heap, onto the gravel.

T·H·I·R·T·E·E·N

JAY DROVE THE MUSTANG, fast, through the iron gates, which were half open. Obviously, Jack Virgo had bribed a key from somewhere, to get the Mustang inside the drive. Jay had no way of knowing whether Jack Virgo had any more backup around the house. He ducked low as he drove the Mustang, without lights, but all that happened was that the side-view mirror was crumpled in a collision with the ironwork. No shots. No shouts. Nothing. Jay put on his lights and sped down the drive toward the main road. He wondered how much time he had. If Virgo did not know things had gone wrong yet, he soon would.

Jay, his shirt wet to his body, numb, feeling nothing yet, slowed the car down and tried to think clearly.

One fact was certain.

He had been set up.

Jay tried to figure out how. First, method: technically, it was very simple and very good. Jay blew away the man in the library and, as arranged, ran out of the house, through the front door, intending to run down the drive toward the waiting Mustang at the gates. But by that time the Mustang had been parked in the darkness of the drive for several minutes. Marty had driven it there. At some earlier point, she had picked up the Scorpion submachine gun, from Virgo, or from an arranged point. It had not, Jay was sure, been anywhere in the Mustang.

Another thing he remembered: Marty's face as she lay on the

gravel, the blood seeping through her blouse, the Scorpion still hot in her hand. The security man, lying a few feet away, had been smart. He'd seen Jay in the house, or heard him. He'd tried for a hit at Jay, missed, and then run. Marty, of course, had thought he was Jay. Poor devil, thought Jay, but better him than me.

So, where in all of this was Virgo?

Not far, probably, but wherever he was, he was on the other end of the radio that had been hidden behind the dashboard and was now clearly visible. Had Marty known it was there? Jay doubted it. All she had said and done, before the operation began, could have been an act, but somehow, at a sexual-emotional level, Jay knew it had not been. Marty *had* wanted to leave Virgo, she *had* wanted to leave the Company. But not enough.

He was possessed of an insane desire to pick up the radio and call Virgo, tell him there had been another fuck-up, but he needed all the time he could get, and gestures like that were out. A sudden thought struck him: did Virgo have any backing *at all*, or was this an entirely maverick operation? Jay slowed his speed, feeling safer by the mile. If it was a maverick operation, masterminded by Virgo alone, if all his talk about other conspirators in the Company was bullshit, then Jay was safe. Virgo's sole backup had been Marty, and now she was dead.

If all that was true, Jay reasoned, then Jack Virgo had been very sure of Marty. Very sure, when he called in all her loyalties, mixed with threats, yes, certainly with threats, being Virgo. Poor bitch, she'd had no choice. She was always Virgo's woman, bought and sold, dead or alive.

There was no trouble at the Canadian border. Jay's British passport was hardly glanced at. The Mountie wished him a pleasant trip, and told him to drive more carefully—he'd noted the shattered side-view mirror. Jay had said sure, and pleaded left-hand drive he wasn't used to. The Mountie had grinned and waved him on. Jay had, before that, stopped at an all-night garage, disposed of the Browning behind a toilet cistern, and cleaned the mud off his face and hands. He had bought a bottle of scotch and drunk half of it, very slowly. He was still numb and cold, and he was trying not to think too much. Jay drove on, through the night and into the dawn. He was not tired; the adrenaline was still running. When this was all over he would sleep. But not yet.

It was a bright fall day when Jay drove the Mustang into the airport at Toronto. He left it in the airport parking lot, after searching it thoroughly. There was, of course, no sign of the money. Presumably Marty had given it to Virgo when she picked up the Scorpion submachine gun at some point not too far from the house.

Jay found a quiet telephone booth and dialed the backup number he had insisted Virgo give him, during the briefing. Virgo had seemed reluctant, but Jay had asked, when did anybody ever go into a thing like this without a backup number to ring, if things went wrong? Virgo's reluctance was understandable now, but he had probably reasoned that the number would never be used.

Jay wondered if it would turn out to be a dud. There was a dial tone. A man's voice answered. It was Virgo's.

"Hello, Jack."

There was a pause, some static, and Jack Virgo's voice, very faint, said, "Who is that?"

He liked the picture. Virgo, holed up in some motel, sitting by the shortwave radio, waiting for the television news. There would be nothing on it, since there had been no news flash on the Mustang's radio, and Jay had kept it on the whole journey. Virgo, sleepless, sweating, and wondering what had gone wrong. Jay liked that. He said, "Marty blew it, she's dead, and you're facing big trouble, but you know all that by now."

There was a very long pause and a lot of static, then the faint, gravelly voice said, "And the target?"

"Very much alive, and asking a lot of questions, I imagine. I see why you wanted him hit. He's no friend of the Company, he's no friend of any gung-ho faction in the Company, or in the Pentagon for that matter, he's an East Coast liberal who might be soft on defense, he's a dove, not a hawk, and he might even make a good president. But I didn't have to do the job. So I didn't. I hope you survive the investigation."

There was a longer silence. "Marty did it for me, you know that? I'll see you again one day."

And Virgo hung up.

Jay walked through the counter area and the customs checks unchallenged. Plainly, the man in the house did not want any nationwide search for the intruder. If the airport security men were looking, they weren't looking hard, and there had still been nothing at all on the car radio. No, the hunt was not on. The man in the house or his advisers had decided it would not help his presidential credibility to have attacks made on his life.

Carrying a cheap bag containing toilet necessities he'd bought at the airport shop, Jay joined the passengers boarding the 747. He reflected that Virgo must have sold Marty a fine bill of goods, sweet-talked her into his own paranoid dream: that the man in the library represented a charismatic liberal presence that must never be allowed in the White House while the world was the dangerous place Virgo knew it to be.

Virgo had known better than anybody what was good for these United States and had been ready to kill to prove it.

Jay had booked a direct flight to Paris and was sitting in his seat on the aircraft before the certainty came to him that he would never do anything like this ever again. The underground war, as a part of his life, was over. He would not even try to get the money from Jones. He grimaced sourly. There was no chance of that anyway. Jones must have had some inkling of what was in Jack Virgo's mind. Or perhaps not. It didn't really matter, now.

South Africa, too, was out. Ten thousand dollars, less the air fare, was better than no dollars, but it was hardly enough to start a life in a new country, and anyway, Jack Virgo might, when things had calmed down a little, go looking for him there. If he survived, which, being Virgo, he just might.

A terrible aching weariness and sense of loss came over Jay. He recognized it well. He'd had it before, often enough—when his mother had stood on the back-to-school train platform, waving helplessly; after his first, bloody SAS action, in the burning sands of the Radfan; after his first hit, the old workman in the leather coat in the pissoir in West Berlin; after the bomb blast that had taken Angie from him, the white tweed cap lying on the grass verge. So many desperate actions, so many black dreams to come, so many wakeful nights. He could only pray, without hope, that sometime they would cease.

Jay closed his eyes and slept, high above the Atlantic. His last waking thought was how surprised Willa would be to see him when (if his calculations were right) he arrived at the marina in Cannes and stepped onto her boat, sometime the following morning.